THE TIME OF THE GHOST

Diana Wynne Jones

ILLUSTRATED BY DAVID WYATT

Collins

An imprint of HarperCollinsPublishers

First published by Macmillan Children's Books 1981
First published in paperback by Collins 2001
Collins is an imprint of HarperCollins*Publishers* Ltd
77-85 Fulham Palace Road, Hammersmith,
London, W6 8JB

The HarperCollins website address is:
www.**fire**and**water**.com

1 3 5 7 9 8 6 4 2

Text copyright © Diana Wynne Jones 1981
Illustration by David Wyatt 2001

ISBN 0 00 711217 3

The author and illustrator assert the moral right to be
identified as the author and illustrator of the work.

Printed and bound in Great Britain by
Omnia Books Limited,
Glasgow

THE TIME OF THE GHOST

Other titles by Diana Wynne Jones

To my sister Isobel and to Hat

CHAPTER ONE

There's been an accident! she thought. *Something's wrong!*

She could not quite work out what was the matter. It was broad daylight – probably the middle of the afternoon – and she was coming down the road from the wood on her way home. It was summer, just as it should be. All round her was the sleepy, heavy humming of a countryside drowsing after lunch. She could hear the distant flap and caw of the rooks in the dead elms, and a tractor grinding away somewhere. If she raised herself to look over the hedge, there lay the fields, just as she expected, sleepy grey-green, because the wheat was not ripe by a long way yet. The trees were almost black in the heat haze, and dense, except for the bare ring of elms, a long way off, where the rooks were noisy specks.

I've always wanted to be tall enough to look over the hedge, she thought. *I must have grown.*

She wondered if it was the heavy, steamy weather that was making her feel so odd. She had a queer, light, vague feeling. She could not think clearly – or not when she thought about thinking. And perhaps the weather accounted for the way she felt so troubled and anxious. It felt like a thunderstorm coming. But it was not quite that. Why did she think there had been an accident?

She could not remember an accident. Nor could she think why she was suddenly on her way home, but, since she was going there, she thought she might as well go on. It made her uncomfortable to be reared up above the hedges, so she subsided to her usual height and went on down the road, thinking vague, anxious thoughts.

What's happened to me? she thought. *I must stop feeling so silly. I'm the sensible one. Perhaps if I ask myself questions, my memory will come back. What did I have for lunch?*

That was no good. She could not remember lunch in any way. She realised, near to panic, that she could not remember anything about the rest of today at all.

That's silly! she told herself. *I must know!* But she didn't. Panic began to grow in her. It was as if someone was pumping up a very large balloon somewhere in the middle of her chest. She fought to squash it down as it unfolded. *All right!* she told herself hysterically. *All right! I'll ask something easy. What am I wearing?*

This ought to have been easy. She only had to look down. But first she seemed to have forgotten how to do that. Then when she did—

Panic spread roaring, to its fullest size. She was swept away with it, as if it were truly a huge balloon, tumbling, rolling, bobbing, mindless.

There's been an accident! was all she could think. *Something's awfully wrong!*

When she noticed things again, she was a long way on down the road. There was a small house she somehow knew was a shop nestling in the hedge just ahead. She made herself stand still. She was so frightened that everything she could see was shaking – quivering like poor reception on the telly. She had a notion that if it went on shaking this way, it would shake itself right away from her, and she would be left with utter nothing. So she made herself stand there.

After a while, she managed to make herself look down again. There was still nothing there.

I've turned into nothing! she thought. Panic swelled again. *There's been an accident! STOP IT!* she told herself. *Stop and think.* She made herself do that. It took a while, because thinking seemed so difficult, and panic kept swelling through her thoughts and threatening to whirl her away again, but she eventually thought something like: *I'm all right. I'm here. I'm me. If I wasn't, I wouldn't even be frightened. I wouldn't know. But something has happened to me. I can't see myself at all, not even a smear of shadow on the road. There's been an accident! STOP THAT! I keep thinking about an accident, so there must have been one, but it does no good to say so, because every time I do, things just get vaguer. So I must stop thinking that and start thinking what's the matter with me. I may be just invisible.*

On that not altogether comforting thought, she took herself over to the hedge and – well – sort of leant into it. She had, as she leant, strong memories of the way a stout prickly hedge bears you up like a mattress, and sticks spines into you as it bears you.

Not this time. She found herself in the field on the other side of the hedge without feeling a thing. She could not even feel anything from the clump of nettles she seemed to be standing in. *Seemed is the right word,* she thought unhappily. *Let's face it. I'm not just invisible. I haven't got a body at all.*

She had to spend another while squashing down bulging panic after this. *It does no good!* she shouted at herself. In fact, she was beginning to see that the panic did positive harm. Each time it happened, she felt odder and vaguer. Now she could hardly remember coming down the road, nor why she had been coming this way in the first place.

It probably comes of not having a proper head to keep my thoughts in, she decided. *I shall have to be very careful.* She half put a non-existent hand to what she thought was probably her head, but took it away again. *If I put my hand right through, I might knock all the thoughts out,* she said, forgetting she had already been through a hedge. *Where am I?*

The field had a path winding through it, and there was a stile in the hedge opposite, leading to somewhere with trees. As she looked at that stile, she had a very strong feeling that, beyond it, she would be able to get help. She went that way. Now she knew herself to be bodiless, she was almost interested by the way she moved, dangling and drifting, with her head about the height she was used to. She could rise higher if she wanted, or sink lower, but both ways made her uncomfortable. When she reached the stile, she started to climb it, out of habit. And stopped, feeling foolish. For a moment, she was glad no one was there to see her. Of course she could just go straight through. She did. Then she was in an orchard, a rather messy place that she seemed to be used to. The nettles, and the chickens pecking about, were rather familiar, and, as she passed a hut made of old doors and chairs and draped with soggy-looking old carpet, she had almost a twinge of recognition. She knew there would be a mildewy rag doll inside that hut. The doll's name was Monigan.

How do I know that? she wondered. *Where am I?*

The fact that she did not know confused her. She dangled sideways across the orchard, avoiding trees out of what seemed to be habit, and found herself faced with a hedge again – a tall hefty hedge, which looked as impenetrable as a wood.

Well, let's see, she said, and went through.

Here, she was more confused still. For one thing, she had a very strong sense of guilt. She was now somewhere she ought not to be. For another thing, it was all much less familiar here. It was a very sparse, open garden, much trampled, so that the grass was mostly bare earth. Beyond that, behind a line of lime trees, was a large red-brick building.

She drifted under the lime trees and inspected the red building. Bees buzzed among the flat, wet, heart shapes of the lime leaves, and little drops of lime liquid pattered down around (and through) her. Oddly enough, the bees avoided her. One flew straight at her face, and swerved off at the last minute. This comforted her considerably. *There must be something of me for it to dodge*, she told herself, staring at a church-like window in the red house. From behind the window came a buzz, quieter than the bees, but quite as perpetual. There was also a smell, distinct from the smell of lime trees, which she found she knew.

This is School, she said.

Maybe this was why she felt so guilty here. Perhaps she should be at school. Perhaps, at this moment, a teacher was looking up from a register and asking where she was.

This was alarming. It caused her to speed along the front of the red house to a small door she somehow knew would be there, and dart through it, to a dark space full of blazers and bags hung on pegs. No one was there. They were all in lessons, evidently. She sped on, through tiled corridors, wishing she could remember which was her classroom. She knew there was a rule about not running in the corridors, but she was not sure it applied to people without bodies. Besides, she was not running. It was more like whizzing.

She could not find her classroom. It was like a bad dream. And here she had an idea which made her much, much happier. It *was* a dream, of course. It was a bad dream, but a dream definitely. In dreams one could run without really running and often could not feel one's body, and, above all, in dreams one was always urgently looking for something one could not find. She was so relieved that she slowed right down. And there, beside her, was a door labelled IV A.

That was her class, IV A. She was more relieved than ever, even though she did not remember the door looking like this. It was pointed, like the school windows, with thick ribs and long iron hinges on it. But behind the door she could hear a teacher's voice droning on, and the voice was definitely one she knew. She put out her hand to turn the ring-like handle of the door.

Of course the handle went right through the part that seemed to be her hand. She stood back. A strong pricking where her eyes ought to have been suggested she might be going to cry disembodied tears. She knew she could go through the door by leaning into it, but she did not dare. Half the class would laugh and the rest would scream. The teacher would say—

Dreamlike, she had entirely forgotten she could not even see herself. *I will do it! I will, I will!* she said.

She put her non-hand to the handle again. This time, by exerting enormous effort, she managed to make it flip, and rattle gently.

The handle turned fiercely under her not-fingers. The door was wrenched open inwards from her. A voice roared, "When I ask you to decline *mens*, Howard, I do not mean *mensa!* Come!" the voice added, and a man's bristly head looked round the door.

Uncertainly, she slipped through the opening into the sudden light of the classroom. It was more dreamlike than ever. They were all boys here, rows of boys, some leaning forward writing busily, some leaning back on two legs of their chairs looking anything but busy. There was not a girl in the room.

"Nobody there," said the teacher, and clapped the door shut again.

She looked at him wonderingly. For some reason, she knew him enormously well. Every line of his bristly head, his bird-like face and his thin, angry body were known to her exactly. She felt drawn to him. But she was afraid of him too. She knew he was always impatient and nearly always angry. A name for him came to her. They called him Himself.

Himself rounded on the class, glowering. "May I remind you, Howard, that *mens* means the mind, and *mensa* means a table? But I expect in your case the two things are the same. No, no. Don't scratch your head, boy. You'll get splinters."

The boy Howard seemed untroubled by the glower and the roar of Himself. "Not to worry, sir," he said comfortingly. "I don't think splinters are catching."

"Fifteen all," murmured someone at the back of the room. This caused a good deal of not-quite-hidden laughter.

She found she knew Howard too. He had a round, bright-eyed face like an otter's. In fact, most of the boys at the desks were people she had seen before. She knew names: Shepperson, Greer II, Jenkins, Matchworth-Keyes, Filbert, Wrenn and Stinker-Tinker, to name just the front row. But she was beginning to think this was not her class after all. There should have been girls. And this was probably a Latin lesson. She had never learnt Latin.

I think I'd better go, she said apologetically to Himself.

"A test tomorrow on the Third Declension," said Himself. "Make a note in your rough books."

He had not heard her. To judge from the way everyone was behaving, no one could see her or hear her. She might just as well not have been there. Maybe that was not such a bad thing. Very much ashamed of her embarrassing mistake, she leant into the door and was in the corridor again, hearing Himself still, dimly, from behind the door.

Puzzling about how she knew everyone in that strange class so well, she wandered on. And, because she was not trying to remember where to go, she found herself going very certainly in a definite direction – downstairs, past a room with rows of tables, past a shiny door which gusted out smells of cooked cabbage and washing-up liquid, into a dark wooden hall with a green-covered door at the end of it. The green was the felty kind of cloth you find on billiard tables. She knew that door well. She suddenly wanted badly to be on the other side of it.

Before she got there, a lady came quickly through the shiny door, which bumped loudly and let out a gust of old gravy smell to join the smell of cooked cabbage. The lady hurried to a side table and picked up a pile of papers there, frowning. She was a majestic lady with a clear strong face. Her frown was a tired one. A bright blue eye between the frown and the straight nose stared at the papers. Fair hair was looped into a low, heavy bun on her head.

"Ugh!" she said at the papers. She looked like an avenging angel who had already had a long fight with the devil. All the same, the papers should have withered and turned black. The bodiless person in the corridor felt yearning admiration for this angel lady. She knew they called her Phyllis.

Under the frown, Phyllis said wearily, "Your father's told you, I've told you. How many times have you been told to stay behind the green door, Sally?"

Warmth and comfort and pleasure swelled, as huge and swift as the balloon of panic had swelled earlier. Mother had seen her. Mother knew her. Mother knew who she was. She was Sally. Of

14

course she was Sally. Everything was all right, even though she had gone and done an awful thing and interrupted Father while he was teaching. It was true she should have been on the other side of the green door. Coming into School was quite forbidden. Sally — yes, she was sure she was Sally — stood guiltily by the green door, wondering how to explain as Phyllis turned her blue eyes and tired frown towards her.

The blue eyes narrowed her way, and widened, as if Phyllis had suddenly focused on a distant hill. The frown vanished, and came back, deeper, making two little ditches at the top of Phyllis's straight nose.

"Funny," said Phyllis. "I could have sworn—" Her creamy face became reddish in the darkness. The words turned to mere moving of the lips. Phyllis twitched her shoulders and turned away uncomfortably.

Sally — she must be Sally, if Phyllis had said so — was astonished to find that other people besides herself could get embarrassed when they thought they were all alone. That embarrassed her. It was even worse to realise that Phyllis could not see her after all. Sally — she knew she was Sally now — turned and plunged desperately through the green door. She went so fiercely that the door actually lifted inwards an inch or so, and bumped back into place. Sally thought that Phyllis turned and stared at it as she went.

Beyond the door was the right place. First, a stone-flagged passage, which was chilly now and freezing in winter, where four coathooks held a mound of many coats. The open door at the end led to the room called the kitchen, also stone-flagged, but warmed by the sun that rippled in through the apple trees outside.

It was in its usual mess, Sally saw wearily. Books, newspapers and bread and jam were cast in heaps on the table. Someone had spilt milk on the floor. Sally longed to lift the front page of one of the newspapers out of the butter, but she was not sure she would be able to. She wondered whose turn it had been to do the washing-up. She could see a mountain of white school china sticking up out of the sink.

Well, this time I can't do it, she was saying, when she saw what she took for a hideous dwarf standing on the draining board.

The dwarf had a tangle of dark hair and was wearing what seemed to be a bright green sack. The sack stuck out so far in front that Sally thought the dwarf was hugely fat at first, until she saw its long skinny arms propped on the edge of the sink. The dwarf was leaning forward, propped on its arms, so that a sharp white nose smeared with freckles stuck out from among the tangled hair, and so did two large front teeth. From between those teeth came a jet of water, squirting on to the white crockery in the sink. The dwarf appeared to have tied two knots in the front of its tangled hair to make way for the jet of water.

The dwarf squirted solemnly until the mouthful of water was used up. Then it relieved Sally's funny vague mind considerably by standing up on the draining board. Two skinny legs with immense knobs for knees unfolded from under the green sack, making the dwarf about the right height for a small ten-year-old. Some of the bulge in front of the sack had been those knees, but quite a large bulge still remained. Fenella – she knew its name was Fenella now – took another mouthful of water from a mug in her hand and tried the effect of squirting the crockery from higher up. The jet of water hit a cup and sprayed off on to the floor.

That's no way to do the washing-up, Fenella! Sally cried out. *And what have you tied your hair in two knots for?*

There was no sound, no sound at all, except the gentle hissing of Fenella's spray on the cup and the floor, and the mild buzzing of flies round the table.

No one can hear me! Sally thought. *What shall I do?*

But Fenella said, "Look at this, Sally." The white face, the freckles and two large shrewd eyes under the knots of hair turned Sally's way. "Oh, I forgot," said Fenella. "She's not here." At that, Fenella raised her sharp nose and her voice too and bellowed, "Charlotte – Cart! Cart, come and see this!" Fenella had the loudest possible voice. The window rattled and the flies stopped buzzing.

"Shut up," said someone in the next room, obviously answering without listening.

"But I've invented something really horrible!" Fenella boomed.

"Oh, all right."

There were sounds of movement in the next room – sounds like a heavy creature with six legs. The creature came in about level with Sally's head. It looked like two people under an old grey hearthrug.

It's only Oliver, Sally told herself quickly. She found she had backed almost into the passage again. Seeing Oliver suddenly often had that effect on people. Oliver was probably an Irish wolfhound, but he was larger than a donkey, and blurred and misshapen all over. He looked like a bad drawing of a dog. And he was almost impossibly huge. *Oliver wouldn't hurt a fly,* Sally told herself firmly.

Nevertheless, it was alarming the way Oliver shambled straight towards the passage door and Sally. His huge heavy-breathing head – more like a bear's head or a wild boar's – came level with Sally's non-face and sniffed loudly. His shaggy clout of tail swung, once, twice. A distant whining came from somewhere in his huge throat. Then, even more distant, a rumbling grew inside his shaggy chest. He stepped backwards, still rumbling, and sideways, and his tail dropped and curled between his legs. He could not seem to take his great blurred eyes off the place where Sally was. The whine kept breaking out on the rumble and then giving way to a growl again.

"Whatever's the matter with Oliver?" Charlotte said from the door of the living room.

Charlotte was just as much of a shock to Sally as Oliver had been. She was built on the same massive scale. Like Oliver, she was huge and blurred. Blurred fair hair stuck out round her head. A blurred face, like a poor photograph of angel Phyllis, floated in the hair. She was the size of a tall fat woman, and cased in a dress that had clearly been designed for a little girl. There was about her, blurred and vast, the feeling of a powerful personality which, like her lumping body, had somehow got itself cased in the mind of a little girl. She was carrying a book folded round one finger. "Oliver's scared stiff!" she said.

"I know," said Fenella. Oliver was trembling now, rattling the things on the table.

Nobody bothered with Oliver after that, because the door behind Sally crashed open. Sally was barged aside like a kite in a stiff wind, and Imogen stormed in.

"Mr Selwyn turned me out of the music rooms *again!*" Imogen yelled. "It's impossible! How am I going to perfect my art? How shall I ever be famous like this?"

"You could win a screaming competition," Fenella suggested. "Except that I'd beat you."

"You little—" Imogen turned on Fenella, at a loss for words. "You *Thing*! And why are you wearing that green sack? It looks terrible!"

"I made her that green sack," Charlotte said, advancing on Imogen and looming a little. And so she had, Sally remembered. Fenella's clothes had been handed down three people before they reached Fenella, and they had all fallen to pieces. It was a pity, Sally thought, looking at the sack, that Cart was so very bad at sewing. It was not even a straight green sack. It puckered one side and drooped the other. The neck sort of looped over Fenella's skinny chest.

Imogen realised her mistake and tried to apologise. "It was only an insult," she explained, "chosen at random to express my feelings. I was thinking about my musical career."

Which was typical Imogen, Sally thought, in the dim, remembering way she had been noticing everything so far. Imogen had set her heart on being a concert pianist. Very little else mattered to her. Sally looked at Imogen. Imogen, like Charlotte, was tall and fair, but, unlike Cart, Imogen was an unblurred version of Phyllis and very pretty indeed. This was unfair on Cart and Fenella, and unfair on Sally too, because Imogen was bigger and cleverer than Sally, and over a year younger.

What a hateful family I've got! Sally thought suddenly. *Why did I come back here?*

Oliver meanwhile, seeing that nobody noticed him, passed his great nose gently over the table. The butter was coaxed from under the newspaper, deftly magnetised, and slid away inside Oliver. This seemed to help Oliver get over the phenomenon of Sally a little. He advanced towards her, trembling a little, whining slightly, and gingerly swishing his tail.

"What *is* the matter with that dog?" said Imogen.

"We don't know," said Fenella.

All three of Sally's sisters stared at her, and not one of them saw her.

CHAPTER TWO

Their name was Melford, Sally suddenly remembered. They were Charlotte, Selina, Imogen and Fenella Melford. But she still did not know what she was doing here in this state.

Perhaps I came back here to get revenged, she thought.

It was rather a horrible thought and one, Sally hoped, that would not have come to her in the ordinary way. But no one could deny that this was not the ordinary way. They were all three looking at her and she hated them all: big formless Cart in that babyish blue dress, and self-centred Imogen — it was a mark of Imogen's character, it seemed to Sally, that Imogen had somehow got hold of a bright yellow trouser suit which would have fitted Cart better. On Imogen, it was so large that the top half hung in downward folds like a curtain, and the bottom half was in crosswise folds like two yellow concertinas. Imogen had great trouble in not treading on the ends of the trousers all the time. And she had evidently felt the suit needed brightening up. She was wearing mauve plastic beads and orange lipstick. As for Fenella, Sally thought angrily, she looked just like the little Thing Imogen had called her. Those knob-knees were like joints in the legs of insects, and for antennae she had those two knots of her hair.

I hate them so much I've come back to haunt them, Sally decided.

At that, the whirl of misty notions – which was all Sally's non-existent head seemed able to hold – took a sharp turn in the opposite direction and almost stopped. *This is a dream after all,* she told herself tremulously.

But was it? Where had Sally come back from, after all? She had no idea, except that there had been some kind of accident.

Oh good gracious, am I dead? Sally cried out. *I'm not dead, am I?* she asked her sisters.

It did no good. Unaware that anyone was asking them anything, they all went back to their own concerns. Then all at once it became very important to Sally that they should know she was there. It was even more important to her than the reason why she was here. She was sure at least one of them could explain everything, if only they knew she was here to be explained to.

Fenella! she shouted. Fenella, after all, had almost known she was there.

But Fenella climbed from the draining board, through the open window, and jumped down outside. Sally fluttered after her, towards the sink. Oliver followed, whining uneasily, but gave up with a huge sigh when Sally sailed away through the window after Fenella.

Fenella was walking this way and that through the orchard when Sally caught up with her. She seemed to be making sure nobody else was there.

There is someone, Sally said, coming to a halt in a clump of nettles in front of Fenella. *Look! There's me.*

Fenella walked straight past her, frowning. Fenella's frown was the one thing about her that was like Phyllis. It gave Fenella the angel look too – a fallen angel. "Weaving spiders come not near," Fenella said to the air beyond Sally and walked on. She came to the hut made of old chairs and knelt down in front of the opening in the soggy carpet. At once, she became a large-fronted dwarf again, with spindly arms. The spindly arms stretched towards the hut. "Come forth, Monigan. Come forth and meet thy worshipper," Fenella intoned. "Thy worshipper kneeleth here with both arms outstretched. Come forth! She never does come forth, you know," she remarked to the air above Sally.

I know, Sally said impatiently. The Monigan game had gone on far too long, it seemed to her. She knew she had thought it was pretty boring when Cart first invented the Worship of Monigan a year ago. *Fenella, listen, look! Notice me!*

"Monigan, thou hast but one worshipper these days," Fenella intoned, unheeding. "Thou hadst better look out, Monigan, or I shall go away too. Then where wouldst thou be? Come forth, I say to thee. Come forth!"

Fenella! Please! said Sally.

But Fenella simply swayed around on her knees, intoning. "Come forth! Monigan, thou mightst do me a favour and come forth just this once. Canst thou not understand how boring thou art, just sitting there? Come forth!"

It would teach you if she did! Sally said, unheard and soundless. Then she had an idea. If she could flip a latch and barge a door, she might be able to move something as light as a rag doll, if she tried very hard. Fenella would notice that at least. Sally drifted to the hut and ducked in through the old carpet.

She only had the part of her that seemed to be head and

shoulders inside it, but even that was almost too much. It was dank and stifling in there. And it smelt. Sally had a moment's wonder that she should mind a smell so much, when she seemed to have no real nose to smell with. *But I can hear and see too,* she thought. *Mostly what I can't do is feel.* She could not feel the sopping carpet, though she could smell the mildew on it, and smell Monigan herself, leaning soggily against the table leg at the back of the hut. There was a sharp mushroom smell from the pale yellow grass. But the worst smell came from the four or five little dishes in front of Monigan. The stuff was too rotten for Sally to tell what it had once been, but it smelt worse than the school kitchen. In front of the dolls' plates, someone had carefully planted three black feathers upright in the pale grass.

Hm, said Sally. *I wonder if Fenella is the only worshipper. Or did she do that?*

She leant further in to push Monigan. She did not want to in the least. Monigan was hideous. A year in the wet hut had turned the rag face livid grey, and fungus had puckered it until it looked like a maggot. The rest of Monigan was misshapen before she went into the hut. One time, Cart, Sally, Imogen and Fenella had each seized an arm or a leg — Sally could not remember whether it had been a quarrel or a silly game — and pulled until Monigan came to pieces. Then Cart, in terrible guilt, had sewed her together again, as badly as she had sewed Fenella's green sack, and dressed her in a pink knitted doll's dress. The dress was now maggot grey. To make it up to Monigan for being torn apart, Cart had invented the Worship of Monigan.

Sally did not like to go near Monigan, but she made one half-hearted attempt to push her. But she had forgotten how a rag doll, sitting in the wet, soaks up moisture like a sponge. Monigan was too heavy to move. Gladly, Sally came up out of the hut. It was unbearable in there.

"I shall go and check the hens now," Fenella remarked to the air, as Sally emerged.

No — notice me first! Sally cried out.

Fenella simply unfolded her insect legs and went wandering off. "Spotted snakes with double tongue," Sally heard her say. "I wonder, do goddesses know how boring they are?"

Sally left her to it and went to find Cart or Imogen. They were both in the living room. Sally drifted in there, with Oliver anxiously trudging behind her.

"Can't you play this piano?" Cart was saying. She had one hand keeping her place in her book and the other vaguely pointing to the old upright piano against the wall.

Imogen and Sally both looked at the piano, Imogen with contempt, Sally as if she had never seen it before. It was a cheap, yellowish colour and very battered. Its yellow keys looked like bad teeth. Sally could see nobody ever used it because of the heaps of papers, books and magazines all over it. There was a box of paints on the bass end, with a paste pot full of painty water balanced crookedly among the black notes. A painting was propped on the yellow music-stand — a surprisingly good painting of Fenella standing in a blackberry bush. Sally wondered who had done it.

"Play that!" Imogen said contemptuously. "I'd rather play a xylophone compounded of dead men's bones!" She collapsed her full yellow length on a dirty sofa, which gave off a loud twang of springs as she landed. "My career is in ruins," she said. "Was Myra Hess ever tormented in this way? I think not."

Why does she talk like a book all the time? Sally wondered irritably. Cart seemed busy with her reading again. Since there seemed little chance of either of them noticing her, Sally roosted dejectedly on the back of an armchair. Oliver, seeing her settled, flopped down himself with a deep groan and lay like a heaped-up hearthrug. But he was not asleep. Every so often he whined and turned one morbid eye in Sally's direction.

"What's wrong with him?" said Cart, looking up. Her blurry look was stronger when she was reading. It was as if she had faded into her book.

"His lunch, probably," said Imogen. "You're always fussing about that wretched animal."

"Well, he's my dog — or supposed to be," said Cart. "I show a natural concern."

"You show total, besotted devotion," declared Imogen.

"I don't! Why do you talk like a book all the time?" retorted Cart.

"It's you that does that," said Imogen. "You're a walking dictionary."

Cart went back to her book. Imogen stared stormily at the yellow piano. Sally tried to muster courage to attract their attention. She knew why she could not. They were both bigger than she was. *Though why it should matter to me in this state, I can't imagine*, she said to herself.

Cart looked up again. "Isn't it peaceful? I suppose it's because the boys are in lessons. It's hard on them breaking up a week after us, isn't it?"

"No," said Imogen. "I could use the music room if School term was over."

"No you couldn't," said Cart. "Mrs Gill told me there's a Course for Disturbed Children as soon as term ends. They're coming to overrun the place on Tuesday."

"Oh my Lord!" Imogen looked up at the ceiling and twiddled her mauve beads, faster and faster, so that they clattered viciously. "I *hate* the way we never get any holidays! It's not fair!"

Oh, thought Sally. Her bodiless mind became clearer. Her parents kept a school — or rather, she seemed to think, they kept

School House of a large boys' boarding school. Yes, that was it. The girls went to quite a different school, some miles away. *Oh dear!* said Sally. She had been very silly looking for her class in the boys' school. She was glad no one had known. Why had she not remembered she had broken up already? Because she had lived in the boys' school all her life, she supposed, and it was much more real to her than her own. And Cart had supplied another memory: School was never empty. Almost as soon as the boys went home, more children came for courses. There were, as Imogen said, never any holidays.

Next second, Sally found herself jumping to attention. Her movement made Oliver raise his head and rumble unhappily. Cart said, "I feel really envious of Sally — a horrible yellow envy, like the colour of that piano. Why did we agree it should be *her*? Why Sally?"

"That's why it's so quiet, of course," said Imogen.

"So it is!" said Cart, sitting forward as if Imogen had made a truly exciting discovery. "No whining and grumbling."

"No arguing and quarrelling," agreed Imogen, stretching as if she was suddenly very comfortable. "No stream of remarks about squalor. No tidying up."

"No hysterics and crashing about," said Cart. "No criticisms. I sometimes feel I could bear all the rest of Sally if she wasn't always going on about the way we speak and walk and dress and so on."

"The thing about her that really annoys me," said Imogen, "is her beastly career, and the way she's always on about it. She's not the only one with a career to think of."

There was a slight pause. "Well — no," said Cart.

Sally looked from one to the other, wondering which she hated most. She had just decided it was Imogen, when Cart started again.

"No – it's Sally's pose of being good and sweet that drives me up the wall, now I think. And, if I venture the slightest criticism of Phyllis or Himself, she springs to their defence. She can't seem to believe they're not the most perfect parents anyone could have."

Well, I think they are! Sally shouted. Neither of them heard her. Without question, it was Cart she hated most.

"That's not quite fair, Cart," Imogen said. She exuded justice and fair-mindedness. Sally remembered she always wanted to hit Imogen when she went like this. "Sally," Imogen explained seriously, "truly does think this family is perfect. She loves her father and mother, Cart."

Imogen's saintly tone maddened Cart as well as Sally. Cart's large face took on a blur of pink. Her eyes glared like holes in a mask. She roared, louder than Fenella, so that the windows buzzed, "Don't you give me that nonsense!" and flung herself at Imogen. Oliver saw her coming just in time and lumbered to his feet to get out of the way. But Imogen, with the speed of long practice, catapulted off the sofa in front of him. Oliver was forced towards Sally, and he did not like that. He growled. But he also wagged his tail and lowered his head in Sally's direction as he growled, because he could not understand what made her so peculiar.

Imogen and Cart took no notice. They dodged round Oliver, howling insults. And Sally forgot this was not the usual threesome quarrel and screamed unheard insults also. *Talk about arguing and quarrelling! Talk about hysterics! And you can talk about careers, Imogen! How dare you criticise me behind my back!*

"I think Oliver's gone mad at last," Fenella's largest voice boomed behind them. Fenella was standing in the doorway, looking portentous.

Cart and Imogen – and Sally too – looked at the growling,

27

wagging Oliver. "Well, he never did have any brain," Imogen said.

"There really is something wrong with him, I think," Cart said anxiously.

"I'll tell you something else wrong," said Fenella. "The black hen is still missing. I counted all the hens and looked everywhere. It's gone."

"There must be a fox," said Cart. "I told you."

"I didn't mean that," Fenella said meaningly.

"Then what *did* you mean?" said Cart.

Imogen said, "Cart, she's tied her hair in knots. Look."

Fenella dismissed this with magnificent scorn. "Of course Cart knows. It's all part of the Plan." Imogen, at this, looked surprisingly humble. "I meant the hen and Oliver."

"You mean Oliver's eaten it!" Cart exclaimed. She rushed to Oliver and tried anxiously to open his mouth. This was impossible. Oliver, as well as being very large, very strong and utterly thick, was also rather more obstinate than a donkey. He never did anything he did not want to, and he did not want his mouth open just then.

"I don't think you'd be able to see the hen, even down Oliver," Imogen objected.

"But he might have feathers on his teeth," Cart gasped, wrenching at Oliver's muzzle. It could have held two hens easily. "Think of the row there'll be!"

"Then it's better not to know," said Imogen.

"If you're ready to listen to me – I didn't *mean* that," Fenella said, and, still very portentous, she turned in a swirl of crooked green sack and marched away.

"Then what *was* it about?" Cart said to Imogen.

Imogen spread her hands. "Fenella being Fenella." She raised her hands to the ceiling. "Oh why am I cursed with sisters?"

"You're not the only one!" snarled Cart.

Sally left them beginning another quarrel and drifted miserably out into the orchard. The hens, like Oliver, seemed to know she was there. They were all gathered pecking at some corn near the gate, which Fenella must have put down so that she could count them, but they ran away chanking and squawking as Sally floated through the bars of the gate. Sally stared after their striding yellow legs and the brown sprays of tail-feathers jerking away from her in the grass. Silly things. But, as far as she could tell, the black one was indeed missing. She felt she ought to have known. She knew those hens as well as she knew her sisters.

That was the funny thing about being disembodied. Her mind did not seem to know anything properly until she was shown it. Drifting in and out among the trees, where hundreds of little pointed green apples lurked under the broad leaves, Sally tried to recall all the things she had been shown. Somewhere, surely, she must have been given a clue to what had made her like this – an inkling of what had happened at least. Well, she knew she lived in a school. She had three horrible sisters, who thought she was horrible too – or two of them did. Here, Sally broke off to argue passionately with the air.

I'm not like that! I'm not hysterical and I don't go on about my career. I'm not like Imogen. They're just seeing their own faults in me! And I don't grumble and criticise. I'm ever so meek and lowly really – sort of gentle and dazed and puzzled about life. It's just that I've got standards. And I do think Mother and Himself are perfect. I just know they are. So there!

But before all that started, hadn't Cart shown that she and Imogen knew where Sally was supposed to be? They had. Cart had envied Sally – *envied!* That was rich! They were certainly not worried about her – but that proved nothing. Sally could not see either of those two worrying about anyone but themselves. But if Cart envied her, why should Sally have this feeling that there had been an accident? A mistake – something had gone wrong –

there had been an accident—

Before Sally was aware, the balloon of panic had blown itself up inside her again. She whirled away on it, tumbling and rolling...

When at last it subsided, she found herself drifting along the paths of a slightly unkempt kitchen garden. She gave a shiver of guilt. This too was a forbidden place. There was, she remembered, a perfectly beastly gardener called Mr McLaggan, who hit you unpleasantly hard if he caught you, and shouted a lot whether he caught you or not. All the same, as she drifted past a hedge of gooseberry bushes, Sally had a firm impression that she and the others often came here, in spite of Mr McLaggan. Those same bushes, where a big red gooseberry or so still lingered among the white spines, had been raided when the gooseberries were apple green and not much larger than peas. And they had picked raspberries too, in a raid with the boys.

Sally saw Mr McLaggan down the end of a path, hoeing fiercely, and prudently drifted away through a brick wall. There was a wide green playing field on the other side of the wall. Very distantly, small white figures were engaged in the ceremony of cricket.

I think, Sally said uncertainly, *I think I like watching cricket.*

But it made you very shy, she remembered, being one girl out in the middle of a field full of boys. They stared and said to one another, "That's Slimy Semolina, that girl." Some said it to your face. And being boys, they were of course quite unable to tell you and your sisters apart, and called all four of you Slimy Semolina impartially. But now, when she was in the ideal state for not being noticed, Sally somehow could not face all that wide green space. She was afraid she would dissolve to nothing in it. There was little enough of her left as it was. She kept along beside the wall and the buildings, past an open cycle shed, across a square of asphalt with nets for basketball at either end, and – quickly – beside a row of tennis courts. Here, the balls sleepily went phut-phut. The ones in white, playing tennis, were all from the top of the school, who looked and spoke exactly like men. It was unnatural, somehow, that they should be schoolboys, when you could not tell them from masters. They alarmed Sally too, when they suddenly broke into bellows of deep laughter. She always thought they were laughing at her. This time when they did it, she imagined them saying, "Look at that girl – got nothing on – not even her body! Ha-ha-ha! Oh ha!"

Ha-ha to you! Sally said angrily, speeding past. *I can't help it!*

Of course, she thought – it was as if embarrassment had churned up new ideas – this was probably only a dream. But just in case it was real, Mother and Himself would know what to do. Mother had really, very nearly, seen her by the green door. She need only wait until school was over for the day and they would be able to tell her what had happened. *Probably everybody knows except me*, Sally said, with the pricking of not-real tears in her non-existent eyes. *I'm always left out of things.*

Almost at that moment, school was over for the afternoon. Sally found herself mixed, tumbled and swept back again, in a running grey crowd of boys. She was surrounded by laughing – "Did you listen to what Triggs said to Masham in Geography?" – and arguing – "No it isn't! They have four-wheel drive!" – jeering – "Don't give up, Peters! Just hit me and see what you get!" – and wordless fighting. BANG.

Ow! said Sally. *I felt that!*

It was very curious. She began to wonder if she had some kind of body after all. She had definitely been caught just then, between somebody's fist and somebody else's body. And it was as difficult to go forward against the crowd as it would have been in the ordinary way. Though Sally pushed and shoved, and expected with every push that she would go right through one of the chattering, running boys, she found that this was one thing she could not do. Each boy seemed to have, around his solid body, a warm elastic quivering field of life, which held Sally off. It was as thin as tissue paper, but it was there. Sally could feel it crackling faintly, every time she bumped against a boy.

That's peculiar, she said. *I wonder if all living things are like this. I must remember to try walking through a hen sometime.* Oliver would have made a bigger target, but the idea of walking through Oliver was too alarming.

While Sally said this, the crowd of boys surged off past her and left her on her own, feeling strange and shaken. It was like being breathless – except that she had no breath to start with. She went on, round into the school garden beside the lime trees. More boys were coming out from under the lime trees and wandering about there. Sally hovered above the trampled earth, watching them. It was strange how few of them walked like human beings should. They went shambling, or knock-kneed, or with one shoulder up and the other down, and it almost seemed they did it deliberately. One boy was going up and down a space twenty feet long, walking with his toes digging into the earthy lawn and his knees giving gently. His jaw was hanging and he was muttering to himself. Every few steps, one of his knees bent sharply, as if he had no control over it.

"Ministry of Silly Walks," Sally heard him mutter. "Ministry of Silly Walks." It was Howard, the boy whose splinters were not catching.

Near him, another boy with gingery hair was going about with one arm bent like a cripple's and jerking about. At each step he made a different hideous face. "Quiet, please, gentlemen!" he muttered from his contorted mouth. This one was Ned Jenkins, Sally remembered, and she did not think there was anything wrong with his arm usually.

Honestly! You'd think they were all mad, to look at them! she said wonderingly. She could not believe boys usually behaved like this. The boys at this school were clean-limbed young Englishmen. Yet, as she watched the stumbling, muttering, jerking figures, she knew that they often did this – or something equally peculiar. Cart had once told her that all boys were mad. Sally had protested at the time, but she now thought Cart was right. And she went on watching, trying to fix all of their bizarre antics in her strange, nebulous mind, hoping that something – anything – might give her a clue to how she came to be like this. *Because I can't stay like this for the rest of my life,* she said. *I shall go as mad as Jenkins.*

Panic began bulging again. The idea hovered – just behind the name Jenkins – that it was nonsense to say *the rest of my life*. It was quite possible Sally was a ghost, and her life was over already. Sally fought to keep this idea behind Jenkins' name, safely hidden, and the idea fought to come out. In the battle, Sally herself was tumbled off again, through the thick hedge, back into the orchard where the hens fled cackling, and then whirled towards the house. There she stopped, hanging stiffly against the branches of the last apple tree. A new idea had been let out in the fight.

Suppose, Sally said, *I left a letter – or made a note – or keep a diary.*

The notion was a magnificent relief. Somewhere there would be a few lines of writing which explained everything. Sally did not quite see herself doing anything so methodical as keeping a diary, but, right at the back of her transparent, swirling mind, she found a dim, dim notion that she might have written a letter. Alongside this notion was a fainter one: if there was a letter, it was to do with the Plan Fenella had talked about.

The house quivered with Sally's excitement as she whirled inside it.

CHAPTER THREE

In the kitchen, Cart was actually doing the washing-up. She was standing at the sink with her heavy feet planted at a suffering angle, slowly clattering thick white cups. Her face had a large expression of righteous misery.

"Penance," Cart said, as Sally hovered by the kitchen table, wondering where to look for a letter. "Utter boredom. I do think the rest of you might help sometimes."

Now you know how I feel, Sally said. *I always do it.* Letters were more likely to be in the sitting room. She was on her way there when she realised that the only other being in the kitchen was Oliver. Oliver was asleep in his favourite place – vastly heaped in the middle of the floor – with three feet stretched out and the fourth – the one with only three toes – laid alongside his boar's muzzle. Oliver was snoring like a small motorbike, jerking and twitching all over. *That means Cart was speaking to me!* Sally said, and hovered to a halt in the doorway. *Cart?* she said.

Cart plunged a pile of thick plates under the water and broke into a song. "I leaned my back up against an oak, thinking he was a trusty tree—" It sounded as if there was a cow in the kitchen, in considerable pain.

CART! said Sally.

"First he *bended* and then he *broke!*" howled Cart. Oliver began to stir.

Sally realised it was no good and went on into the sitting room, just as Fenella shut its door to keep out the sound of Cart singing. She brushed right by Fenella, feeling again the tingle of the field of life round a human body. But Fenella seemed to feel nothing. She turned away from Sally and went to crouch like a gnome in an old armchair. Imogen was still lying on the sofa. The room was hot and fuggy and dusty.

You both ought to go outside, Sally said disgustedly. *Or at least open a window.*

There was a desk and a coffee table and a bookcase in the room, each covered and crowded with papers. There were rings from coffee cups on all the papers, and dust on top of that. Sally could tell simply by hovering near that it was several months since any of the papers had been moved. That meant there was no point looking at them. The notion was very firm – though dim – in Sally's mind that, if there was a letter, it had not been written very long ago. She went over to try the papers on the piano.

It was the same story there. Dust lay, even and undisturbed, over each magazine and each old letter, and only slightly less thickly over a school report. This last term's, Sally saw from the date. "Name of pupil: Imogen Melford." A for English – A for almost everything except Maths. Imogen was disgustingly brilliant, Sally thought resentfully. A for Art too, which made a change. Only B for Music – which made a change also, a surprising one, considering Imogen's career. Underneath: "An excellent term's work. Imogen has worked well but still seems acutely unhappy. I would be grateful for an opportunity to discuss Imogen's future with Imogen's parents. B.A. Form Mistress."

But Imogen always seems unhappy! Sally said.

The papers on the treble end of the piano keys were actually browning with age. Nothing there. The picture – it *was* good – was more recent, but still slightly dusty. There was a film of scum on the water in the crookedly balanced paste-pot at the other end.

Here Sally noticed that Imogen had turned on the sofa to stare at her. Imogen's eyes were large and a curiously dark blue. They had a way of looking almost blank with, behind the blankness, something so keen and vivid that people often jumped when Imogen looked at them. Sally jumped now. They were, as she remembered agreeing with Cart, unquestionably the eyes of a genius.

Imogen? Sally said hopefully.

But it was the picture behind Sally that Imogen was staring at. "I like those brambles particularly," she said. "The stalks are just that deep crimson – brawny, I call them. They almost have muscles – tendons, anyway – and thorns like cats' claws."

"My self-portrait," Fenella said smugly.

"It's not a self-portrait. You didn't paint it," said Imogen. "And it makes you look too brown." She sighed. "I think I shall take up writing poetry." A large tear detached itself from the uppermost of her dark blue eyes and rolled down the hill of her cheek, beyond her nose.

"What are you grieving about now?" Fenella enquired.

"My utter incapacity!" said Imogen. A tear rolled out of her lower eye.

Imogen's grieving was so well known that Sally was bored before the second tear was on its way. There was going to be no letter down here. The place to look was the bedroom. She flitted to the stairs at the end of the room, as Fenella said, "Well, I won't interrupt you. I'm going to steal some tea."

Sally was halfway upstairs when the door was barged open under Fenella's hands. Oliver's huge blurred head appeared on a level with Fenella's face.

"Get out, Oliver," Imogen said, lying with a tear twinkling on either cheek.

Fenella pushed at Oliver's nose. "Go away. Imogen's grieving." Oliver took no notice. He simply shouldered Fenella aside and rolled into the room, growling lightly, like a heavy lorry in the distance. Where Oliver chose to go, Oliver went. He was too huge to stop. And he had detected that the peculiar Sally was here again. He shambled past Imogen to the foot of the stairs, alternating growls with whining.

"Sorry," Fenella said to Imogen, and went out.

Sally hung at the top of the stairs, looking down at Oliver. He filled the first four steps. She did not think he would come up any farther. Oliver was so heavy and misshapen that his feet hurt him most of the time. He did not like going upstairs. But she wished he would not behave like this. It was alarming.

"Imogen's grieving again," Fenella said to Cart in the kitchen.

"Damn," said Cart.

Sally gave Oliver what she hoped was a masterful look. *Go away.* The result was alarming. Oliver growled until Sally could feel the vibrations in the stairs. The hair on his back came pricking up. Sally had never seen that happen before. It was horrifying. He looked as big as a bear. Sally turned and fled to the bathroom, where Oliver's growls followed her but, to her relief, not Oliver himself.

The bathroom was in its usual mess, with a bright black line round the bath and dirty towels and slimy facecloths everywhere. Sally retreated from it in disgust, into the bedroom. Here, as seemed to keep happening, she found herself being startled by something she should have known as well as the back of her hand. *Perhaps it's because I haven't got a back to my hand at the moment*, she thought, trying to make a joke out of it.

The bedroom was airless and hot, from being up in the roof. It was the size of the kitchen and sitting room downstairs, with a bite out for the bathroom, but that space did not seem very big with four beds in it. Three of the beds were unmade, of course, with covers trailing over the floor. The fourth bed, Sally supposed, must be hers. It had a square, white, unfamiliar look. There was no personality about it at all.

Another reason why the room looked so small was that it was as high as it was long. Three black bending beams ran overhead. You could see they had all been cut from the same tree. The twists in them matched. Above them was a complex of dusty rafters, reaching into the peak of the roof, which was lined with greyish hardboard. Sally found herself knowing that this part, where they lived, was the oldest part of School House. It had been stables, long before the red buildings went up beside it. She also knew it was very cold in winter.

She turned her attention from the roof and found that the walls were covered with pictures. By this time, from under the floor, through the rumbles from Oliver, she could hear Cart in the sitting room. Cart was beginning on another unsuccessful attempt to stop Imogen grieving. "Now look, Imogen, it's not your fault you keep being turned out of the music rooms. You ought to explain to Miss Bailley."

Sally paid no attention, because she was so astonished by the number of pictures. There were pen and ink sketches, pencil drawings, crayoned scenes, water colours, poster paintings, stencils, prints – bad and wobbly, obviously done with potatoes – and even one or two oil paintings. The oil paints and the canvases, Sally knew guiltily, had been stolen from the school Art Room. Most of the rest were on typing paper pinched from the school office. But there were one or two paintings on good cartridge paper. That brought a dim memory to her of the row there had been about the typing paper and the oil paints. She remembered Himself roaring, "I shall have to pay for every hair of every paintbrush you little bitches have thieved!" Then afterwards came a memory of Phyllis, desperately tired and terribly sensible, saying, "Look, I shall give you a pound between you to *buy* some paper." A pound did not seem to buy much paper, by the look of it.

This was supposed to be an Exhibition. Sally discovered, round the bathroom corner, first a bell-push, labelled FOR EMERGENCY ONLY, and then a notice: THIS WAY TO THE EXHIBITION. The notice was signed "Sally". But Sally had not the slightest recollection of writing it. Why was that? After staring at it in perturbation for a minute, she thought that it must have been written very recently, perhaps just after the end of term – and it was always the things in the last few days she seemed to have the greatest difficulty in remembering.

She followed her own arrows round the walls, drifting through beds and a chair in order to look closely at the pictures. Cart had signed all hers with a flourishing "Charlotte". Imogen had signed some of hers neatly, "I. Melford", but not all. Sally could not tell which of the rest were Imogen's, or which were her own – if any. Then there were three signed "WH", including one of the oil paintings, and several labelled simply "N". N's pictures leapt off the page at you, even though N could not draw. There was a drawing of Oliver N had done, which was a bad drawing of a bad drawing. But it was Oliver to the life, in spite of it.

I simply don't remember any of these! Sally said. A view of the shop-cottage, unsigned. The dead elms, with blodgy rooks, also unsigned. A splendidly dismal dream-landscape by Cart. Cart went in for funereal fantasies: a coffin carried past a ruined castle in a black storm; cowled monks burying treasure; and a horrendous one of a grey, bulky maggot-like thing rising out of mist in a meadow. That one made Sally shudder and pass on quickly. Imogen, on the other hand, seemed to paint more strictly from life: flower studies, fields of wheat, and a careful drawing of the kitchen sink, piled full of thick crockery. That seemed very like Imogen. She could hear Imogen at that moment: "But I must face *facts*, Cart. It doesn't matter how unpleasant they are. I can't turn my back on reality."

"Why can't you?" Cart demanded. "It seems to me that enough facts come up out of life and hit you, without you going and facing all the other ones. Why can't you turn your back on a few?"

"Don't you see? It's a matter of Truth and Art!" Imogen declared. The strong note of hysteria was in her voice.

Sally signed and turned to the next picture in the row. And laughed. Oliver seemed to hear her. He rumbled hard from the bottom of the stairs. Sally was laughing too much to care. The picture was signed "And Fenella did just this one awful one". The picture was a terrible wicked jumble of everyone else's. N's badly drawn Oliver snuffled at Cart's cowled monk, who fled for protection past WH's spaceship to Imogen's sink piled with crockery, where — Sally found she remembered this one all right. It was a large, simpering Mother figure, stretching out both arms towards the sink.

She made tracings, the little beast! Sally said.

The Mother was the next painting. She was stretching out her arms, not to a sink, but to a fat simpering baby. Sally could remember painting this. And it was awful. It embarrassed her, it was so bad. The faces simpered, the colours were weak and bad, and the shapes were floppy and pointless. The Mother was like an aimless maggot with a pretty face on top. Sally could even remember the row she and Cart had had over it. "Oh leave it out, for goodness sake!" Cart had yelled. "It's fat and squishy! It's absolutely yuk!"

And Sally had yelled back, "You're the one who's yuk! You don't know a tender emotion when you see one. You're afraid of *feelings*, that's your trouble!" That was true in a way, about Cart. Cart's body may have been large and blurred, but she tried to keep her mind like a small walled garden. She would let no wild things in – though she was ready enough to let them out if it suited her. Sally's talk of tender emotions drove Cart wild at once.

"Don't give me that sentimental drivel!" she roared, and she had chased Sally round the bedroom, waving a coat-hanger.

Cart was saying much the same at the moment to the sobbing Imogen, though she said it in a kinder way. "Imogen, really, I do think you're working all this up out of nothing."

"No, I'm not! What good would a letter do? A letter, when my whole personality is at stake!" Imogen rang out dramatically.

Oh! said Sally. She had quite forgotten she was looking for a letter. It was awful the way her mind seemed to point to only one thing at once. It was like the narrow beam of a torch.

The obvious place to look was in the old bureau wedged in the corner. Its top had been cleared for the Exhibition and pictures propped on top of it. But it had four drawers below, one for each of them. Sally, of course, could not open the drawers, but that was not exactly a problem in her condition. She lowered herself at the bureau and pushed her face into the top drawer.

This drawer was Cart's. It was dark in there, but light came in through the keyhole – and through Sally – so that she could see. There was nothing to see. Cart had cleared the drawer out along with the top of the bureau. Sally remembered her doing it now. Cart had said, "I shall put away childish things."

"Pompous ass," said Fenella.

Nevertheless, Cart had thrown everything away – stamp collection, raffia, modelling clay, old drawings, the maps and lists of kings from her imaginary country, and the rude rhymes about her teachers – and had kept only schoolbooks. "I do O levels next year," she told the others. They felt the importance of that.

One exercise book of a childish nature had survived, however. That, when Sally moved her face down into the next drawer, was lying on top of the jumble of her own things. It was pale green and labelled *The Book of the Worship of Monigan*. It was there because Sally must have begged it off Cart. Sally wished vaguely that she remembered what was in it, but she could not, and there was no way she could think of to get it open. As for the rest of the things, Sally found herself exclaiming, *What on earth do I keep all this junk for?* If it had been possible, she would have done as Cart had and thrown the lot away. Pencils, rubbers and scissors she could see the use of, but why had she kept six broken necklaces and half a cardboard Easter egg? What was the pink seaside rock doing, stuck to somebody's old sock? Whose was the button carefully wrapped in tinfoil? And who wanted a collection of old hens' feathers?

Among all this, there was no sign of a letter. The only paper was a drawing she had done when she was six, now covered all over with the scores of a card game. A, N, J and S had played. J had won every game.

Sally sank lower still to push her face into Imogen's drawer. It was full of piano music, stuffed so full that Sally had trouble seeing more than the first layer. The lower she sank, the darker it became. But it was clear that this drawer was devoted to Imogen's career.

"My career," Imogen said at that moment, "is in ruins!"

"If that's what you call looking facts in the face," said Cart, "I'm going away."

"I don't think you believe in Truth," Imogen said reproachfully. At least she had stopped crying now.

"Rather hard not to, don't you think?" said Cart.

Typical of both of them, Sally thought. Cart, walling herself in, buttoning up, making a joke of things, refusing to let Imogen have feelings – though there was a case for it over Imogen, Sally had to admit. Imogen's feelings were vast and continuous.

Fenella's drawer was full of dolls, packed in a dirty jumble, and the remains of several dolls' tea-sets. Sally was a little touched. Fenella had, in a way, put away childish things too. She no longer played with dolls, even if she could not bear to throw them away. There was a piece of paper on top. "Poem," it said, "by Fenella Melford."

I have three ugly sisters
They really should be misters
They shout and scream and play the piano
I can never do anything I want.

The poem had been written at school. The teacher had written underneath, "A poem should be about your deeper feelings, Fenella." And Fenella had written under that: "*This is.*"

Nothing here, Sally said. She came out of the bureau and floated face down at floor level, staring at the worn-out pattern of the rug. It looked like Oliver's tufty coat, except that the pattern was in orange triangles. Imogen hated that rug. She said it offended her. Fenella called it the Rude Rug after that. There must *be* a letter. Sally was now quite sure there had been. She began floating to more her usual height, and stopped, with her torch-beam attention fixed on the wastepaper basket beside the bureau. It was stuffed and mounded with papers.

Ah! said Sally.

She dived towards it like a swimmer in her eagerness. And there, sticking sideways out of the top, was a sheet of blue writing paper with round, ragged writing on it which could well be hers.

"Dear Parents," she read. "When you find this I shall be far away from here."

There was no more, nothing but a doodled drawing of a face. Sally guessed she must have drawn it while she was thinking what else to say. Then of course she could not use that paper. The real letter must be elsewhere.

But where was I going? What was I doing? she wondered frantically.

Desperately, she pressed her face down among the other papers. Thank goodness! Here was another, on paper decorated with roses this time.

"Dear Parents, This is to inform you that I have taken..." Taken what? Sally wondered: the family jewels, a short holiday, leave of her senses? She had no idea. But here was more rosy paper.

"Dear Parents, Let me break this to you gently. I have decided, after much thought, that life here has little to offer me. I have..."

I think I was going to run away from home, Sally said. *But I don't think I had anywhere to go. Both grannies would send me back at once. Why didn't I say more? Oh, here's another one.*

"Dear Parents, My life is in ruins and also in danger. I must warn..."

Shaken, Sally withdrew her face from the basket and hovered like a swimmer treading water, staring at the papers. So there had been danger. That matched her feelings of an accident, though not her feeling that something had gone wrong. But what danger, and where from? And now she came to look, the whole top of the waste basket was packed with the same rosy writing paper. She must have used the whole packet, trying to explain whatever it was to Phyllis and Himself. Perhaps if she read every single one, together they would tell her what had happened. She plunged her face among the papers again.

But it was impossible; they were packed in so tightly, some sideways and some upside down, some rolled into balls, some torn in half, and all so mixed up with old drawings and things Cart had thrown out, that Sally's bodiless eyes could pick out hardly any of it. The ones she did see were only variations on the first four. And it got darker – too dark to read – more than four packed layers down. It was the merest luck that, when Sally was about to emerge from the basket and give up, her sight came up against a larger paper wedged upright against the side of the basket. At the top was her own writing – the now-familiar "Dear Parents" – but the next line was, to Sally's wonder, in writing that had to be Cart's. Cart's writing was neat and unmistakable.

"We think Sally has come to a sticky end."

Underneath that, the spiny writing with the angrily crossed Ts was surely Imogen's. Sally brought her face up, backed away, and drove in again, right through the basket and the papers, so that her non-eyes were right up against the paper. It was dim, yellowish gloom, nearly too dark to see.

"Her bed has not been slept in and we have not seen her since—" Imogen had written. It was too dark to see any more. All Sally could gather was that Cart's writing and Imogen's alternated, line by line, all down the page, from yellowish brown gloom to night black. Horribly frustrated, Sally backed out and hovered.

I am going to see that letter!

There was a deal of noise downstairs. Imogen had seemed calmed by Cart, but, in the irritating way it had, her grieving now sprang up again like a forest fire, loud and wild, in a new place.

"But don't you see, I may be using these difficulties as an *excuse* to hide the truth from myself! I'm hiding away behind them! I know I am!"

"Now Imogen," Cart said soothingly. "I think that's just tormenting yourself."

Oh shut up! Sally called out. *Imogen enjoys grieving. She doesn't need sympathy, she needs shaking. It's me that needs the sympathy!*

Furiously, she threw herself at the heaped wastepaper basket. She went right through, and found herself looking at the wallpaper beyond. But she was so determined that she backed away and threw herself forward again, and again, and again. She still went right through, but, ever so slightly, the basket rocked. The papers rattled and crunkled. *Oh good!* said Sally. She threw herself at it once more. There was such a rustling that Oliver started to growl again. But Sally knew she was making some impression. *If I try hard,* she said. *Trying does it. I am made of something after all. I'm not quite nothing. I'm probably made of the life stuff that was all round the boys. I shall think of myself like that.* Bash, slide, crunkle. Sally thought of herself as strong, crackling, flexible, forceful, and bashed forward again. Bash, crunkle, crunkle.

She had done it. Instead of going into the basket, she was bounced off from it. The basket, already swaying, swung sideways, tipped and fell heavily, sending a slither of paper out across the Rude Rug. Oliver's growls rose to sound like a small motorbike.

Imogen's voice, bloated and throaty with crying, said, "What was that?"

"There must be a mouse in the bedroom again," said Cart.

"Ugh!" said Imogen. "Send Oliver up."

"He won't go," said Cart. "Besides, he just makes friends with mice."

Sally was hovering, hovering, over the scattered papers. She had done it wrong. The vital letter was still in the basket, packed in by other papers, lying against the floor. And now she found she could not get in to read it. She had made herself so forceful that she kept bouncing off. She could get no further than the letter on top. Wait a minute! This top letter was in Fenella's writing.

"Dear Parents, We have killed Sally and desposed of the boddy. We thouhgt you ouhgt to know. You are neckst of kin. Love, Fenella."

What! said Sally. *They haven't. They didn't. They can't. So I did come back for revenge!*

Downstairs, Fenella herself had come in. "Oh, is Imogen still grieving? I nicked four buns for tea."

"You needn't have nicked one for Sally," said Cart.

No, you needn't, need you! Sally yelled out, unheard.

"I didn't. I need two myself," said Fenella. "Why is Oliver growling up the stairs like that?"

"There's a mouse up there," Imogen said, still throaty.

"I'll go up and catch it then," said Fenella.

Sally could not face this. Ever since she read the letter, anger and panic had been swelling in her. Now those feelings swept her away, dissolved her through the wall, then over the field, turning and twisting and hardly knowing where she went.

CHAPTER FOUR

The next hour or so was more like an unpleasant dream than ever. Sally found herself now here, now there, with very little knowledge of how she got to places or what happened in between. From the fact that everywhere she noticed was filled with the ringing mutter of boys, she thought she was mostly in school. First, she was among the smallest boys queuing up somewhere, each with a brown sticky bun in his hand. Next, she was in a dismal room, with grey ringing distances, in which two or three grey, dismal boys sat writing. Detention. Himself was there, grey as granite. He was sitting marking exercise books. Sally hovered round him, wondering if he was hating Detention as much as the boys did. He looked very grim. The way his hair bunched, iron grey, at the back of his head, put her in mind of the ruffled crest of an iron-grey eagle, brooding on a perch, with a chain on its leg.

"Please sir," said a dismal distant boy.

Himself said, without looking up. "What is it now, Perkins?" His hand, holding a red ballpoint pen, swiftly crossed out, and out. Wrote "See Me" in the margin.

"I need to pee, sir," said the boy.

"You went five minutes ago." Himself slapped that book shut. Slapped another in front of him. Slapped it open.

"I know, sir. I have a weak bladder, sir."

Himself crossed out, crossed out. Made a tick. "Very well." His eagle face lifted, and caught the boy half standing up. "You may be excused, Perkins, on the strict understanding that for every minute you spend out of this room, you spend half an hour in it. Off you go."

"Yes, sir." The boy hesitated and sat down again. He would have to go down two long corridors, and then come back up them, not counting the time in between. That was three hours more in Detention, even if he ran. He looked annoyed.

Himself lowered his beak and made three swift ticks. A slight moving under the iron skin of his face showed his satisfaction. He was enjoying himself. He loved detecting a try-on. Sally realised it, and realised she did not dare try to attract his attention just then.

A vague ringing while later, she was in a warm brown room, with thick brown lino on the floor. This room was provided with an iron bed, a white cupboard with a red cross on it, and a desk. Phyllis sat at the desk, dealing with a line of boys. She screwed back the top on a bottle and passed a small boy a pill. "There, Andrew. Are you still wheezing?"

The small boy put his head back, expanded his chest, and took several long croaking breaths. He seemed to be trying very hard to breathe.

Phyllis smiled kindly, an angel of judgement. "No wheeze," she said. "You needn't come again tomorrow, Andrew. Now Paul, how's that boil?"

A large boy with a red swelling by his mouth stepped up as Andrew dwindled away. Phyllis put up a kind cool hand and felt the boil. The tall boy winced.

"I think we'd better get the school doctor to look at that tomorrow," Phyllis said. "I'll give you a dressing if you wait. Now, Conrad. Let's have a look at your finger."

Mother was very busy just now, Sally realised guiltily. She must not try to interrupt her.

Later again, she found she was with Himself once more. He was sweeping down a corridor among a crowd of boys. One of them was carrying a metal detector.

"We're not going to use that again, Howard, unless we find ourselves in any doubt," Himself was saying. "Untold harm has been done to archaeology by wild metal detecting and wilder digging. We must behave responsibly. Are you sure you marked the place, Greer?"

A boy assured him that he had marked it. Himself swept on, talking eagerly. He was in his whirling mood, when his coat fluttered behind him like wings and seemed to catch up and carry people in the excitement of his progress. He looked younger like this, Sally thought tenderly.

"Who knows what it may be?" said Himself. "Possibly a cannonball. Unquestionably, School House was once the site of Mangan Manor, where Cromwell's army besieged the Royalist forces during the Civil War. We may have lighted on their camp. Yes," he said, as they thumped through a door, whirling Sally with them, "I plump for a cannonball as the most likely thing."

They were out in the gold-green of early evening. The playing field stretched towards faraway trees in faint white mist, flat as a lake, bright as water. The ringing mutter of School went suddenly distant.

"Neither can we rule out the possibility of something earlier," Himself continued, whirling out on to the flat green space. "Round here, we have some of the earliest British settlements — but I doubt if those would yield much metal. It's more likely to be metal from the Roman occupation. I must say I fancy finding a hoard of Roman coins. In which case it would be a treasure trove. Which boy knows the law about treasure troves?"

Sally paused. Once again, the wide open green space made her uncomfortable. In spite of the hurrying group, she was defenceless. She thought she might dissolve. Besides, Himself was still thoroughly busy.

"Of course," he was saying, as they whirled away from her, "we mustn't discount the possibility of a complete sell. It may be a cache of Coca-Cola tins."

Sally faded back into the ringing, muttering school. By now, there was a strong gusting of gravy from the kitchen. Phyllis was hurrying towards the kitchen with a lady wearing a white overall and a bent cigarette stuck to her lower lip.

"Well, you must do what you think best, Mrs Gill," Phyllis was saying. "Haven't we a tin of processed peas left that we could eke it out with?"

The bent cigarette wagged. "Those all went last week," said white-coated Mrs Gill. "Did you order more in, Mrs Melford? I can't see how I'm going to manage for the Disturbed Course without, if you didn't."

"I'll see to that tomorrow," said Phyllis. THUMP went the silver door behind them both, and a gust of gravy.

Still busy, Sally realised, hanging heavily in the corridor.

But they must notice me! she was saying to herself before long. *I must tell them I think I'm dead. I think it's important. It has to be more important than cannonballs and processed peas. They have a right to be worried about me.*

A battering bell shortly summoned battering feet and furious gusts of gravy to a high brown place full of tables. Sally was sucked in by the rush. And then hung quiet, because everyone hushed. Himself stood up to say, "For what we are about to receive, may the Lord make us truly thankful. Amen." Again he had a different manner, more like a priest. Himself's voice rolled out the few words like organ music. Chairs scraped. Cutlery clattered. Voices blared, and Phyllis and Himself were again immersed in talking to the boys at tables where they sat.

Sally became desperate. She tried battering herself, fluttering and hovering, first round Himself, then round Phyllis. *Look at me! Notice! It's Sally. It's Sally and I'm DEAD!*

"Would you care for some salt?" Himself asked Paul with the boil. Paul, looking shamefaced, hurriedly passed Mr Melford the salt.

Phyllis laughed. "Julian, tell Ned he can't do that. It's not possible."

I give up, Sally said. *No, I don't. They're bound to pop in and see how we are later on. I'll get them to notice me then. And until then I'm going to HAUNT my beastly sisters. I'm going to scare them thoroughly.*

On that thought, she shot back towards the green-covered door. Imogen was just going through the door too. She flung it wide as Sally arrived, and flung both herself and Sally through into the passage beyond. There, Imogen tripped on the ends of her yellow trousers and fell into the kitchen.

"What's up? Or rather down?" said Cart. She and Fenella were standing, looking expectant, beside the kitchen table. There were three places laid on it.

Imogen heaved herself up on to her elbows. "Oh nothing," she said bitterly. "They've forgotten to leave us any supper again. That's all."

There was silence. Imogen lay there, Cart and Fenella stood, looking depressed. None of them behaved as if this was unexpected. Indeed, Sally knew it was not. It happened fairly often. *I don't think I'll start haunting them just yet,* she decided. She knew too well how they were feeling.

Below her, Imogen's eyes bulged waterily. "This is the last straw," she said. Her voice croaked. "I think I shall simply starve and die."

Cart and Fenella leapt towards Imogen and hauled her off the floor. "Oh, Imogen, don't cry *again*," Cart said. "The rest of us have to listen to you."

Fenella said, with menace, "*I'll* go to the kitchen." Sally had expected that. It was usually Fenella who went to deal with School for them. Since Sally felt she had had enough of Imogen grieving that afternoon, she went with Fenella. Fenella marched down the passage, swung wide the green door and marched to the silver door. THUMP. Fenella let the silver door swing shut behind her and stood meaningly, waiting to be noticed.

School kitchen was a hot vista of gravy steam, white enamel, shiny taps and greasy black floor. Three white-coated ladies were standing in the steam by the serving hatch. They had finished their own supper, as the three plates covered with scraped gravy on the table showed, and were drinking out of thick white cups. They were laughing loudly and did not notice the thump of the door. Nevertheless, Fenella did not move. She did not do anything that Sally could see, but, somehow, she became steadily more and more noticeable. Her green sack became shriller, her buck teeth seemed to grow larger and her whole self, with its wriggly dark hair and insect knees, shortly seemed to fill the whole end of the kitchen, vengeful and brooding and waiting. Sally much admired this. It was a gift Fenella had.

Two seconds later, Mrs Gill's bent cigarette turned that way irritably. "You," she said, "have been told often enough not to come in here bothering us when we're working."

Fenella simply stood and looked at her.

"I shall tell your mother," said Mrs Gill. She put down her cup and ran at a saucepan of steaming custard, which she shook vigorously, to show how busy she was.

Fenella spoke, deep and loud. "I came," she said. Really, Sally thought, it was as if Fenella was doing the haunting and not Sally at all. "I came because we haven't got any supper again."

"Well, there's no need to look at me like that!" Mrs Gill retorted. "I've got enough to do without running after four great girls that ought to be able to look after themselves. You've got a kitchen in there. You ought to cook for yourselves. When I was your age——"

Icily, Fenella cut through this. "There isn't a cooker in our kitchen."

"Then there should be!" Mrs Gill said, scoring a triumph. "Your mother should ask for one to be put in, and then——"

"Our supper is paid for," said Fenella. "Tonight."

"I can't help that!" shrilled Mrs Gill. "It's none of my business who pays for what. I'm only the cook here. And how your mother expects me to manage on the provisions I get, I just don't know!"

The other ladies, looking nervously at Fenella's brooding face, seemed to feel Mrs Gill needed support.

"There wasn't hardly enough meat to go round, dear," said one.

"And the veg was off. We had to eke out with frozen," said the other.

Fenella smiled at them. It was a ghastly sight. It was as if her face had split open. "Never mind. You'll both be interviewed on television when we die of starvation."

The two looked at one another. Fancy!

"Oh all right!" snapped Mrs Gill. "I'll see what's left in the fridge. You'll find some bread and some cheese in that cupboard. And I can spare some custard."

Mrs Gill flounced to the cupboards and the fridge and clattered out bowls and plates. Fenella stood silently by, accepting everything Mrs Gill offered. She accepted twice as much as there would have been in the ordinary way, and a bowl of custard. Shortly, her skinny arms were braced round almost more food than she could carry.

"Thank you," she said at last. It was royal.

"I don't know why your sister can't carry some of it," Mrs Gill said fretfully, heaving the custard saucepan off the stove. "She's twice the size you are."

Fenella's chin was lowered to keep a block of cheese in place. She gave Mrs Gill a quick, shrewd look from under her knotted hair. "If you mean Sally," she said, "she's dead."

Mrs Gill's mouth opened, with the cigarette stuck to its lower lip. She spun round, holding the saucepan. She looked straight at Sally, hovering at Fenella's side. Her open mouth stiffened, until it went almost square. She screamed, "AHA-aaaaa-a-a-a!" a long fading scream, like someone falling off a cliff, and dropped the saucepan. Custard flew. It went in yellow dollops and strong gouts, through Sally, across Fenella's insect legs, and along the kitchen floor right up to the silver door. The other two ladies screamed as well, at the sight of it.

"Oh dear," Fenella said briskly. "What a pity." She turned and picked her way, slithering a little in the river of custard, to the door. She pushed through the door. THUMP. Sally dived after her.

Mrs Gill broke out screaming again behind the door. *"Oh look at that! It went through the door! Did you seeeee? It went throoooough!"*

She was clearly audible beyond the green door as Fenella eased herself and her armful of food carefully through that. Imogen and Cart sped to meet her.

"Oh good!" said Cart, seeing the food. "What's that noise?"

"Fenella, you are clever," said Imogen. "Who's screaming?"

"Mrs Gill," said Fenella. "She's covered me in custard. I think she must be psychic."

"What do you mean?" asked her sisters.

"Psychiatric then," said Fenella, who was never sure about difficult words. "Physical. You know." She went carefully to the table and eased her armful down on it. Cart caught a skidding bowl full of tinned tomatoes. Imogen caught the block of cheese as it toppled from under Fenella's chin.

"Yes, but what *happened?*" they demanded.

"She thought Sally was with me," said Fenella.

Neither Cart nor Imogen showed the slightest sign of guilt. They laughed. Cart heartily, Imogen waterily. "But Sally's not here! What do you mean, Fenella?"

Fenella never explained anything properly. She had once told Sally she didn't know how. She peeled a slice of corned beef off a cold fried egg and did her best. "She thought Sally was a ghost and threw custard all over the floor."

This puzzled Imogen. "I didn't know you got rid of ghosts with custard."

Cart was puzzled too. "But Sally can't be a ghost."

"Can't she?" asked Fenella. "Look at Oliver."

The smell of food had roused Oliver, and he had woken to discover Sally here again. He heaved up rumbling, and dribbling a little, and waltzed towards the table, looking rather menacing. *He can't bite me, even if he tried*, Sally said uneasily.

"He walks just like a camel," said Imogen. "He swings his legs out sideways."

"That's his deformity," said Cart. "I think he's just hungry."

"Doting fool!" said Fenella.

Oliver took advantage of the situation to pass his nose across the table and work his magnetising trick again. After an almost unnoticeable pause for swallowing, he was growling again.

"It's not fair," said Fenella. "Cold fried eggs are almost the only thing I like!"

Cart pushed Oliver's nose away and began sorting out what food he could eat. She had to supplement cold roast potatoes and tinned tomatoes with four tins of dog food. Oliver took a lot of feeding. When Cart dumped the plates down on the floor for him, it seemed to reconcile Oliver somewhat to Sally's peculiar presence. His growling subsided. The tail end of him swayed sedately, while the blurred fore end bent busily to pushing the plates around the floor. The other three settled to supper. Sally watched wistfully. She did not exactly feel hungry, but it would have been nice to eat something too, for company. And it did irritate her, the way Fenella, after picking at everything on the table, refused to eat anything but cold baked beans.

No wonder your stomach sticks out so! Sally said to Fenella. *You're like a starved savage in a famine poster!* Savage indeed. She recalled Fenella worshipping Monigan, and Fenella's letter: "Dear Parents, We have killed Sally…" *I think I shall start haunting you now,* Sally announced.

There was, Sally knew, a kind of ghost which threw things about. After her success with the wastepaper basket, she was sure she could do that. She reached for the salt cellar. To her surprise and exasperation, nothing happened. She reached for it again. Still nothing. She could make no impression on it at all. She could not seem even to move Imogen's handkerchief, which Imogen had prudently crumpled beside her plate in case she cried again.

Oh bother! Sally cried out. *I've forgotten how!* Oliver responded to that with a sudden growl. He seemed to have resigned himself to Sally, but he did not like her shouting. *I hate you all!* Sally shouted, and flounced off, bobbing and whirling, to perch on the draining board.

"You know," remarked Cart, "if Sally was here, she'd just have got to the part where she shouts out that she hates us all."

Sally glowered at Cart from the draining board. *You wait*, she said. *People can see me. Mrs Gill did. And I can move things. Just wait till Mother and Himself come in, and then I'll shrivel you all with guilt!*

She was certain both parents would come and see them as soon as School was over for the evening. Hopefully, she watched the big wall clock for nearly an hour. There was a bell, and distant shrill bustling from School. *Now*, she thought.

However, no parents appeared. Sally had to move from the draining board then, because Imogen cleared the table. Even bodiless, Sally did not fancy sitting on dirty dishes. She thought it might be a hopeful sign that Imogen was clearing up. Himself got very irritable if he saw the mess they lived in. But Imogen was not behaving as if she was expecting Himself. None of the sisters was. Imogen was tidying in a vexed, restless way, as if she felt more grieving coming on. Cart was reading. Fenella was lying on her bulging stomach under the table, spitting chewed-up pieces of paper at Cart's feet. She missed every time.

The latch of the outside door clacked. Sally sprang up. So did Oliver. Imogen turned round from the sink, and Cart laid down her book.

"Hallo," Cart said cheerfully. "Come on in."

Ned Jenkins slid round the door, clutching a paper bag, grinning rather guiltily. "We brought the jar of coffee," he said. "Have you any spare food?"

"Because," said Will Howard, sliding in after Ned, "there was practically nothing for supper again and we're starving."

"Drat you!" Fenella exclaimed from under the table.

"Why?" asked Ned Jenkins, bending down to look at her.

Fenella looked accusingly up at him. "You made me jump, opening the door, and I swallowed the piece of paper I was chewing."

"Paper doesn't kill you," said Ned Jenkins.

"Yes, it does," Howard said cheerfully. "It wraps itself round your appendix and you die in agonies."

Fenella gave him the look which had defeated Mrs Gill. It had no effect on Will Howard at all. "How many more of you are coming?" she said witheringly. "I'm not going to chew any more paper until you've all arrived."

"Stinker's up to his ears in Physics," Ned said, rubbing Oliver's back with his paper bag. "Greer, Wrenn and Shepperson are all prancing around in wire helmets, waving swords. And Howard told Nutty Filbert we weren't coming here tonight——"

"Why?" said Fenella.

"Because Filbert's mad," Howard said blandly.

"But we're pleased to see you two," Imogen said kindly.

She said it so grandly that Howard bent down under the table and whispered to Fenella, "Is your sister saying Hallo, or is she letting me know my socks smell?"

"You *are* stupid!" said Fenella.

Ned Jenkins said awkwardly, "Julian's coming. He went to scrounge some buns from Perry's."

Cart turned round from plugging in the electric kettle, beaming. Sally could see this was good news to her. "Let's have that coffee here," she said. "I saved enough milk, I think."

"I brought some powdered milk too," said Ned. "By the way, where's Sally?"

"Gone to visit a friend," Fenella said, grinning up at him from under the table. She looked like a green goblin in a cave.

CHAPTER FIVE

This was another thing Sally had forgotten, it seemed — these almost nightly visits of the boys. She watched Imogen stumbling over her trouser legs to draw the curtains, even though it was not dark yet. Nobody switched on the light until the windows were covered, because the boys were here quite illegally. Will and Ned both had a slightly guilty look and kept grinning at one another like conspirators, while Cart stirred mugs of coffee and Fenella, with great dignity, crawled out from under the table. Everyone settled round the table with their mugs.

Now Sally knew who did the pictures signed WH and N. The spaceships were Howard's, of course. And it was no wonder Ned Jenkins had done his surprisingly good bad drawing of Oliver. He really liked him. Oliver was rolling amiably and hugely from person to person, joining in the sociability, but he kept returning to Ned. Ned rubbed his back energetically each time, as if he was scrubbing a hearth rug, and chuckled.

"That dog is so ridiculously huge that I have to laugh every time I look at him," he said.

"I know. Something went wrong with his genes and he turned out nearly twice as big as he should be," Cart said. "He ought to have been an Irish wolfhound really."

"You've told him that before," said Fenella. "Why is Filbert mad?"

"He thinks he's got two heads," said Will Howard. Everybody looked incredulous, even Imogen, who did not care for coffee much and was not being very interested in anything. "Really," Howard assured them. "Stinker started it yesterday. 'Nutty,' he said, with an absolutely straight face, 'Nutty, we think you may not have noticed your other head. We thought we ought to tell you, because you forgot to comb its hair. It looks a sight.' And Nutty says, 'What do you mean? I haven't got another head.' 'Oh yes you have,' says Stinker. 'You mean you've gone all these years and not noticed!' And Nutty said, all puzzled, 'If I'd got two heads, I'd have seen them in the mirror, wouldn't I?' 'Oh no,' says Stinker. 'The one behind's behind the one in front, you see.' And Nutty, being Nutty, believes him! Ever since then, he's been turning round suddenly about once a minute, trying to catch a glimpse of his other head before it dodges out of sight. Honestly – I swear it!"

"Boys are all mad," said Fenella.

"Ah," said Howard. "Is that so? Girls only do sane things like lying under tables eating paper, don't they?"

There was silence, while Fenella turned her most phenomenal glower on him. Out of it, Imogen said violently, "I think that's a very cruel and barbarous story!"

The silence deepened uncomfortably. Imogen would not look at anyone. She sat leaning forward stiffly in her chair, with her head bent at an odd, listening angle, staring into her mug of coffee. Sally found herself saying, *Imogen really is terribly unhappy!* Imogen's face, with its strong angel features, was somehow bloated from behind, with tears she was waiting to cry. The boys could see it too. They could not understand it, and it embarrassed them. Sally wondered, *Is that how Imogen would look if she knew I was dead?*

"Fiddle-di-dee, Imo!" Howard said, forcing the natural expression of cheerfulness back to his face. "I'll tell him tomorrow it was only a joke." Imogen did not answer. She just sat, leaning and bloated. "I promise," Howard said. When Imogen still would not answer or even look at him, he leant back with an artificial sigh of pleasure and gazed round the kitchen. "I do like a taste of home life!"

Though that sounded sarcastic just at that moment, Sally knew Howard meant it. He was trying, in the only way he could think of, to remind Imogen he was grateful to her. Imogen had started the visits of the boys. One day, two years ago now – Sally thought it was – Imogen had discovered a homesick new boy crying in the hedge between the school garden and the orchard. It was Howard, of all people. Though he was a year older than she was, he had inspired Imogen to mother him. She had brought him into the kitchen and fed him cups of tea mixed with condensed milk stolen from Mrs Gill's cupboard, until Howard felt better. Howard came back the next day, and the next, and, when he made friends, he brought his friends. They had worn a well-beaten secret path down the middle of the orchard hedge.

The latch of the door clicked again, and everything changed except Imogen's misery. Julian Addiman strode in laughing and dumped a bag of buns on the table.

"Two nicked, one sponged, and three paid for," he said. "How's that?"

"Brilliant!" said Cart.

"Out of character. What made you *pay* for three?" said Howard.

"I only promised him the money," Julian said.

"Then I let you off," said Howard. "Hey! They're jam doughnuts! My favourite!"

"Perry's House have doughnuts every Tuesday," said Julian. "Why do you think I went there? You can trust your Uncle Julian, you know. He thinks of everything."

"Keep the bag away from Oliver!" Cart shouted, banging up from her chair to turn the kettle on again. Oliver's blurred nose was sweeping in over Ned's shoulder to work its magnetising trick on a doughnut or so. Julian and Fenella plunged on the bag, both laughing, and shoved it out of reach. But Ned seemed to have worked Oliver's magnetising trick for him. Sally saw him pass Oliver a jammy lump over his shoulder, smiling secretively. What an odd boy Ned Jenkins was. You would never catch Julian Addiman being that secretive, nor making faces and jerking an arm, like Ned had been doing in the garden.

Sally had forgotten Julian Addiman completely until now. She wondered how she could. He was dark and striking-looking, with brows as black as Fenella's and eyes nearly as blue and luminous as Imogen's, and he had a wide, curiously red mouth, which looked as if it was laughing all the time. Julian Addiman laughed a lot. But what people noticed most about him was that, wherever he was, he took control. He was not bossy. Nor was it the fact that he was a fifth former and older even than Cart. It was just that when Julian Addiman was there things ran Julian Addiman's way.

He took control now, in the easiest possible way. Ned moved his seat, Oliver was pushed out of the way and Julian Addiman sat down with a mug of coffee, next to Cart and facing Fenella. He looked at Fenella and laughed. There was nothing particular to it, but Sally found herself staring at Julian Addiman and feeling very strange. Everything seemed to quiver when she looked at him, as if she was about to be swept away by panic again. It seemed almost as if she was terrified of Julian Addiman.

"Fenella," said Julian, "do my eyes deceive me, or have you tied your hair in two granny-knots, one over each eye?"

"I've been dying to ask that too," said Howard, "but I wasn't sure it was polite."

Fenella sat up haughtily. "It keeps the hair out of my eyes. But, if you must know, it's part of the Plan."

"Nature's Holy Plan?" asked Howard. "Or something else?"

"A Plan we devised to shake our parents up a bit," Cart explained. "We wanted to prove to them — and to Sally too, actually — that they wouldn't notice if — if something awful happened to one of us."

"If one of us *died!*" Imogen said savagely, without looking up.

"I'm going to time how long it takes them to notice my knots," Fenella explained. "If they haven't noticed by Christmas I shall fall seriously ill instead."

"How are you going to do that? Drink poison?" Julian Addiman asked, laughing.

Fenella sat up even haughtier. "I don't need to do anything so crude," she said, lifting her chin. "I shall just lie in bed and groan and think pale."

"Pretend to be ill then, you mean?" Ned suggested.

Fenella was genuinely scandalised. "It's not pretending! When I'm ill, Mrs Gill has to bring me dinner, and she scolds me for being ill when she's so busy. She says it's only psychological. That means in your mind. And if I think pale, that's in my mind like a real illness, isn't it?"

"I still call that pretending," said Ned.

Howard was looking unhappy. "You don't know," he said, "how lucky you are to have so much independence. I wish I had."

"It's all right for *you!*" Imogen said fiercely. "You just come along in the evenings and enjoy yourself. You don't have to live with it."

Julian Addiman was finding this boring. Sally could see him shifting about, even though she was avoiding looking at him. She did not like the feeling he gave her. "Oh come on," he said impatiently. "When are we going to start the séance?"

Séance? said Sally. And at that, the whole room, the electric light, the faces, the furniture, and the bulk of Oliver asleep by Ned's feet began to shake and quiver apart for Sally. *This is wrong!* she said. *There's been an accident!* Everything she could see was falling into upright, waving strands, as if she were looking through a bead curtain. Voices were filmy threads in a different dimension. Something very terrifying and grey and formless was appearing in the space behind the threads. Sally was so much afraid of the formless thing that she clung with all her might to the waving, stranding, fraying kitchen. She heard Ned and Howard, in distant voices like filaments, protesting that spiritualism was "a load of crap" and Julian Addiman replying, in another strand of sound, "I thought that's what we came for."

No it wasn't. It was something else I came for, Sally said.

And she clung again to the threads, as they threatened to billow apart and leave her with the formless thing; Cart, she noticed, evidently knew all about the proposed séance. She bounced up – Cart was so clumsy that two chairs spun about as she went, twirling from thread to thread as they moved – and fetched a set of Scrabble letters, which she dumped on the table with a thick glass tumbler. Howard's otter face, swaying like water-weed, examined the letters nervously. Ned and Fenella began picking out an alphabet from them, and Cart wavered across half the threads like a blue bolster, to put the alphabet in a ring in the middle of the table.

The thread of Julian Addiman's voice said something. Cart turned and smiled at him. Sally saw, with what seemed to be a sense of enormous relief, that Cart was keen on Julian Addiman. A formless face like Cart's, swaying and billowing from thread to thread, ought to have had no shape at all just then. Yet, because of the way she felt about Julian Addiman, Cart's face showed more firm and angelic than Imogen's, whose face was destroyed by misery. But Julian Addiman had been pointing out something wrong. The table was sticky. Cart moved all the letters and bent over, a blue bolster again, rubbing the table hard with a cloth. Julian Addiman's hand swung casually out and came down on the bolster's rear. SMACK.

Sally jolted. The threads drew firmly back into place and the kitchen, with everything in it, was solid again. There was an uncomfortable silence in it. Everyone was sitting and standing like a tableau, except for Oliver, who was heaving himself to his feet and looking enquiringly at Cart's too-pink face.

Imogen scraped back her chair and stood up. "Are you quite settled on this stupid séance?" she asked. Nobody answered. They were trying to move their attention from Cart and Julian to Imogen. "Very well," said Imogen. She was speaking in a hard, hacking gabble, by which Sally knew she was very angry. "I'm not doing it! I think it's stupid, mean-minded and vicious. It's playing with something nobody understands. It's — it's immoral!"

"It doesn't do any harm!" Julian Addiman exclaimed. "It's only for fun."

"You've no business doing a thing like that for fun!" Imogen snapped.

"So you're not doing it?" said Julian.

"No," said Imogen. She took up her mauve beads in a trembling hand and bit them. "Nobody must do it."

Julian Addiman gave Cart an exasperated look. Cart said wearily, "Imogen's always been like this. The first words she ever spoke were" — Cart put on a squeaky, jeering voice — "I'm not play-ying!"

Sally found herself swooping towards the table. *Cart, that was thoroughly unkind! How dare you hurt Imogen just to please Julian Addiman!* Of course, no one heard her except Oliver. He growled.

"Look, if we get a ghost," Ned said diplomatically, "and it spells something out, we're going to need someone to write it down. Couldn't Imogen do that?"

"Yes, Imogen," Cart said unkindly. "Do that or go away."

Imogen bit her beads, not knowing what to do.

Julian Addiman laughed. "She'd better go. The presence of an unbeliever could be fatal."

"I'll stay and write it down," Imogen said defiantly, which was what Julian Addiman had intended her to do. Sally could see it in his face.

I can't think how I ever liked you! she said to Julian, and Oliver growled again.

"Calm down," Ned said to Oliver. "What do we do, Julian?"

"Everyone sits round and puts one finger on this glass," Cart said briskly. "After a bit, it should start to move. Then we ask it things and it spells out the answers."

"I *don't* think!" said Howard. "I'm another unbeliever in your midst. Shouldn't we turn out the light?"

"Stupid! How do we see the letters?" asked Fenella.

Sally hovered over the table, above the bent tops of five heads and five arms stretching star-shaped out to rest a finger on the glass. This was decidedly where she did some haunting. The first thing she would do was to give Cart a piece of her mind, she thought, looking at Imogen, sitting bowed over a pad just beyond the table. Slowly, a little fearfully, Sally descended towards the fingers and the glass.

"What happens if your parents come in?" Julian Addiman laughed.

Everyone's arms at once went tense. Even if Sally had had the strength to move the glass against their five stiff arms, she could not have gone near it. Their nervousness crackled in the field of life round their fingers. It was like an electric shock. Sally bounced up from it with a yelp. The rumbling of Oliver vibrated the letters on the table.

"They never do come in," said Imogen beyond the circle.

Nonsense, said Sally. *Of course they do. It would serve you all right if they came this moment!*

"Cool it, everyone," said Cart. Her face was still firm and glowing with her feelings about Julian Addiman. "Nothing's going to happen unless we all relax. Sit quiet. Somebody tell a silly story or say something interesting."

"The ghost of marmalade," Ned Jenkins said suddenly. "There was a rhyme when I was a kid, see. I think it went 'I am the ghost of Able Mabel, This parrot cage goes on the table,' but I didn't know what it was about. I thought it said 'the ghost of marmalade'."

This caused a mystified silence. Sally nervously descended. The glass, in the middle of the fingers, was quite bearable to touch now. She gave it an experimental shove. Her hand – or what seemed to be her hand – went down inside it, in the midst of five sizzling, living fingers. It was like being inside a gas-ring. But this gas-ring was fixed in place by five stiff arms and would not move.

"Just what does that mean?" Howard said to Jenkins.

"I was thinking of the sticky table," Ned said apologetically.

"Were you indeed?" said Howard. "Now I'll tell you something really interesting. You know, don't you, that I'm the proud possessor of a metal detector? Usually I use it to go round picnic places on the Downs, and you'd be surprised how much money people lose there. Now, today at lunchtime, Greer borrows my metal detector, just for kicks, and goes pottering off with it along the trees across the playing field. And the thing shouts at him. There was obviously a whole heap of metal hidden in the ground there."

Sally felt the glass sliding gently away with her. *Help! There's a ghost!* she exclaimed, and nearly snatched herself away from it. Then she realised that the muscles were slyly flexing in the longest arm. Julian Addiman's finger was fizzing just a little harder than the others, and that finger was bearing the glass softly sideways.

No you don't! said Sally, and pulled against the finger. Between them, she and Julian brought the glass to a trembling standstill. The smile which had been curling Julian Addiman's red mouth faded to a look of surprise.

"It's moving!" Ned whispered.

"Take no notice," Fenella said reprovingly. "You were saying, Will?"

Howard's eyes were very round and fixed on the glass, but he went on. "Well, Greer knew he'd found something big, but, being a prat, he doesn't dig it up himself or even tell me. No. He reports it to Himself. And Himself steams off there this evening with all of us and tells us we may have found a hoard of Roman coins."

I see how to do it, said Sally. *You have to brace yourself against the fingers. The fizzing-thing round them is quite good for pushing at. Here goes!* She heaved the glass over in the direction of C, meaning to begin on Cart.

"And was it a Roman hoard?" Cart asked breathlessly, as the glass stirred.

"No," Howard said distractedly, mesmerised by the glass. "I mean I don't know. Himself forgot to bring anything to dig with."

"It's definitely moving," said Ned. It was. Sally was exerting all the force she had. And still the glass only crept.

"Here's where we ask," said Julian Addiman. His eyes were glowing with excitement, very blue, and so luminous that they looked odd. He said, very loudly and precisely, "Is there anybody there? Move to Y for Yes if there is."

"And N for No if there isn't," murmured Ned.

If you insist, said Sally. She looked over her non-existent shoulder and found the Y. It took a mighty heave. The five arms were not ready to give way at all. Then they did, and the glass slid with a rush.

"Z," said Julian Addiman. "Got that, Imogen? I think we take it that means Yes. Put Y-query. This really is working, isn't it?" He spoke loudly and precisely again. "Would you spell your name please."

If you say so, said Sally. *I wish I knew the alphabet better.* She stared round in search of the S.

"It's stopped," said Fenella, bitterly disappointed.

"SHSH!" said the others.

The S was not far from the Z, of course. Sally dragged the glass round there.

"S," said Julian Addiman. "Next letter please," he added loudly.

All right, snapped Sally. *I'm doing my best. This is hard work.* Heave on the fizzing fingers and heave. They had the idea now. The arms were yielding more easily. She heaved towards the other end of the alphabet. And stopped. *How do I spell my name, anyway? A vowel next. There's one.*

"E," said Julian Addiman. "Next letter please."

The next part was no one's fault exactly. It was simply that excitement seized them all, Sally included. She was really communicating! It was the best thing that had happened all day. When she pushed the glass, the arms yielded swiftly, readily — too readily. She had been aiming for the L. *Never mind. There's two Ls in Sally. Bother — missed again! They're letting it go too hard. Ah, got it. Now I know the rest. There, there, there.* Exhausted, Sally pulled away from the ring of fingers and hovered towards the ceiling. *Wow, that was hard work!* The five round the table took their fingers off the glass and rubbed aching elbows, almost equally exhausted.

"Imogen, can you read that back?" Julian Addiman said, puzzled.

Imogen's voice shook. "S-E-M-O-L-I-N-A," she said. Then she gave a squawk of laughter and covered her face with the pad.

"It's a ghost called Pudding," said Fenella.

"Ask them to spell it again," Ned said urgently.

"Yes, do," Howard said, catching the urgency. Sally could actually feel the surge of worry coming from them both. It piled upward out of them like smoke from a bonfire.

"Why?" said Cart. "Oh, we might as well, but it seems to have gone dead." She shoved the glass with her finger and nearly toppled it over.

"See if it will come back again," said Ned. "Howard and I will if you don't want to."

Ned Jenkins and Will Howard looked at one another. Both of them put their fingers back on the glass.

"What's the fuss?" said Julian Addiman. "We've got a ghost with a strange sense of humour, that's all."

Cart and Fenella put their fingers to the glass again. Julian Addiman sighed and did the same, with a flourish.

"There," he said. Then, loudly, "Spell your name again, please."

Oh, very well! said Sally. *You're trying to bore me, aren't you? But it's the only way I've got to talk to you, so I'll have to do it.* She descended once again and pushed her non-fist into the gentle heat of the gas-ring of fingers.

"Ah!" said Julian Addiman, and his eyes glared laughing excitement. Ned and Will, however, were entirely serious. Their eyes flickered nervously to each letter in the circle as the glass trundled off towards it. This time, it was easier. Sally was getting to know where the letters were. The others were ready for the movement of the glass when it came, and there was less excitement to interfere. With very little trouble, Sally spelled out S-A-L-L-Y.

"I thought so!" said Ned, and Cart burst out, "It can't be! It must be some other Sally!"

"Everyone in School House calls your Sally Semolina," said Howard. "Because of her being Selina."

"I tell you it *can't* be!" Cart said vehemently. "Our Sally's all right! She's just gone to stay with Audrey Chambers – just up the hill."

This was news to Sally. She stared at Cart to see if she was telling the truth. She seemed to be. Cart was a bad liar. Then she stared at Fenella, as Fenella said, "But don't tell anyone. That's the other part of the Plan." Fenella was a good liar. There was no way to tell if this was the truth or not. Sally turned to Imogen, as Imogen added, "We hope the parents will think she's dead, or kidnapped – if they notice at all, that is." Imogen was a rotten liar. This was obviously the truth.

Then what's going on then? Sally cried out.

"Come on," said Ned. "Before it goes away again." He spoke clearly to the air in front of him. "Prove to us that you're Sally Melford."

"By saying something we know only you could know," Howard added.

Sally could think of one thing — only one. It seemed a pity it was going to embarrass Howard, but she had to make them sure. She heaved on the fizzing space between the fingers again. *Where's the H? Down that side.* The glass travelled easily to H to O to W, but after that Sally lost her way again. She stopped beside the W, looking at everyone's intent faces, wondering where she was supposed to be taking the glass next. Nobody spoke. Somebody breathed heavily. Beyond Cart and Ned, Imogen sat bowed towards the pad of paper, pencil ready, still with that odd listening look. Again Sally was struck with how miserable Imogen was. She was supposed to be talking about Howard and Imogen, of course. *Where was the I now?*

"I-M-O," everyone murmured as the glass slid. Sally was rather put off her stride by it. When people spell a thing out as you write it, you feel you have to hurry to provide them with the next letter. *Hurry!* thought Sally. *What comes after Imo? Obvious, really.* "G-R-I-V-I-E-N-G," everyone murmured. Sally paused, rather pleased she had remembered to put the E in grieving. It was so easy to get lost between letters.

"That doesn't prove much," Howard murmured to Ned. They both seemed disappointed, but oddly relieved at the same time.

That reminded her. *Oh, this is bothersome!* She set the glass trundling again. W-L-L — there should have been an I in that, but too late now. H-O-M-S-J — *Bother! Missed!* — K-I-N-H-E-D-G-I-M-O-G—

"Oh, good gracious!" Imogen shrieked, jumping up. "It really *is* Sally!"

Sally hovered, resting from her labours, watching two round heavy tears roll across Imogen's cheeks. Howard's otter face glowed dark pink.

"Why is it Sally?" Julian Addiman asked, leaning back and stretching. "What's Homsjkin? Somewhere in Holland?"

Cart explained, "Imogen found Will being homesick in the hedge. But Imogen—" Julian Addiman looked round at Howard and chuckled, not kindly.

Imogen clenched her hands and dug the air with her elbows for emphasis. "I *know* it's Sally! She's reminding me about Will *and* she's worrying about me. That's just Sally all over!" She spoke to the air above Julian Addiman's head. "It's all right, Sally. You mustn't worry about me. You tell us what's the matter with you. Move up, Cart. I'm sure she'll find it easier to talk if I'm holding the glass too." And Imogen thrust Cart sideways to plunge one of her fingers down on the glass. "Now, Sally," she said. "Tell me all about it."

Sally was touched. Another tear was trickling down Imogen's face. All the same, she was a trifle annoyed. She had not meant to ask about Imogen, and she did wish everyone would not speak to her so loudly and slowly, as if ghosts were deaf or very stupid.

"It's not moving," said Ned.

"It was a mischievous ghost playing a trick, I expect," said Fenella.

Shut up, Fenella, said Sally. *Here we go again, then.* Imogen's finger made the glass harder to push, not easier. Sally put her whole force into it and heaved. The trouble was, she thought as she heaved, she could not tell Imogen all about it because she did not know herself. It seemed easiest to ask a question. A-M, spelled Sally, with great effort, M-*no*-J-*no*-N – *Oh I give up!* – D-E-A-D.

She was thoroughly startled by the effect this had. Cart, Will and Ned jumped up beside Imogen. At least two chairs fell over and somebody must have trodden on Oliver too. He sprang up with a yelp. There was such a babble of worried talk that Sally went right up to the ceiling and hung there to avoid the noise.

Imogen was shrieking, "Oh, what's happened, what's happened?" and Ned was shouting, "I knew it was!" Howard was saying, "Look here, this is serious. I think your practical joke misfired somehow." And Cart was bellowing, "Shut up, everyone! Keep calm! This is serious!"

Julian Addiman scraped his chair and coughed for attention. "Look, if this nonsense really worries you, all you've got to do to disprove it is to telephone Sally's friend."

"Stupid," said Fenella. "If Sally's dead, she can't talk on the phone."

"I don't think this was Sally," said Julian. "Not for one moment. Come on, Cart. You go and phone. I'll come with you."

"It *was* a ghost though!" Fenella called after Julian as he and Cart hurried to the door.

Julian Addiman held the door open for Cart and answered as he followed her through it. "Don't believe in them."

What do you think I was then? Sally yelled after him.

CHAPTER SIX

Julian and Cart were gone a long time. For the first ten minutes, everyone sat quiet and tense. For the second ten minutes, everyone fidgeted. Howard built a pile of Scrabble letters, and Imogen made a swift bold drawing of him doing it. It was quite like him, Sally thought, watching over Imogen's shoulder. Then Imogen threw down her pencil.

"Whatever are they doing?"

"Perhaps they ran into Himself," Ned suggested uneasily.

Fenella turned in her chair to give him her most scathing stare. "They're kissing," she said, with deep contempt.

This caused another silence, an embarrassed one. During it, Sally wondered if Fenella was right. She had a strong feeling that Julian Addiman might kiss people, when it was dark, as it was by now. She could not understand why this should make her feel so relieved. She had just decided to set off and find out the truth, when Howard said, "This Plan of yours — does Sally just disappear indefinitely, or what?"

"Until a parent notices," said Imogen.

"But," said Howard, "wouldn't it have made more sense to have sent your parents some kind of letter?"

"We tried that," said Imogen, "but none of us could think of the right thing to write. So we decided just to wait until they noticed."

"It seems a bit strange to me," said Howard.

"We *are* strange," said Fenella.

At that point, Cart came back. She was alone. She crashed through the door into the kitchen like an advancing tank, and her face was radiant with relief. "It's all right!" she said. "Sally *is* at Mangan Farm. They'd gone up to bed — Sally and Audrey — but Mrs Chambers said she could hear them talking. So. Phew! I was worried for a moment, but it really is all right. That couldn't have been Sally."

There was a certain amount of laughter and some exclaiming from the others, but it was short and troubled and rather sheepish. Howard and Jenkins said they would be going now. While Fenella was seeing them through the green door, Imogen swept the Scrabble letters back into their spongebag. "Good," she said. "It must have been an evil spirit then. Where's Julian?"

"He didn't bother to come back. It's almost time for the bell," Cart said, dismissing Julian without a trace of self-consciousness, and even with some impatience.

Sally found herself looking at Cart in dismay. Cart was no longer keen on Julian Addiman, nothing could be plainer. Whatever had happened over the telephone, it had been final. Some of Cart's obvious relief was due to this. What Sally could not understand was why Cart's relief should make her heart sink so. She felt doomed, as if there was something she must go through with now. And that was as inexplicable as the fact that Cart so clearly believed that Sally was at Mangan Farm with Audrey Chambers. There must be some mistake, surely! Yet Cart was just not capable of lying and looking relieved at once. Sally did not know what to think.

A bell began to ring beyond the green door, meaning it was bedtime in School. Howard and Jenkins had only just left in time. "Bedtime," said Cart. "I'm tired out."

From sheer habit, Sally went upstairs with the other three. She felt tired and depressed after her efforts at pushing the glass — efforts which had come to nothing, too, except to give Imogen the idea she was an evil spirit. Sally's disembodied mind hurt that Imogen should think that. *I'm Sally*, she told herself. *I know I am. When Mother comes in after School bedtime to tuck us up, I shall make her notice me and get her to realise I'm not an evil spirit. But I wish I understood how I can be in two places at once!*

While she waited for Phyllis, she hung around watching her sisters undressing. None of them troubled to wash, not even Imogen, who took more care over undressing than the other two. Fenella was ready first. She put on a short greyish nylon nightgown, out of which her stomach bulged crudely, and went wandering round the room surveying the pictures on the walls.

"Can mice knock over wastepaper baskets?" she asked, when she came to the Rude Rug.

"Probably not," said Cart.

To Sally's disgust, nobody bothered to pick the basket up, or made the slightest attempt to gather up the fallen papers. Cart stood in the middle of the torn letters with only a pair of pants on, looking down at her large wobbly body rather critically.

"Do you think Phyllis would let me wear a bra?" she asked Imogen.

"No. Himself would say it was too expensive," said Fenella, and climbed on the bureau.

Imogen was carefully arraying herself in a wilted pair of pale green pyjamas. Sally knew those pyjamas. They had once belonged to Phyllis. Imogen had rescued them from the dustbin. Like the yellow trouser suit, they were far too big for Imogen. They were decorated with grimy green lace, most of which was torn, and hung off Imogen's wrists and ankles in loops. Imogen, however, carefully slid a mirror out from behind one of the beds and looked at herself in it with some complacency. Her tear-swollen face looked happier at what she saw. "You don't need a bra," she said to Cart, "if you intend to be a properly liberated woman."

"I don't think I *am* that liberated," said Cart, still surveying herself.

"No, Imogen," said Fenella. "Cart means will it please boys."

Fenella's voice came from above somewhere. Sally looked, and found that Fenella had climbed on to one of the three wavy beams that ran across in the roof. As she spoke, Fenella set off to walk along the beam, spreading her bony arms wide and swaying like a banking aeroplane. *Stop it!* Sally shrieked, quite horrified. *You'll break your neck!*

Fenella, of course, did not hear. She continued to shuffle and sway along the length of wavy black timber. Neither of her sisters seemed alarmed. Cart said coldly, "Shut up, Fenella," and put her head inside a great bag-like nightdress. Imogen lay down on the unmade bed nearest her. She put her arms behind her head and stared up at Fenella without seeming very interested. Sally had a strong feeling that Fenella had walked along that beam many times before. But she was still terrified. Suppose Fenella fell! She was so frightened that she found she had zoomed up beside Fenella and was flittering round her, before she was aware.

Sally's presence seemed to disconcert Fenella. Her thin arms whirled. She leaned out sideways. Next second, she was hanging upside down, with her knees hooked over the beam. Her face looked exasperated.

"You look like a monkey," remarked Imogen.

"The evil spirit knocked me off," Fenella said crossly, upside down. "Throw me up a skipping rope. I want to play Tarzan."

"Get one for yourself," said Cart. She was climbing into bed and, to Sally's astonishment, it was the one bed which was neatly made. So that meant that one of the two remaining unmade beds must be Sally's.

In her disgust, Sally descended to the Rude Rug again. *I don't think much of your Plan!* she said. *If you don't make my bed, how on earth is Phyllis to know it hasn't been slept in when she comes?*

She need not have spoken. Imogen and Cart were both laughing at Fenella's attempts to climb back on the beam again. Fenella was laughing too. In fact, as Sally saw with exasperation, they had all three suddenly become very silly. This happened quite often. Usually they got silly after something upsetting had happened. In this case, it must have been the séance. Now it was as if a gale of idiocy swept among them, whirling Imogen's grief away, forcing high neighing giggles from Fenella's upside down mouth, and carrying Cart into such gusts of hilarity that not one of her fenced and careful thoughts remained. It was maddening. The room rang with screams and squeals of silly laughter.

Sally hovered up and down on the Rude Rug, shouting, *What about ME? If Phyllis comes to tuck us up and finds you like this, she's never going to NOTICE your beastly Plan!*

"No, no!" Cart shrieked, lying heaving and red faced on her neat bed. "No – a pantomime!" Sally had no idea what she was talking about.

"With all the fairies flying upside down!" giggled Fenella.

"Let's try!" howled Imogen. "Bags I try! I've always wanted to know how it feels!"

"All right! Let's try it!" screamed Cart, bouncing from her bed.

At the same moment, Fenella, screaming "*Whoopee!*" whirled out from her beam and landed with a jangle on the bed Cart had just left. It was a miracle that she hit the bed and did not collide with Cart on the way. But, Sally recalled shakenly, Fenella always did jump to Cart's bed. Sometimes she hit Cart, sometimes not, but she never hurt herself, and she always looked as if she was going to miss the bed entirely. And Sally always protested.

Fenella! You could kill yourself! she was saying, when Cart arrived on the Rude Rug too and shoved her aside. Sally found herself squashed against the paintings on the wall, watching the ballooning Cart heave at the second drawer down in the bureau. *Hey!* Sally complained. *That's my drawer!*

"It's all right," Cart said over her shoulder to Fenella. "I know she had at least two."

"That should be long enough," Fenella agreed.

Imogen was still lying staring up at the beams. Her face had become suffused with silly dreaminess. "I think it will be the most exquisitely beautiful experience," she said.

Irritably, Sally wondered what was going on. She suspected it was something idiotic, and that Phyllis would arrive in the middle of it and be angry — too angry to notice Sally was missing. She watched anxiously as the loaded drawer was heaved out.

"Feathers!" said Cart, and began laughing again.

"Off the black hen," said Fenella. "She keeps picking them up."

"Oh, Monigan I suppose," said Cart and dug beneath the feathers. Her hand came up holding the old sock. She held it in the air, laughing helplessly. After a bit, she managed to speak in weak squeaky jerks. "Look – guess what? – think whose?"

Her sisters rolled about, screaming with mirth. "Julian Addiman's!"

Sally watched, perplexed and embarrassed. She could not think why she should want to keep a sock belonging to Julian Addiman and she was exceedingly hurt that her sisters should think it so funny. She was also a little outraged at the way Cart was going through her private drawer – but not as annoyed as she might have been. After all, if you lived close up against three sisters, this kind of thing was only to be expected. She had done it herself that afternoon. But she hoped Phyllis would come in and catch Cart at it.

However nothing happened to stop Cart, who delved and dug and heaved at the numbers of things in the drawer and finally came up triumphantly with two neatly rolled skipping ropes. "Here we are! I knew she still had them!"

"Oh good." Imogen jumped up and stood on her bed, majestic in her withered loopy pyjamas, and took command. "Tie them together. Tightly." Cart did so. "Now you and Fenella pull on the knot," Imogen ordered. "Hard. I don't want to plunge to my death."

"You would fly through the air with the greatest of ease," said Cart.

"I intend to," Imogen assured her gravely, hitching the wide green trousers up with an air of greatness. "All my life," she said, "I have dreamed of being a pantomime fairy. I've yearned to swoop across the stage in a spangled dress, and now I shall have an inkling of what it will be like. My dreams are about to come true. Now throw one end over the beam."

"Would you like us to stick silver paper on your pyjamas first?" Fenella asked kindly.

"No," said Imogen. "This is an imaginative experience."

Gloomily, Sally watched Cart sling the wooden handle of a skipping rope over the beam and Imogen reach up and pull it down level with her waist. Now she knew what was going on, and it was as idiotic as she had feared. She hoped Phyllis would not come yet. She watched Cart help Imogen to knot the rope round her waist and Fenella taking a firm grip on the wooden handle of the longer end. Cart took a grip on the rope further up.

"Ready?"

"Get on with it," said Imogen.

Fenella heaved. Cart threw her head back, braced her great feet and heaved too. Slowly, with a lot of creaking, the skipping rope slid over the beam. Imogen's feet rose from the bed and vanished inside the loopy green legs of her trousers. It seemed that, as Imogen went up, her trousers were going down. Fenella and Cart puffed and staggered. Imogen's sturdy body went creaking upward again and, quite suddenly and surprisingly, bent in two. Her red, irritated face was now dangling level with the descending grey lace of her trousers. "Ow!" she said.

"You don't look very graceful," Fenella panted.

"Stand up in the air," puffed Cart.

"I can't!" snapped Imogen. Her legs kicked, in an irritated swirl of green nylon. "Let me down. The rope's tied too low."

Cart and Fenella obediently let go. Imogen descended to her bed in a creaking rush, where she floundered about, imprisoned in loopy trouser. "Help me!" she said. "I want it untied and tied round under my arms instead."

No! said Sally. *Stop!* As Imogen plunged down, it had looked unpleasant, rather like a hanging. She knew what Phyllis would think if she had happened to come in at that moment.

Of course no one heard. Cart moved the skipping rope up Imogen, taking quantities of flowing green nylon with it, until it was under her arms. There was a bright red crease round Imogen's square waist where the rope had been. "Are you sure you want to try again?" said Cart. "That looks painful."

"Naturally," Imogen said haughtily. "One is bound to suffer in the cause of Art." She pulled her trousers almost up to her armpits and stood waiting. "Pull."

Obediently, Fenella leant backwards, pulling on the wooden handle. In front of her, Cart leant backwards too, almost on top of Fenella, and heaved on the rope. Creak-creak-creak. The rope travelled over the beam until Imogen was raised on tiptoe. Then it stuck.

"What are you *doing?*" raved Imogen, swaying this way and that on her toe tips. "Pull me *up*, you great weak things!"

"We're trying!" gasped Fenella.

"Your centre of gravity's different or something," Cart said breathlessly.

"Then use your huge weight," commanded Imogen. "You're twice as heavy as I am."

This was true. Cart nodded and tried to brace herself with one foot against the bed. The bed promptly shot away from under Imogen, sending Cart backwards into Fenella. Since Cart and Fenella both hung on to the rope in order not to fall in a heap, the result was that Imogen rose in a rapid set of creaking jerks, until she was hanging about a foot under the beam. There, for some reason, she started to twiddle round and round. Her feet rotated, mauve and drooping, almost in Cart's face. Her hands clutched at the green nylon trousers to stop them coming down. Her face, every time it twirled into view, looked less and less happy.

Let her down! shouted Sally. It looked exactly like a hanging now.

But Imogen's sisters hung on to the skipping ropes and stared critically upwards.

84

"You still don't look graceful," Fenella said. "Stretch your arms out."

Imogen, whose blue eyes now had a curious wide, bulging look, spared first one hand, then the other, from her trousers. The trousers at once fell down. Imogen held her arms out stiff and straight and swung slowly round and round like a rather unhappy scarecrow.

Cart shook her head. "Smile," she suggested.

After a moment when she seemed to have forgotten what smiling meant, Imogen succeeded in baring her teeth. Her head twiddled like a Hallowe'en lantern. Her face was beginning to look a curious colour.

"You still don't look pretty," Fenella said discontentedly. "Try doing something graceful with your legs."

Imogen tried. Probably she intended to stretch one leg backwards like a ballerina. But what happened was that both her legs spread stiffly apart and bent at the knees, causing a great green web of stretched nylon to form between them. She twirled like a grinning wrestler frozen in mid-leap, and the dangling end of her trousers hanging from her feet made her look as if she had an extra pair of knees. Her face was a muddy mauve.

Sally was suddenly sure Imogen was not breathing. She shot into the air to see. For a moment, she was twiddling dizzily with Imogen under the beam, with sickening glimpses of unmade beds and childish drawings whirling round her, and, beyond the taut, creaking rope, the wide interested balloon-face of Cart, with Fenella's insect legs and skinny white feet sticking out behind. She could see the skipping rope cutting into Imogen's chest under her arms.

Help! Sally bawled. *Mother! They're hanging Imogen and Imogen hasn't noticed!*

"She *still* doesn't look nice," Fenella said.

Imogen tried to improve matters by stretching her grin to a sort of leering simper. But Sally was right. She had given up breathing.

Sally wondered frantically what she could do, when even Imogen herself did not seem to see she was strangling. And Phyllis was not going to come. Sally suddenly knew that. Phyllis never did come to see them these days. She was too tired after a day in school. Sally had been thinking of the far-off days, when they were all four little, when Phyllis had managed to come in most nights to tuck them up. So what was she to do? Imogen was still stiff and twirling, and her face was an odder colour than ever.

I know! Sally found herself whizzing through the room towards that bell-push labelled FOR EMERGENCY ONLY. *Because,* she said as she whizzed, *if this isn't an emergency, I'd like to know what is! Oh, the idiots!* She flung herself on the chilly little white button with even more force than she had used on the wastepaper basket.

Downstairs, her worry had somehow communicated itself to Oliver. After a few rumbling, questioning growls, he burst out barking, each bark like a clap of thunder. And, at almost the same time, Imogen reached the end of her endurance. With what was probably the last breath in her body, she managed to make her grinning mouth utter a long grating squeak. "Ee-ee-eeeh!"

"I think she's dying," Fenella said, hushed with shock.

"Get her down – quick!" said Cart.

Sally turned from hurling herself at the bell-push to find them hurriedly lowering Imogen. They tried to do it too quickly and burnt their hands. Fenella let go and fell over backwards. Cart let out a roar. Imogen flopped to the floor and folded there in a green nylon heap, with her face a dense mauve, breathing in small shallow shrieks.

"Christ!" said Cart, with her fingers on the knot in the skipping ropes. "This rope is practically *embedded* in her! Scissors, quickly!"

Fenella leapt up and thudded on knobby feet to Sally's drawer again. Feathers came out in a black cloud to join the waste paper on the Rude Rug. And, to Sally's relief, the scissors toppled out with them. Fenella scudded back with them and hung anxiously over Cart while Cart hacked at the rope round Imogen. All the while, from below, Oliver kept up a thunderous howling bark.

"Oh do go and shut him up, Fenella!" said Cart.

The rope came apart. Sally saw Imogen's chest enlarge. She made a great noise like "Hoom" and began breathing properly again. Her face turned a more normal colour almost at once. Tenderly and gently, Cart and Fenella heaved her into bed, where she lay gasping.

"I don't think I shall be a pantomime fairy," she said tearfully. "Their life must be perfect hell."

"I think they may wear some kind of harness, you know," Cart said.

"All the same," Imogen gasped dolefully, "I think I shall have to stick to my music. I'm – not fitted – for a strenuous – stage career."

Downstairs, Oliver's barking turned abruptly to shamed whining. Impatient angry feet in high heels clattered on the stairs. Imogen, Cart and Fenella exchanged looks of horror. Fenella kicked the skipping ropes and the scissors under Imogen's bed and dived for her own. Cart dithered, and finally decided to sit on Imogen's bed in the attitude of a sister exchanging confidences. There was no point in putting the light out, Sally knew. Phyllis would have seen it shining from the stairs.

The next second, Phyllis burst into the room. She looked like an avenging angel that has done too much avenging for that day.

Tired, so tired, Sally thought. There were deep lines under the angel eyes, and even deeper ones beside the angel mouth. The electric light seemed to bleach her pale face and hair to tired white. Sally took one look at that face and found herself up on the beam over Imogen's bed, out of harm's way.

"What is going on?" Phyllis enquired. It was her terrible flat tired voice. "Is this a practical joke? Is your father to have no peace in the evenings?"

"I — I'm sorry, Mother," Cart said, in a subdued childish whisper. "Oliver just started barking for no reason at all."

"I didn't mean Oliver," said Phyllis. "How many times have you been told that the alarm bell is only to be pressed in a real emergency? And here am I, dragged away from the one peaceful time I get in the whole day, and your father thoroughly startled in *his* quiet time, thinking there was a fire, or one of you was ill. And when I get here, I can see at once you've just been larking around again. Which of you was it that pressed that bell?"

Nobody answered. Cart turned her head so that Phyllis could not see her face and gave Fenella a wrinkle of the nose and eyebrows, meaning "Eh?" Fenella, whom Phyllis could see, looked blank and stupid in reply.

Me, said Sally from her perch on the beam. *And I had to, Mother.*

Nobody heard. Phyllis turned the tired majesty of her anger on Fenella. "Was it you?"

"Of course not!" Fenella said.

Phyllis turned to Cart. "You?"

"No it was not!" said Cart. She sounded as if she was lying in her anxiety. "Honestly," she added.

The beam of Phyllis's tired anger moved on to Imogen. "Imogen?"

Imogen had reached the second stage of suffering, when you feel it worse. Her face was now white, making her hair look green

— a different green from her pyjamas. She had trouble speaking at all. "Not me," she managed to say huskily.

And then, suddenly, the room was full of tension. Fenella, Cart and Imogen were all waiting for the beam of Phyllis's anger to move on to the other empty tumbled bed where Sally should have been. They were all avoiding looking at it. Cart's neck was trembling with the strain of not looking.

"Very well," said Phyllis. She turned wearily back to the door. "I shall expect one of you to confess to me tomorrow," she said, leaving.

She had not come very far into the room. She would be gone in a second. *Mother!* shouted Sally, and swooped down to the papers and feathers on the Rude Rug. Fenella and Cart shot looks at one another, meaning, "You!" "No – you do it!"

"Mother," said Cart.

Phyllis turned back in the doorway, plainly anxious to be gone. She was almost too tired to look at Cart. "What is it?"

"Well – actually," said Cart, "Imogen isn't very happy at the moment. I expect you've noticed."

Evidently the Plan meant that nobody should directly mention Sally. Fenella jerked her face at Cart in an approving nod. Phyllis turned her weary beam of attention towards Imogen. "But that isn't an emergency, Charlotte."

"Oh yes, but—" Cart began, rather desperately. It was important to keep Phyllis here, since, the longer she was in the room, the more likely she was to notice Sally's empty bed. "But it is an emergency that her mark for Music was so low this term," Cart said. She was evidently relieved to have thought of this to say. "We don't think it's only because she's always being turned out of the music rooms here, Mother. We think she's genuinely not as good as she used to be. We think she ought to choose another career. Don't you?"

Phyllis turned to Imogen in mild astonishment. Imogen managed to give a sick and rather self-conscious smile. The smile evidently meant more to Phyllis than the paleness of Imogen's face. Sally saw her muster herself and then smile in return, a weary warm comforting smile. Sally relaxed. Mother was really trying now. "Nonsense," said Phyllis, and she had mustered a warm comforting voice too. "Imogen's artistic temperament means she always builds things up. Every career has its ups and downs. Of course Imogen is going to go on with music. She has enormous talent. Every time I see her seated at the keyboard—"

"About once a year," muttered Fenella.

Phyllis shut her eyes in order not to hear this. It was one of Fenella's stupid remarks. "Every time," she repeated, "I'm impressed by the serenity and passion of her profile. It reminds me of Myra Hess. I know Imogen is cut out to be a concert pianist. Your father would be so disappointed if she gave up."

At this, Imogen turned her weak smile on Cart. She seemed comforted.

Phyllis noticed Cart and seemed to feel Cart might feel left out. "Just as," she said kindly, "Charlotte has all the brains and none of the looks in the family, so Imogen has both the looks and the musical talent. Charlotte must go to University. She's cut out to be a teacher."

"What about me?" said Fenella.

Phyllis turned her golden gaze on Fenella. "Well—" she said. She was rather at a loss.

"I shall be an acrobat," Fenella said earnestly.

Phyllis ignored this. It was another of Fenella's silly remarks. "It will be something quaint and unusual, that I do know."

Cart, meanwhile, had been considering, in a slow, puzzled way. "You know, I don't think I *am* cut out to be a teacher," she said. "People don't listen to what I say."

Phyllis ignored this too. It was one of Cart's silly remarks. She gave them all a tired smile and turned to leave.

Sally jumped – or rather hovered – up and down on the Rude Rug. *What about me?* Such was her anxiety to be noticed that she actually caused one or two feathers to drift up from the floor, but, if anyone noticed them, they must have thought they were blown in the draught from the door as Phyllis held it open.

It was Imogen who, typically, broke the rules of the Plan. "What about Sally?" she asked. She still could only speak in a husky gasp.

"Sally?" Phyllis paused in the doorway. She did glance at Sally's bed. She seemed surprised – but only mildly surprised – to find it empty. "Well, people who are not brainy are usually very good at Art, you know. I think Sally has a great career as an artist." By now she was nearly through the door.

A great black feather whirled halfway to the ceiling as Sally called out despairingly. *But I'm NOT HERE!*

"Mother," Fenella said abruptly, in the deep commanding voice she used on Mrs Gill. "Mother, don't you think we are all rather neglected?" Phyllis turned and frowned at Fenella over her shoulder. Fenella twisted her beaky face somehow into an improbably enchanting smile. "We suffer from lack of attention," she said. She took up one of the knots her hair was tied into and twiddled it meaningly. "You look after the boys, but you don't look after us," she explained, twiddling.

Cart and Imogen were aghast at Fenella's daring, but Phyllis was merely wearily amused. It was another of Fenella's silly remarks. "Oh Fenella! The boys are all away from home and they need attention. Besides, boys are helpless and girls know very well how to look after themselves. Now be a good girl and go to sleep."

She went away downstairs as she said it, leaving them all

speechless. Downstairs, they heard her golden voice murmuring to Oliver in the way which always made Oliver try to lick her face. Then they heard the green door shut behind her.

"I made sure she was going to notice my knots," Fenella said, mortified.

Imogen husked, "At least we didn't get into trouble."

"Wait a moment!" Cart exclaimed. "Who *did* push the panic button? It couldn't have been me, because I was hanging on to the rope."

"So was I," said Fenella. "So."

"And I was strangling," husked Imogen.

"That's just what I mean!" shouted Cart. "But the bell rang, because Phyllis heard it. So who *did* push it? There's only one person I know who'd do a stupid thing like that."

Sally's sisters stared at one another, frightened, annoyed and astonished. "Sally!" they all said together.

CHAPTER SEVEN

"Do you mean the ghost was really Sally after all?" Imogen quavered. She gripped the edge of her bedclothes, ready to pull them over her head.

"No," Cart said thoughtfully. "We know Sally's with Audrey, so it can't be *really* Sally. But what's to stop it being a poor lost spirit that *thinks* it's Sally?"

Fenella chuckled, the deep dirty chuckle which she called her Evil Laugh. "And, what's more, it's here at the moment, listening to every word we say!"

Imogen uttered a husky scream and slid under her bedclothes.

"What did you want to say that for?" Cart said to Fenella. "Imogen's had an awful day, one way and another. Keep your big mouth shut, or I won't let you help me get rid of it."

"Do you know how to get rid of it?" Fenella said.

"Yes," Cart said tightly. She got off Imogen's bed and lumbered over to the chest of drawers again. This time, she opened her own tidy, nearly empty drawer and took out a small red leather book. Sally, fluttering by her shoulder, saw that it was a Prayer Book and felt suddenly peculiar. "Fenella," said Cart. "I'll need your cowbell."

Fenella's mouth came open, showing two large gappy front teeth. And well might Fenella be astonished, Sally thought, remembering that cowbell. Fenella had gone about clanking it for a whole fortnight, and intoning, "Unclean! Unclean!" at the top of her large booming voice. Fenella had intoned and clanked until all three of her sisters, driven to three different distractions, had threatened Fenella with three different dreadful fates if that bell was ever seen or heard again. And how, Sally thought, suddenly indignant, could a person remember that bell and not be Sally? Of course she was Sally, ghost or not!

"And we'll need your Monigan candle too," Cart said to the quaking heap that was Imogen.

A cautious flap of sheet peeled back. Imogen's face appeared, looking – maybe because it was flushed from being under the bedclothes – rather healthier than before. "You're going to exorcise it," she said, "with bell, book and candle, aren't you? I think it's an extremely intelligent idea."

No it isn't! Sally said, angry and unheard. *I refuse to be exorcised! I've as much right to be here as you have!*

As she said it, Cart's drawer and Sally's own were being pushed heavily in, releasing a further cloud of black feathers, and Fenella was rather helplessly turning over wads of music in Imogen's drawer.

"It's down the left-hand side," Imogen said, sitting up warily.

Fenella found the candle. Sally remembered the candle as well as the cowbell, which Fenella next dug out from among the dolls in her own drawer. Cart had made the candle a year ago, when she invented the Worship of Monigan, out of stumps of other candles and the lace of a gym-shoe. She had tried to dye it blue by melting poster paint in the wax, and she had tried to scent it by pouring in some perfume Imogen had bought at Woolworth's. The result was a grey knobby thing, like a monster fungus, with a most peculiar smell.

"Where are the matches?" said Fenella.

There was a short silence. "Downstairs," said Imogen. "And," she added in a gabbling shriek. "I'm not going. There's a ghost down there! I'm *scared*!" Upon which, she vanished under the bedclothes again.

"Bags I not either," Cart said hastily.

Fenella stood up with scornful grandeur. "I sometimes think," she said, "that I do all the dirty work round here. Of course I'll go." She marched to the door and then turned, so that only her nose and her grey nylon stomach showed beyond the door frame. "Stupids," she said. "The ghost was what Oliver was growling at all day. And he's not growling now, so the ghost is up *here*." The nose and the stomach vanished. Fenella's bony feet went thudding downstairs.

Sally had half a mind to go after Fenella so that Oliver would growl. On the other hand, she had two people to scare up here. The lump in Imogen's bed was quivering and uttering low howling sounds. Cart's face was pale and her fingers shook as she turned over the little thin pages of the Prayer Book.

"Oh dear," Cart said, trying to sound natural. "The Order of Baptism for Those of Riper Years, The Catechism, The Form of Solemnisation of Matrimony. They don't seem to give exorcism. Do you think the Litany would do? Or should we use The Order for the Burial of the Dead?"

"Ooh-ow! Ooh-ow!" went the lump that was Imogen.

"The Thanksgiving of Women after Childbirth," said Cart. "No, that won't do. A Commination — what's that? — or Denouncing of God's Anger and Judgements against Sinners. That looks more like it. I think we'd better use that. The rest is all Prayers at Sea and ordaining Bishops."

Sally made a gesture she hoped was folding her non-existent arms and stayed hovering among the feathers on the Rude Rug. Nothing they could do would induce her to leave. She was their sister, for goodness sake!

Nevertheless, when Fenella thumped upstairs with the matches, and Imogen was induced — by means of a very unkind prod from Cart — to sit up shakily holding the smoking flickering fungoid candle, Sally had a sudden feeling of uneasiness. It was not serious. It was as if she had lost something just a little important, like a book or a pen. But it was definite. When Fenella took up the fat cup-shaped cowbell and began to clank it backwards and forwards, the feeling increased. Sally felt frightened and lost and somehow desperate.

"Will it work without a priest?" Fenella said through the clanks.

"We have to will it to," said Cart. She began to read in a pompous priestly voice. "'Cursed is the man that maketh any carved or molten image, to worship it. And the people shall answer and say, Amen.'"

"Amen," said Imogen and Fenella obediently.

"'Cursed is he that curseth his father or mother. Cursed is he that removeth his neighbour's landmark.'"

"Are you sure that's right?" said Imogen.

"That's what it says," said Cart. "Perhaps I'd better skip that and get on to the solid stuff. Here we are. 'It is a fearful thing to fall into the hands of the living God: he shall pour down rain upon the sinners, snares, fire and brimstone, storm and tempest; this shall be their portion to drink. For lo, the Lord is come out of his place to visit the wickedness of such as dwell upon the earth..."'

The now familiar panic began to grow in Sally. She looked from face to face. Cart's was set and concentrated, so that the big features were no longer blurred, but clear and implacable. Fenella's face, as she swung her bell, looked older, intense and beaky and ferocious. Imogen stared at her wavering candle with a little clear crease in her brow. She looked worried, as she always did when she was exercising her will power. Sally knew they were all willing, willing mightily, the ghost to go away. The panic went on rising in her, and with it a sense of loss and desolation.

Cart intoned, "'But who may abide the day of his coming? Who shall be able to endure when he appeareth? His fan is in his hand, and he will purge his floor, and gather his wheat into the barn; but he will burn the chaff with unquenchable fire. The day of the Lord cometh as a thief in the night..."'

And suddenly, as it had before the séance, Sally found the scene was splitting apart. Shreds of Cart, of Fenella, of Imogen and the candle, swung this way and that.

"'But let us,'" intoned Cart, "'while we have the light, believe in the light, and walk as the children of light; that we be not cast into utter darkness, where is weeping and gnashing of teeth. Let us not abuse the goodness of God, who calleth us mercifully to amendment...'"

Now, with every word Cart intoned, with every clank of the cowbell, the splits in the scene grew wider. And behind the splits – Sally screamed, a soundless scream. There was a fat, shapeless grey thing there, in the darkness behind, like a cocoon, or a mummy, or a beetle grub. It was huge, and it was trying to draw her in, through the widening splits, into itself...

NO! Sally shrieked. Anything rather than be drawn in by that fat grey grub. She let herself be whirled by her panic, out, along, away, through the night, she had no idea where, whirling and tumbling, until at last the panic faded. She found herself out in the dark countryside, going up the road she had first come down.

Perhaps I shall just go away again, the way I came, back into nothing, she said miserably. But there seemed no reason in that. Maybe her sisters did not want her, but there were still so many things she did not understand. She still had no idea why she was a ghost like this. She wanted to know. And while she was considering how she might find out, she was drifting steadily — almost purposefully — up the road. It was a still, mild night, scented with hay and indistinct flowers. Sally felt soothed by it. But it was so dark that she was scared at first.

Silly! she told herself. *Ghosts aren't scared of ghosts!*

Besides, she soon realised, it was not utterly dark. The road glimmered, a faint greyish white between the jetty black rustling hedges. The stars blazed overhead, like diamonds strewn on blue-black velvet, so bright that some were clearly green, or orange, or faintly blue — not the twinkly silver things Sally had always supposed they were. Some were pearly in places where small wisps of cloud hung in front of them. And when Sally raised herself above the hedges, the fields beyond were pearly too, silvered with damp, scented mist, with black trees standing expectantly about in it.

Raised like that, Sally could clearly see the trees on the hill ahead, black against the lighter blackness of the sky. Among them was the orange square of a lighted window. Someone was in a bedroom of the farmhouse up there. Almost as Sally saw it, the orange square flicked out, leaving her dazzled. Someone had gone to bed up there. At the same time, softly tolling across the pearly fields, she heard the school clock striking midnight.

Midnight, Sally said. *Ghost time. I'm legal now. And that's Audrey's house up there. Why don't I go and see if I'm really there?*

It was a tempting thought, but an alarming one. Sally knew still — more clearly than she knew anything else — that there had been an accident. Suppose she got to the farm only to look down on her dead body? Because, look at it how you would, *something* must have happened to make her a ghost.

But the obvious thing seemed to be to go and find out. Sally continued to drift between the hedges and on up the hill, where the trees reduced the road to the faintest of glimmers, until she came to the farm gates. Beyond the gates was the hot dungy smell of farmyard. And it was a little frightening. All the animals seemed to know she was there. Sally wafted aside from the fierce grunt of a big white hunk of angry flesh, which turned out to be a white sow, and then from a spitting kitten, and from the snarl of the sheepdog. Finally, a splitting whinny from Audrey's pony sent her through the farmhouse walls into the safety of the close air indoors. It was fuggy in there, and smelt of polish.

Here she was bewildered. She could not remember ever being in this house in her life. She found the stairs, old and dark and covered with new carpet, smelling of newness, and more new carpet lining a crooked corridor upstairs. She stopped, suspended at the head of the stairs, with no idea where to look. A faint idea she had had that her body would naturally draw her to it drizzled away from her. It was obviously not like that.

Then two things happened. First, it was suddenly lighter. Long silver rays fell through a window somewhere off to the right and reached down the crooked corridor. The moon had risen. Its light was not clear. The shapes of the swaying trees outside tumbled within the beams, but it gave enough light to turn the corridor into somewhere Sally remembered faintly. Instead of being fuggy, the smell of new carpet seemed clean and pungent. On the walls and on tables at the sides of the corridor, the white rays were picked up and turned yellow in the surfaces of polished brass ornaments. There were horse brasses, oil lamps, ship's wheels, a stand of bells, and flat shapes of sailing ships. Sally remembered these. She remembered Fenella – why was Fenella there? – looking at the brass things with admiration.

"Isn't it posh?" Fenella had said. "Fancy having your upstairs as pretty as your downstairs! When I'm a lady, I shall have things like these all over my house."

Remembering this, Sally had a dim feeling that Audrey's house had inspired the exhibition of paintings in their own bedroom.

Then the second thing happened. Down at the end of the corridor, a toilet flushed. The noise was so loud and so sudden that Sally whirled away half downstairs again. There, through the noise of rushing water, she was just able to hear footsteps – footsteps which set the old boards under the new carpet creaking – but not too much or too many. Just four or five light footsteps, followed by the creak of an old door not quite shutting.

Sally was upstairs and along the corridor in a flash. Those footsteps had to belong to someone young. Probably to Audrey. At the end of the corridor, the toilet cistern was still gushing and glopping away and, nearly opposite, an old door was still slightly moving. Sally slid through the dark wood into a warm airy room. She was aware of pretty print curtains fluttering against the dim moonlight of an open window, and then of two sets of quiet breathing.

Two people. Definitely.

Sally hung there while she located the breathing and then the warmth and the electric life-feeling from two beds, one at the dark end of the room, the other in the moonlight under the window. The one in the dark bed was Audrey. Sally recognised her – though not as someone she knew particularly well. Audrey had a large warm presence, that of a person comfortable within herself, and a surprising amount of straight black hair spread out on a floral pillow. Looking at the hair and listening to the slight gentle breathing, Sally recollected why it had been Fenella admiring the brass ornaments. Audrey had been Fenella's friend at first. Fenella had struck up an acquaintance with Audrey because Audrey had a pony. Fenella was mad on horses. Then her sisters had been brought along to be shown the pony and the posh house. Audrey was the same age as Sally, though not in Sally's class at school, and Sally had – to put it crudely – taken Audrey over. From the unfamiliar feel of the sleeping Audrey, Sally thought this could not have been very long ago.

But this meant that the person in the other bed was herself. Well, at least she was alive, Sally thought, hovering up to the humped shape under the covers. For some reason, the bodily Sally had pulled the covers up over her head, just like Imogen earlier, and almost nothing of her showed except a tuft of hair. That hair surprised Sally by being much fairer than she expected. She had had a notion that she was dark, like Fenella.

Perhaps I'm not Sally after all, she said.

As she said this, she realised that the person in this bed was not asleep. The breathing was too heavy and irregular. And the fizzing of the life-feeling coming off her was not gentle, like Audrey's, but fierce and gusty. She was the one who went to the toilet, plainly. But now she was not settling back to sleep, she was – waiting for something.

And that time had arrived. A hand emerged from the bedclothes – a hand which was neither familiar nor unfamiliar – crackling so with life and suspense that Sally was forced to move backwards. The hand seized the covers and flung them back, and the bodily Sally got out of bed in one clean rolling movement. Cre-eak went the old floor as she stood up.

Sally hovered away backwards from her in total amazement. She was dressed, in jeans and an old sweater, for one thing. She was obviously planning to do something. But Sally's main astonishment was that this girl looked like a normal person. After seeing her three sisters, she had not expected anyone in the family to look normal. This girl was thin, but she was not a witch-insect like Fenella, and she was quite tall, at least as tall as Imogen, but not as large as Cart. Her face, in the moonlight, was quite pretty, though it was not as striking as Imogen's angel beauty, because the girl had dark eyebrows and a slight hawk-look inherited from Himself. But Sally found her unexpectedly good looking, all the same. Her hair indeed seemed to be fair. The less-than-good-looking thing about her was that she had the awkward figure of a thirteen-year-old, when a person's back curves to make way for hips she has not got, and the rest of her is straight up and down, and instead of a bosom she has a chest with lumps on it. Sally found that made her feel sorry for this unexpected girl. But her main feeling was surprise. She had expected something much more peculiar.

The bodily Sally, after standing for a second, put out a cautious foot. The old timbers of the floor responded at once with a gentle groan. The girl froze. But it was too late. The sleeping shape of Audrey fizzed, heaved, rose up. She said, in a high whining voice, blurred with sleep, "What are you doing *now* Sally?"

"Only going to the loo," the bodily Sally answered. The voice surprised Sally as much as the rest. It was a clear, pleasant voice.

"But you've only just *been!*" grumbled Audrey.

"No, that was an hour ago," the bodily Sally lied, quietly and firmly. "You've been asleep since then. Go back to sleep. I shan't be a moment."

Audrey seemed to accept this. She gave a groan, not unlike the floorboards, and heaved round to face the wall. She was asleep as soon as she lay down.

The ghostly Sally heard the breath come out of the mouth of the bodily Sally, in a gasp of relief. Then she saw her walk firmly and lightly across the creaking floor and slip round the door she had carefully not shut before. Sally followed, out of the room, along the crooked, brass-glinting corridor and down the creaking stairs.

Where am I going? I mean, what are you doing? she said. She was now thoroughly perplexed. Not the least of her troubles was that she could not bring herself to think of this girl firmly creeping through Audrey's house as herself. She knew the girl was Sally. There had been no mistake there. Yet she had no sense of identity with her. She had no idea what this Sally thought and felt. She seemed just someone else she was forced to hover and watch, as she had watched Sally's sisters.

The bodily Sally led her through a living room even more lavishly provided with glinting ornaments than the corridor upstairs, and unlatched a long glass door there which led to the farm garden. Sally approved of this. It was sensible not to go through the farmyard and disturb the grunting sow and the uneasy dog. She also saw from the way the girl carefully wedged the glass door with a tissue that she intended to come back from wherever she was going.

But suppose she never came back! Perhaps that was why Sally was a ghost. Sally had a sudden feeling that, wherever this girl was going, it was somewhere wrong and dangerous. Alarm and foreboding grew in her as she followed the girl between dewy bushes, down to the end of the garden. Perhaps it was a danger which could be avoided. Perhaps, she thought, mercy had been granted to Sally the ghost, so that she could come back and guide herself clear of whatever the danger was. So she followed the bodily Sally faithfully, out through a gate at the end of the garden and down a path among the trees. Beyond the trees, the path went on, over the fields, into the moonlit distance.

Sally knew the path kept on. But the moon, hanging like a coppery gong low in the east, had made such a difference to the landscape that most people would have thought there was no path at all. The pearly look to the fields had been caused by bands of white mist lying low on the grass. With the moon on it, the mist now seemed almost solid. The lower part of the girl Sally vanished in it. You could only tell her legs were there from the rasping of wet grass on her jeans. The ghost Sally found it easier to rise above the milky whiteness. She had a feeling, rather like she had had on the playing field, that she might dissolve to nothing in it.

The bodily Sally began to go faster and faster, and her head began nervously jerking about. The ghost did not blame her. Though the mist mostly lay flat and quiet like bands of milk, there were places, mostly against the dark trees, where it inexplicably rose and bellied up, slow and heavy and thick, into huge white moving shapes. Bear-like, grub-like, rolling, menacing shapes. And, to add to the eeriness, there were cows hidden in the still bands of mist, which only revealed themselves when the bodily Sally was close to them, in a snort of breath, or a huge hidden stamp. The girl Sally put both hands to her face to act like blinkers and broke into a trot, refusing to look right or left.

Owls began hooting, now near, now a long, long way away. Owls, Sally realised, did not say Tu-whit-tu-woo, as one had been taught. half of them let out a long quavering OOOOH, like people pretending to be ghosts. The other half went Tu-whit, tu-whit, sharply and suddenly, like Himself giving peremptory orders to a boy.

The owls increased the bodily Sally's terror. Her hands, as

well as acting like blinkers, were soon trying to cover her ears too. She broke into a run and fled across the fields, half buried in mist, under a moon which, as it rose, put out a foreboding coppery rainbow ring round itself.

She was panting furiously as she scrambled through fallen barbed wire into the tufty grass under the dead elms. There was no mist here. The empty trees stood bare against the moonlit sky, still decorated with the scruffy black blobs of rooks' nests. The rooks in them were stirring and cawing as if something had disturbed them. But the bodily Sally behaved as if she was now feeling safer. She took her hands from her face and stumbled among the brambles to the clearing in the very centre of the dead trees.

A dark figure jumped up from the grass and said, "Ahah!"

The girl uttered what struck the ghost as a very silly giggle and said, "Didn't think I'd come, did you? Mind you, I nearly didn't. I was quite sure there was a ghost in Audrey's bedroom."

"I was sure you wouldn't come," said Julian Addiman. "I was just going back to bed. After the fuss you made when I killed the hen this morning—"

"Well," the girl Sally said defensively, "I did know that black hen rather well."

"It was the blood you minded," said Julian Addiman. "Ready?"

"Yes," said Sally, standing bravely straight.

"Right," said Julian Addiman. "Start invoking Monigan then."

And the girl, still standing bravely straight, began, much as Fenella had done, "Oh Monigan, mighty goddess, come forth and show thyself to these thy worshippers..." Except that this, the ghost remembered, was the proper Invocation which Cart had composed last summer, full of rolling phrases borrowed from the

Prayer Book. And now she was truly terrified. This was really dangerous. These two had no idea what thing they were invoking. And besides, Julian Addiman had no business to be there. He had not been among the original Worshippers of Monigan. That band had been a select few, led by Cart as High Priestess, and consisting only of Cart, Sally, Imogen (always unwilling), Fenella, Will Howard and Ned Jenkins. Sally must have gone on with the Worship of Monigan secretly on her own and taught it to Julian Addiman after that.

They had stopped the Worship – or thought they had – because it made them all so uncomfortable. The ghost remembered that, and remembered Cart saying: "We may call it Monigan and think it's a game, but I don't think it is. I know there really is a dark old female Something, and whatever it is we've woken it up and brought it stalking closer. And we mustn't go on. It's not safe." At that time, the ghost remembered wondering if Cart was saying that just to keep them all believing even though Cart was tired of the game. But now she knew otherwise.

Cart had been right. As the bodily Sally went on with her Invocation, the ghost could feel Something stirring, rising, stalking closer. It closed in towards the dead elms out of the dark like the bellying of the mist, wet and tasteless and shapeless. But it was still very, very powerful. She felt its flat, stealthy vibrations, like but not like the crackle of life surrounding Sally and Julian Addiman, and far, far stronger, slowly drawing in among the dead trees.

She threw herself at the invoking Sally and hovered round her. *Stop it! Run away! You don't know what you're doing! It isn't a joke. Monigan's real! And I think Julian Addiman's a bit mad!*

But, as always, she was ineffectual as a guardian angel. The bodily Sally did not hear and continued reciting under the moon.

The Invocation was longer than it used to be. Sally, or Julian Addiman, must have enlarged it. Now it was full of phrases like "gust thy hot breath through us" and "let thy blood-lust inflame our souls" which Cart would never have dreamt of putting in.

Meanwhile, Julian Addiman was busily lighting a ring of candles round Sally. They were tall fat yellow candles, stolen from School Chapel. As each one flickered alight, it gave a new view of his handsome white red-mouthed face. It was brilliant with sarcastic amusement, and his mouth seemed very wet.

The Invocation finished. Thirteen candles were now burning, and the ghost could feel the thing which was Monigan pressing close round the flickering circle.

"Right," said Julian Addiman. "My part now." He stood up with a flourish and stepped to a spot about a yard off where a spade was lying – stolen from Mr McLaggan. This he planted briskly in the earth and heaved. A large sod of turf, loaded with half-lit closed shapes of dandelions, peeled backwards and flopped over. The ghost could not resist hovering over to see what was underneath. On top of the dim hole was the carcass of the black hen. It was earthy but not long dead. It lay with its neck bent sideways on a heap of rusty iron links. Julian Addiman tossed the hen to one side and took out the iron, which proved to be a clanking armful of chain. He hung the chain carefully, in a heavy loop, over one arm. Then he picked the hen up by its neck and stood facing the moon and Sally and the candles. "These and myself I dedicate to thy use, oh Monigan," he intoned. He was not serious about it. He was grinning all through.

Then he stepped inside the candles and hung the chains on Sally.

Once more the ghost threw herself at Sally and tried to make her run away. But Sally just stood there, her eyes shining and blinking quietly in the light of the candles, letting Julian Addiman drape her in heavy chains, as if she was bewitched. The Monigan-feeling was in among the candles now, hanging its heavy presence on Sally, as heavy as the chains. It knew the ghost was there. It was cruelly amused at the ghost's efforts to frighten Sally. But, to be on the safe side, it threw contemptuously to both the idea that this was just a game. Just a game Julian Addiman was playing. As a result, Sally felt a mixture of disgust and amusement and horror. It seemed awfully silly and gruesome that the clanking chains should be sticky with hen's blood, which shone in the candlelight, mixed with rust and earth. It was a silly touch, when Julian Addiman saved a separate length of chain to hang round his own neck.

"We have bound ourselves to thy service, oh Monigan," he said, and laughed, to show that it was silly.

As a final touch, he took the dead hen and pressed its bloody, feathery side to Sally's forehead. Then to his own. After which, he raised the hen solemnly in both hands and said, "Repeat after me. I, Selina Melford, am now your servant, oh Monigan, and this bargain solemnised this night of the seventeenth of July. Now and henceforward I am yours."

When Sally started to repeat these words, the ghost felt the Monigan-force moving among the candles to take what was hers. Frantically, she tried to go upwards to avoid it. But it was no good. She was caught and pressed downwards above the uplifted dead hen, pressed and pressed, squirming and struggling. Monigan was all round her, like a flat misty blackness.

And the force seemed to say she must feed on the hen. *Feed on the hen*, it told her. *You can speak with mortals then. Feed.*

But she could not feed. She did not know how, and she was too disgusted and too terrified. She knew it would serve Monigan's purpose if she did. She struggled and struggled, and finally broke away from the hen, out as far as the ring of dead trees. But Monigan was still with her. She was held, hanging between two trees, with the mist at her back, unable to go forwards or backwards. She could still clearly see the ring of candles and Sally standing like a statue loaded with chains, and Julian Addiman standing in front of her, triumphant and amused.

The force that held them was cruelly angry, but it was also amused, just like Julian Addiman was. *You refuse to feed.* It was a joke, really. *Very well. You set me aside. I set you aside for seven years. I can afford it.* The joke turned very cruel, with triumph in it. *Those seven years are up now.*

At this, the mist from behind the dead elms rose up and advanced into the open space, slow and bulging and milky. It flowed across Sally and across Julian Addiman and hid them. For a moment, the thirteen candle flames blinked feebly through it. Then they were gone and the mist was rising again, into a fat maggot-like shape which dominated everything else. The trees, the moon and the fields vanished into the maggot, as if it was eating them up. But it was not a maggot. It was a thing swathed in bandages like a rotting mummy. It had a curious head, something like a dog's head without ears. Its face was hideous. It was made of fat pink fleshy lumps, peering out of the bandages. She did all she could not to be drawn towards this thing, and it drew her, helplessly. In seconds, she was face to face with it.

CHAPTER EIGHT

And it was a foot. It was a foot and a leg encased in plaster, raised up in front of her eyes by a sort of pulley. The face which had so terrified her were the toes of the foot, which the plaster did not quite cover.

She lay and stared at it. Is Monigan only a leg? she wondered, in some bewilderment. One of my legs, she corrected herself. Somehow, she had no doubt that the leg was part of her. She could feel it aching, in a dismal, distant way. She could feel the other leg aching too, and just catch glimpses of it, lower down, also in plaster. She was not really able to move. Just trying to see made everything turn grey. She shut her eyes and lay sniffing smells of antiseptic and polish. She could hear machinery humming in the distance, something clattering rather nearer, the squeak of shoes on polished tiles, and brisk voices not very far away.

Before she opened her eyes again, she was fairly sure she was in hospital. Sure enough, when she forced herself to look again, she could see a stand to her right, holding high up a transparent bag of red stuff that looked like blood. Tubes led down from the bag and vanished out of sight where her right arm must be. That seemed to be the arm she could move a little. The other arm, when she swivelled her eyes that way, was raised up and in plaster too. She had a feeling something was also wrong with her head. It hurt, and she could not move it. But nothing hurt very much. It was all remote and dreamy.

No wonder I thought I had an accident! she thought. I wonder how I got this way.

She had to close her eyes again then, and her question was answered almost immediately. Once again she was a floating nothingness, but, this time, it was more as you float in dreams. She knew she was lying in bed. She lay, and she floated, and she saw, driving away from her at furious speed, a small powerful car. She could see the heads of two people through its back window. But, as she saw them, the two people were clearly fighting. The one on the right, who was driving, was bigger. The heads were swaying over to the left as the bigger one won. The car gave a sharp wobble, and its left-hand door came open. It continued to go at a furious speed. The door was blown almost shut with the speed, and then forced open again to let a lady tumble out. She tumbled just like a doll, helplessly, to the rushing road, and, like a doll, went on tumbling for yards and yards, because her foot was hooked in a long black loop of seat belt. When at last her foot came loose, the car door slammed shut and the car sped away, leaving the doll-like crumpled lady lying at the side of the road.

Although she had no sense that this had happened to *her*, it was not a pleasant thing to see. The strong one driving that car had intended to throw the lady out. There was no question about that. She brought her eyes open and again tried to look at the hospital she was in.

This time, she grasped that she was in a small room at the end of a bigger ward. There were no windows in the room, but most of its walls were glass, so that there was sufficient bleak grey light. Beyond, in the ward, the light was warm and sunny. She had glimpses of more white plastered legs and of a nurse walking with a lady.

She had just closed her eyes again, when the nurse came into her glass room. She heard the nurse's voice. "I think she should be awake now. What name did you say it was?"

A very well-known voice, clear and pleasant, said, "Sally. Selina, really, but we say Sally."

Then the nurse was bending over the bed saying, "Try to wake up, dear. Here's your sister Sally to see you. She's been waiting for hours."

Highly confused, the person in the bed opened her eyes on swimming greyness. Then who am I? she wondered.

She heard someone give a distressed noise. No doubt she was an awful sight. "Are you awake? Can you hear me?"

She managed to focus on her sister. It was all a bit grey still, but she could see. It was the lady she had seen walking with the nurse, a grown-up lady. But it must be Sally. There was the fair hair that had surprised her in the farmhouse, now scraped back and done up somehow in a way that did not seem very pretty — although it could have been fashionable. Not that this lady had a very fashionable air. She was drab and depressed and seemed to be trying not to cry. But the depressed face had the right slight hawkiness about it, and there was no question that they knew one another well.

"I can hear you," she mumbled. It hurt a bit to speak, but not too much.

"Then I'm sorry!" Sally burst out, nearly in tears. "This is all my fault! It was me going on at you that did it! It was all my missionary zeal, telling you you really must finish with Julian Addiman. You do know what happened to you, do you?"

She thought. The doll-like lady and the car. "Julian Addiman threw me out of his car," she said. It did not worry her just then. She felt sorry for Julian Addiman in a way, because he had bound himself to Monigan and was going to have to murder her after seven years. "Seven years have passed," she said. It seemed a reasonable guess. But she did wish she could remember even a single one of the things that must have happened in those seven years.

Sally said, "Look, I brought you some flowers. Here."

Flowers were put in front of her face where she could see them. They were lilies. Some were flaming speckled tigerlilies, some delicate pink and gold, some white and some yellow. They were beautiful waxy things with big dusty stamens. She could not imagine them growing.

"Do you like them?"

She tried to nod and found she could not. But she managed to smile. "Lovely. Just as if I was dead."

"Oh *don't!*" her sister cried out. "You're not dead! Listen—" And she embarked on some kind of explanation. It was rambling and it was tearful, and it seemed to be some kind of self-accusation. Perhaps it was about Monigan. But the patient did not know. She found it hard to listen. All that came over to her was a rather familiar dismalness. Her sister blamed herself about Julian Addiman and the accident, it was true, but she was also far more worried and discontented about herself – as one would be after seven years of Monigan, the patient supposed. And she was expecting her injured sister to listen to it all and bear the weight of her discontent as if there was nothing wrong with her. It was all just as usual. And it was exhausting.

"Sally," the patient said at length. "Please. Talking hurts my head."

Sally's reply was to burst into tears. "Oh dear!" she sobbed. "I'm sorry! I'll go. I really have to go. I waited as long as I could, but I have to get hold of one of my teachers before this evening. I'll come back after that, shall I?"

Yes," said the patient, hoping she could stand it by then.

She closed her eyes and floated in greyness, trying to puzzle out what seemed to have happened. She was one of four Melford sisters who had once, as a game, invented the Worship of Monigan. Sally had gone on with the game and taught it to Julian Addiman, and had ended by dedicating herself to Monigan. But, after that, the dedication seemed to have got passed on to one of Sally's sisters. The question was, Which one? If she was not Sally, who was she? She tried looking back at her experiences as a ghost to see if she felt any more fellow-feeling for Cart, Imogen or Fenella. Not really, except for Imogen, when Imogen was dangling like a crazy scarecrow under the beam – and that might only have been because she knew what it felt like to be at the point of death.

A thought struck her: If Sally came to see me, then the others will come too. I shall know that the one who *doesn't* come must be me. That seemed clever, until it occurred to her that she could ask a nurse who she was. But she found she was ashamed to ask. It seemed so silly not to know, even though all the nurses must know she had lost her memory.

It was clear she must have lost her memory. Seven years had passed – or at least enough time for her sister Sally to grow into a drab, depressed lady – out of which she knew one fact: Julian

Addiman had done his best to kill her. All the rest was a blank, except for what she knew from being a ghost. And the funny part was that, apart from the last half hour of that time, Julian Addiman had not seemed important at all. She had not even remembered him. That suggested she must be Imogen or Fenella, for Cart had clearly fancied him, at least for a time. But, the fact was, she did not feel like any of them. Perhaps she was a case of mistaken identity?

No, that could not be true. Sister Sally was familiar, and her discontent was the most familiar thing of all. The home and the parents she had visited as a ghost had definitely been hers. And a funny home it was, she found herself realising: everyone so strange and her parents so busy, and no cooker in the kitchen. Could it have been a mad feverish dream? No. She knew it had been real and true. That School had really existed – perhaps did exist still.

The frightening thing was that the Monigan part had also been real. Which meant that, somehow, after seven years were up, she had been released as a ghost to visit the cause of her death. No. Because she was still alive. It was horribly confusing.

A beautiful thought struck her: Monigan meant to kill her, but, thanks to modern medicine, she didn't manage it.

Soothed by this idea, she went to sleep. But it worked in her head, distrustfully. The result was that, when she woke up and found someone else by her bed, the first thing she said was, "What date is it?"

"Sixteenth of July," the person sitting there replied promptly. "You've been unconscious twenty hours, as near as they can work it out. You was brought in here half past eight last night, and they thought you was a goner, I can tell you! They were half the night doing jigsaws on you. Did you know you had a hundred and ninety-two stitches in you? Fact. I asked in the Office," the visitor said gleefully. And she added, with thoughtful relish, "They won't half hurt coming out, too!"

The patient turned her eyes and gazed at – not a perfect stranger. She knew she had seen this new lady somewhere before, but where she could not imagine. She saw a smart not-quite-elderly lady, who had staved off advancing years by dyeing her hair bright ginger and using quantities of orange lipstick. She was wearing an exotic coat made of alternating areas of bald mauve plastic and curly lavender fur. The patient knew she had never seen *that* before. It was truly memorable. But the fat green and orange shopping bag dumped on the lady's knee was not entirely strange. Nor were the bright gleeful eyes and the dry perky features of the face beneath the ginger curls.

"Here," said the lady, digging busily in the green and orange bag. "I brought you some grapes. Got them on the station when I got in. Awful price they were – but then everything is these days." Her hand, plump and wrinkled, came into sight dangling a mighty bunch of big green grapes. "Like them?" she said. "Green is the best kind for eating, I always say. I thought of getting you flowers, but I didn't dare. I didn't see you, with your artistic tastes, liking anything I could buy."

"Thank you," said the patient feebly. She did not like to say she could not move enough to eat the grapes.

However, her visitor had thought of that. "Don't look as if you could move much, the mess you're in," she said. "Like me to pop one in your mouth?" She seemed to gather that the patient did not welcome this idea. Unconcerned, she laid the grapes down out of sight somewhere and rummaged in her bag again while she talked.

"They had a proper job tracing you, I can tell you, after they brought you in. You don't have to tell me what happened to you. It's common knowledge. That no-good boyfriend of yours threw you out of his car. The trouble was, he went off with your

116

handbag. I hope they've got him by now. There was plenty of witnesses – more fool him for choosing a main road! Someone got to you almost at once, thank the good Lord! But all the hospital had to go on, to find out who you was, was one of those school name-tapes on your old shirt, and all that said was MELFORD. I ask you! They was all night and half this morning trying to trace you – they got you through the Art School in the end. You'd have seen me last night if – well, you weren't in a fit state to see then, but you know what I mean."

The rummaging had at last produced a dingy old tobacco tin and some cigarette papers. The visitor proceeded to roll herself a cigarette, and talk continued to gush out of her. The patient stared. Who *was* this lady? Her landlady? That seemed the most likely idea.

"Just MELFORD," said the visitor, laying tobacco along a fragile strip of paper. "That's your Mum all over, making one set of tapes do for the four of you. If she could have brought herself to get you a set each, then they'd have had that much more to go on. Wouldn't they?" she asked, rolling the paper round the tobacco. "All economy is false economy," she declared, with her orange lips parted ready to lick the paper. She licked it, stuck it down, and continued, "As I've told your Mum, over and over again, skimping only leads to trouble. And don't say I'm not proved right by this!" she concluded. She stuck the withered little cigarette triumphantly in her mouth and lit it with a huge mock-agate lighter.

That proved to be the clue. Many and many a time, on raids to the school kitchen, had the patient seen just such a withered, bent cigarette, usually bearing a long trembling length of ash, sticking straight out of her visitor's face as it bent over a mixing bowl. Now she knew, she could see that there had actually been an expectant groove in the orange upper lip, waiting to be filled by that cigarette.

"Mrs Gill!" she exclaimed.

Mrs Gill crouched guiltily under a wave of blue smoke. "What? Am I going to be in trouble for smoking on the wards?"

"Oh no! No," said the patient. "It's just—" She found she could not bear to let Mrs Gill know how blank her memory was. "I've only just placed you. I don't think I've ever seen you dressed up before."

Mrs Gill laughed, a strong whirring chuckle. That was well known too. Fenella said it sounded like someone trying to start a car. "You'll bet you haven't, dear! I don't wear my good things to work. But I could see you couldn't place me. That's because you're in shock. In shock, they told me when I asked at the Office. I found out all about you. I thought your Mum and Dad ought to know. I've got it all written down here. Like me to read it out to you?"

"No thanks," the patient said hurriedly. One of Mrs Gill's most outstanding characteristics was a love of gory details.

"Yes, you'd be better off not knowing," Mrs Gill said. Her manner suggested that the very least thing wrong was a broken neck. "They'll tell you when you're off the danger list, I expect. Anyway, the hospital phoned through to the school around Break, but it's end of term, you know. Your father's up to the eyes in exams, and your Mum's packing all the boys' trunks – work, work, work. You know how they are. So I phoned your sisters and then said I'd pop up to Town and see you for her. Mind you," said Mrs Gill. She spoke with some viciousness. The patient instantly had dim memories of a thousand rows between Mrs Gill and Phyllis. "Mind *you*, I don't grudge the fare to London one bit, but I'm quite as able to pack a boy's trunk as what she is! Frankly, I nearly said to her, 'Mrs Melford, here's one of your daughters lying at death's door, and all you can think of is packing socks and shirts!' But I held my tongue. I'm not one to pick a quarrel."

"Of course not," said the patient. She was feeling grey again. Mrs Gill had brought back to her the reality of her time as a ghost. "Mrs Gill, do you remember a ghost? About seven years ago?"

Mrs Gill made her starting-motor chuckle. "You mean that time I saw right through one of you and threw custard over the kitchen? You were a wicked lot! Been up to Black Magic, hadn't you? Got half the boys in on it too! Oh yes. I remember the row there was, and all four of you packed off to your Granny's for corrupting the lads. But as I said to Lily at the time, those boys didn't need corrupting. Boys never do. And it was only a silly bit of child's play, when all's said and done. I never saw the harm in that."

"Do you think there was really no harm in it?" she asked eagerly.

Mrs Gill tipped her ginger curls to one side and considered. "I wouldn't say you was little innocents," she said. "Wicked is wicked and harm is harm, at any age. But children get up to things. Kids left to themselves get up to everything. But your father should have laughed it off, to my mind. You don't want to take the idea with you that you're wicked into when you're grown up. That's where the harm is. You don't grow up proper if you think you're wicked. But that's all over and done with now, and I'm worried about your father. He's not well. He ought to retire, really, but you get some that can't do that. My cousin's husband dropped dead the night after he retired. She told me, she said work was his life and— Oh, hallo, Charlotte, dear! Fancy you getting here so quick!"

Cart's voice, as well known as any, answered from somewhere out of sight, "It wasn't very quick, I'm afraid. I was supposed to be going to France with my tutor, to look after her children, and I had to see her and explain I couldn't go."

"Ah, she probably has sisters she's close to, too," Mrs Gill said wisely. "She knew how you felt."

"Yes. She has," Cart said, rather brusquely. "Then I had to hitch up from Cambridge, and that took ages." She came into sight and stood looking over the plaster, the bandages and the bag of blood with evident horror. "This looks an utter mess! How is she?"

"In shock, dear." Mrs Gill leapt up from her chair with a clatter. She and Cart retired almost out of sight and began holding one of those muttered conversations which makes any patient feel they must be at death's door.

This patient did not mind. She knew she was at death's door. It was only July the sixteenth. Monigan would be able to claim her just after midnight. She would have to tell Cart. Chiefly, she was occupied in staring at Cart – Cart whom she remembered as a blue bolster with a blurred face. It brought back a scene, around seven years ago, probably just before their school broke up for the summer holidays, when she and Cart had been coming out of school. At the bus stop had been standing a line of girls, some from Boots across the road, two from the school office, and a group from the Poly down the street. She and Cart had wondered how all these grown-up girls came to be so incredibly slim and pretty. They had wondered what happened in five or seven years to work such a change. They looked at the other girls coming out of school. They looked at one another.

"I don't know," Cart had said gloomily. "It must take a miracle."

The miracle had happened to Cart. She was evidently a student. Her jeans were old and patched. Her check shirt was tied in a knot at her waist. Her fair hair simply hung. And she was one of the prettiest girls the patient had ever seen. It was not only that she was slim and fair and young – and she looked younger now than she had looked as a bolster – she had a clear, glowing, confident look. She looked as if she felt as lovely as she looked. It was awesome.

She watched Cart smile radiantly at Mrs Gill. "Then I'll come and talk to you about it before you go. You'll want to come back and say goodbye anyway, won't you? I tell you what – I came in through Casualty. There were some awfully comfortable seats in the waiting room there. Why don't you wait there?"

"Just the job," agreed Mrs Gill. She leant forward to stare brightly at the patient's face. "Ta-ta for now, dear. At least you're not dead yet, eh?" Uttering her starting-motor chuckle, she vanished.

"Oh Cart," the patient said weakly. "It was naughty of you to send her to Casualty!"

Cart's clear features bunched into a much more familiar look of anger. "She's an old ghoul! Nothing delights her more than broken bones and buckets of gore. She was absolutely gloating over you!"

"I know." Weak tears greyed the sight of Cart's angry face. "I know she was, but you're not being fair, all the same. She came because Mother couldn't, and she paid her own fare, and she bought me a beautiful bunch of grapes."

"Yes. Typical of our parents!" Cart said, swinging herself angrily into the chair by the bed. "They can't be bothered, so they send Mrs Gill instead. And Mrs Gill goes, because then she can tell all her neighbours how they don't come near you even when you're at death's door. Oh – don't cry. I'm sorry. I *know* Mrs Gill was being quite as kind as she was being horrible, but it doesn't make it any less true, and that's what makes me angry! Now tell me how you are and what happened – or don't you know? Is it true that rat Addiman slung you out of his car? Oh *don't* cry! I suppose you're still as crazy about him as ever, even after he does this to you."

"No," she gulped. "Don't – don't think I ever cared two hoots for him." Tears continued to fill her eyes. She knew she was crying because of seeing Cart – Cart so transformed and yet so well known – and because she had suddenly realised that Cart was – and always had been – someone you could tell things to. Who, after all, had always patiently listened to Imogen's grieving?

Cart was staring at her. "Never cared for him? Now she tells me! You ran away from home after him, and actually forced Himself to pay for you at Art School so that you could be near him – and, believe me, no one has ever forced Himself to pay out so much money in his life! And now you say you never cared for Julian! Who's crazy? You or me?"

"Me," she sobbed. She wanted to say many things, but all she managed was, "M-monigan."

"Oh." Cart sat back, almost out of sight, in sudden sobriety. Her face, outlined against Sally's lilies, which someone seemed to have put in a vase, looked very clear and brooding and pale. "Now that's a funny thing," she said. Then, after a moment of brooding, "Yes, I *will* tell you. Do you remember Will Howard?"

"The one with a face like an otter," the patient said.

Cart laughed, a little blurt of merriment. "That's him! You were always so good at describing things! Well, you know he's in Canada now – I thought we'd lost touch with him entirely, but this morning, just before Mrs Gill phoned me, I got a telegram from him. Like to see it?"

"Yes please." She was astonished. Will Howard! What was such a stay-at-home English kind of boy doing in Canada?

Cart stood up to fetch a folded greyish paper from the back pocket of her patched jeans. Holding it spread between both hands, she leant over and displayed it before her sister's watery eyes. The smell of clean hair and health came off her as she leant.

I don't smell like that, the patient thought. I have that funny smell people have when they're ill. For a moment, the typed lines of capital letters danced all over the greyer letters printed behind them. Only the word ONTARIO stood out. She blinked, and the letters steadied.

CHARLOTTE MELFORD GIRTON COLLEGE CAMBRIDGE
REMEMBER MONIGAN CLAIMS A LIFE
JULY SEVENTEENTH THIS YEAR AND WATCH OUT
OR TRY ANOTHER HEN STOP WORRIED STIFF
HOWARD IN THE HEDGE

"He called himself that because he thought we might have forgotten him, I think," Cart said. "As if anyone could forget Howard! And when I read it first, I thought it was just Howard being silly. Then Mrs Gill phoned, and my spine crawled. I thought, It *can't* be! It's a day early. Monigan's cheated!"

"Two days early," said the patient. "It happened last night."

"Yes, I know," Cart said, sitting soberly down again. "But it's occurred to me that there have been two Leap Years since."

A grey chill seemed to settle over the little glassed-in antiseptic room.

"But it's so silly!" Cart burst out. "Monigan was just a stupid game! And I *curse* myself for inventing her – I curse my wretched imagination! I keep on telling myself that Monigan isn't real. Perhaps it's all a matter of belief. Perhaps you should try very hard not to believe in Monigan – because I can see you do, just as much as Howard does." She lifted the telegram up, to stand for Howard. "Stupid boy!" she said. "Stupid humble boy! Fancy thinking we might have forgotten him!"

The water in the patient's eyes welled, and rolled away down the sides of her stitched and plastered face. "But I have," she confessed. "I mean, I haven't forgotten *him*, but I haven't the faintest memory of him going to Canada!" She could see Cart turning to stare at her. "It's seven years since – since I last knew," she explained. "I've been having the weirdest experience. I've been a ghost, and I went home, and you were all there – I saw everyone. Howard was one of the first people I saw. But he was a schoolboy."

"Don't you really remember?" Cart said wonderingly. "It was just after the row over the hen, after we'd all been sent to Granny's. Will Howard suddenly turned up at Granny's and mooned about almost crying, because his parents had decided to take him and live in Canada, and he didn't want to go. We said we'd hide him. But," Cart concluded, remembering gloomily, "Granny phoned his parents and they came and fetched him away."

There was a pause. Then Cart turned to look at her sister again.

"Ghost, did you say? There *was* a ghost – or we all thought there was – just before the hen trouble. I think you'd better tell me."

She told it, hurrying, sobbing a little, and hurrying on. She was suddenly obsessed with the feeling that there was not much time. She told it all, more or less, right up to the exorcism and the farmhouse, and Sally's midnight dedication to Monigan. But what she did not say, and this was the fact pressing behind all the rest which she could not bring herself to tell even Cart, was that she did not know which sister she was. Not Cart. Not Sally, she thought as she spoke. So I'm either Imogen or Fenella. But I can't bear Cart to know I don't know.

Cart listened, bent forward, with two clear creases on her brow – the same clear creases her sister remembered as belonging to Imogen, when Imogen was thinking.

"So that explains the hen," Cart said at length, when the story was finished. "Funny that none of us knew then. But that's wrong somehow, you know. There's more to it than that, I *know* there is. I wish I could remember properly. For instance, I knew exactly what Will Howard was talking about in his telegram. I knew it was seven years, and that Monigan had demanded a life — but I don't know how I knew. What I do know is that we sort of understood then, and took some kind of action."

"Yes, you tried to exorcise me," the patient reminded her.

But Cart shook her hanging fair hair vigorously. "No. I don't mean that. That didn't work. I remember one of us saying — I forget which of us — that it was no good trying to be religious about it, because we were all so very irreligious. And I have a feeling that the things we tried after that were all highly irreligious — I *know* they were, in fact, because that was all part of the hen row — but—" Cart stopped and sat looking at her sister with strong anxiety.

"What?" she asked.

"You can't alter the past," Cart said. "The only thing you can alter is the future. People write stories pretending you can alter the past, but it can't be done. All you can do to the past is remember it wrong or interpret it differently, and that's no good to us. I'd forgotten the whole thing, until you started talking about it. I think I didn't want to remember it because it was so disturbing. I'd forgotten how keen we all were on Julian Addiman, for a start. We were all in a silly sexy flutter about him because he was different from Will and Ned and the other boys, and didn't think he had two heads like — who was it thought he had two heads?"

"Nutty Filbert," the patient supplied.

"Nutty Filbert," said Cart. "And he didn't do silly walks or pretend to be spastic like they did. In fact, I think that meant

Julian Addiman was probably rather insane even then. And," Cart said, looking rather astonished, "the end of that sentence should be 'though we weren't to know it'. But it isn't, is it? We all knew there was something wrong with him, and we knew it was dangerous, and that was why we were fascinated. Were we jealous of one another at all?"

"Yes—" said the patient. "No. Not about Julian Addiman."

"That's the odd thing!" said Cart. "We were in a way, but actually we were so – such a unity, that when one of us got him it almost didn't matter which of us it was."

"You make us sound like vultures – or female spiders," her sister protested.

"Well, we were in a way," Cart said. "I thought as I was talking that if none of us really cared two hoots about him, even you – well, it makes me wonder if Monigan wasn't really a manifestation of our common thirst for excitement, or our suicidal urges, or something."

"Do stop being so clever!" the patient begged her. "What are you trying to say?"

"I don't know," said Cart, slumping rather. She put her face in her hands. "The ghost was definitely there the next day," she said. "I remember that much clearly. It looks as if – you haven't finished yet." Her face came out of her hands. She was full of anxiety again. "Count two days for Leap Years and you've got till midnight tonight. Monigan *is* playing fair after all. Or someone is. It almost looks as if you're allowed to go back and see what you can do about it. But you can't!" Cart suddenly stood up. "Why am I sitting here babbling this bloody nonsense? Even if Monigan exists, no one can alter what's already happened. I know this – I knew it this morning. But even so, I was so damned superstitious that I telephoned Granny when I got Will's telegram, to see if Oliver was all right."

"Oliver!" her sister exclaimed. "Is Oliver still alive?"

"Oh yes," said Cart. "Didn't I——? I keep forgetting you can't remember. He's oldish, of course, and he smells, and he eats like a pig, but luckily Granny adores him, so he lives with her while I'm in Cambridge. I couldn't leave him at home. No one would remember to feed him." Suddenly, without warning or explanation, Cart's face folded together and she began to cry.

"What's the matter?" the patient said. Crying seemed infectious. She started to sob again herself.

"I'm sorry," wept Cart. She pulled out what she thought was a tissue from her pocket, found in time that it was the telegram, and wiped her shirt sleeve over her face instead. "Now I've made you cry too. It's just – I dote on Oliver, but seeing you there like that makes me see how much more I love you. You must – when you get back as a ghost, try and *make* us understand. We may have all been nut-cases, but none of us were fools. And——"

A nurse was suddenly there, a blurred shape beyond the great white leg. She said to Cart, "Do you mind waiting outside for ten minutes? Dr Smythe wants to examine Miss Melford."

"Of course," said Cart. She bent quickly over the patient, and once more brought the smell of health with her. "I've got the key to your flat, so I shall stay in London anyway, until you're better. May I use your bed? I know you'll hate the thought of me tidying your things, but I promise not to touch anything, honestly."

"That's all right," said the patient. She was aware that the doctor was in the room and that Cart was going away. "Just a moment," she called out. Cart paused. "*Are* you going to be a teacher?" Funny thing to ask, but it seemed important.

Cart hesitated, looking at the dim people crowding into the room. She grinned. She knew why it was important. "Just because Phyllis always said I was going to be? Come off it. It was her way of looking after us – telling us all we were bound for those careers made her feel we were taken care of. I haven't decided what to do yet. It's not that easy to get a job."

Then she had slipped away. Her place was taken by the dim people and by a great white leg with a nodding face of fat purplish toes.

CHAPTER NINE

There was peace to think again. Sally – no, she was not Sally, she must be Imogen or Fenella – hung among the buzzing flies in the empty kitchen room, trying to consider some of the things she now knew. But, as before, her intelligence as a ghost seemed as limited as a narrow torch beam. What was outside it hardly seemed to exist. The flies seemed to exist more, and the fading breakfast smells from beyond the green door.

None of the sisters seemed to be awake yet. There was silence apart from the flies and a distant hum from School. Outside the window, the apple trees gusted and the hens pecked in one of those windswept hot grey days when every colour looks bleak and ordinary. It was ominous, as if the day was expecting something. From time to time, the windows were covered with blisters of fine rain.

The ghost hung, trying to recapture some of the seven years between now and the hospital. It was a time of fruitless mistakes. It had been dominated on one hand by Himself, always angry but seldom there, and on the other hand by Julian Addiman, always laughing, always demanding more and more. Between them, she had scarcely been a person. At first she had tried to please them both, until it was obvious she could never please Himself: he was just not interested enough. After that, she had devoted herself wholly to pleasing the demanding Julian Addiman. She had gone to Art School, Cart had said. That seemed to be true. She had a fuzzy memory that Julian Addiman had decided on that. He said it made a good excuse to live near him in London. She could not live with him. He lived with his parents.

But Art School. What was that like? By turning the narrow beam of her attention on that as hard as she could, she recalled a time of being lost and shamed. There were a host of brilliant painters and wildly good young artists, who could all talk intelligently about what they were doing. She could not talk like that. And, as an artist, she knew she was stuck at what was good for a child, but rather feeble in a grown student. She was only there because of Julian Addiman.

She wondered if she had become as dismal and discontented as the grown-up Sally. She rather feared she had. She had blamed Julian Addiman for it. But she had known it was her fault for letting Julian Addiman take her over like this. And she had decided to break with him. She knew she had to, if she was ever to do anything of her own accord. But she was afraid to do it. Julian Addiman had outbursts of frightening violence if she did anything he did not want. That was how he came to fling her out of his car.

He was going to South Africa. His father had found him a job there. His father found him everything, even the car he had thrown her out of. Julian Addiman had wanted her to go to South Africa with him – to drop everything and go. And she knew this was the time when she had to say No. There were a thousand reasons – particularly the fact that South Africa was the kind of country it was. And she had put off saying No, because she was so frightened of him, until they were driving along in his car. Then she had clenched her hands and teeth and her courage, and said No. And Julian Addiman had reacted with more than his usual violence—

She was interrupted by Oliver. Oliver came stumbling sleepily out of the living room, and uttered a faint far-off rumble on finding she was still there. But he was used to her now. She was one of his family, after all. She could make herself useful and let him out for his morning airing. Accordingly, Oliver rolled his mottled donkey-sized bulk to the back door and stood with his head pointed at it patiently. When she did nothing, he uttered a few squeaks, like the whistle of a distant referee, and continued to stand, patient and pointed.

It's no good, she said. *I can't open doors in this state.*

Oliver did not believe her. He put his nose to the crack where the door closed and blew, meaningly. When that failed, he sighed, raised a massive three-clawed foot and hit the door with it. The door leapt about. Oliver waited, looked over his shoulder at her, and did it again.

Stop it, she said. *I told you, I can't.*

Oliver, however, went on hitting the door, and the door went on leaping, shaking the whole building. Five repetitions of this treatment brought Fenella, tramping half awake downstairs in her grey nylon nightwear.

"Oh," said Fenella. "The ghost is back again. Stupid dog. Ghosts can't open doors." She opened the door and Oliver rolled majestically forth.

The ghost went with him, for no real reason except that Cart had been anxious about him. She followed while he ambled forth among the hens and sketchily raised a hind leg against the hut that held Monigan. She followed again when he walked round the buildings and emerged in the wide bleak green of the playing fields. Here, Oliver went on the longest walk he ever permitted himself – to the other side of the field, almost as far as the dead elms.

She did not follow. She hung by the school, watching the shaggy shape, large even at that distance, ambling and prying among the hedge bottoms there.

She could feel Monigan out there. Monigan was waiting, gloating, dwelling out there in triumph. Last night, Sally and Julian Addiman had brought Monigan more life than she had had for centuries, and now the ghost could feel that life in each fleeting dry shower of rain and in each sour scudding patch of sunlight. Seven years away, Cart might have said she had invented Monigan, but that was not true. The school had once been a place called Mangan Manor, and Cart had taken the name from that, out of a mispronunciation Fenella once made. But who was to say Cart had not taken the name of a real being – either by accident or because that being made her take it? No, Monigan was terribly real.

Suddenly terrified, the ghost knew that the only way she could hang on to her little patch of existence – a white patch, seven years away, the size of a hospital bed – was by keeping near to people. People could keep Monigan away. People could stop Monigan moving in and taking her, if only they had long enough to understand in.

How long had she to make them understand? Seven years in the future, it had been – say – three in the afternoon. What was the time here? It was later than the soporific state of her sisters suggested. She could tell by the hum from the red-brick building that it was lesson time. Ten o'clock?

Confirming this, the school clock began to strike. Heavily, it tolled off ten. Then she had nine hours here. Until seven o'clock that evening. It was not much time.

The ghost fled back to their private quarters. *Quick! Wake them up. Get them to UNDERSTAND!* She arrived back with Oliver and was let in by Imogen this time. Imogen and Fenella were getting up. Imogen looked tousled and unwell, and the yellow trouser suit became her less than ever. Fenella was tousled too. The knots jutted at the sides of her face and her green sack hung unevenly. She stood in the middle of the littered living room and boomed to Imogen, "Oliver's feet are killing him and the ghost is back again."

"How do you know?" Imogen called from the kitchen.

"I just know," boomed Fenella.

From Cart, up above in the bedroom, came a wordless snarl of rage. It was like a wild animal. Both her sisters – and the ghost with them – stopped dead where they were and stared nervously at the ceiling. There was an angry rattle of bedsprings from above, but no further noise.

Fenella tiptoed into the kitchen. "I think she ought to get up and look after Oliver at least," she muttered to Imogen.

"Sssh!" said Imogen, staring at the ceiling, with half a loaf clutched anxiously to her chest. They remained like that for a good minute. When it seemed clear that there was going to be no further sound from Cart, Imogen whispered glumly, "There aren't any cornflakes left."

"Let's go and get some," said Fenella.

Remembering that Mrs Gill could see her, the ghost went with them, pushing through the green door and thumping through the silver one into the white, breakfast-scented school kitchen. There was not much going on there. The two other white-coated ladies were sitting face to face at the white-topped table, eating cornflakes. Looking at them now, with the eyes of someone seven years in the future, the ghost saw that one was an elderly nonentity and the other was a girl not much older than Cart. This girl had asserted her grown-upness by dyeing her hair a deep and improbable black. Mrs Gill was the one who mattered here. Mrs Gill was sitting at the table with her back to the door. Her hair, at this stage in her life, was a kind of peppery brown. As the door thumped, her peppery head turned, bringing into view her peaked side face and the cigarette curving from her upper lip.

"Get out of my kitchen," she said.

Fenella simply stumped towards the table and removed the packet of cornflakes from it. All three ladies stared unlovingly, but none of them said anything until Imogen came up too. Imogen, with a nervous duck of her head and a silly polite smile, picked up the jug of milk from the table and started to carry it away. It was clear that Fenella's brazen approach was the right one. There was something about Imogen's apologetic manner which invited trouble. All three ladies reacted.

"Hey!" said the young one. "You just put that back!"

"You got no right," said the old one.

"Coming in here," said Mrs Gill, passing smoothly into a tirade from a standing start, "without so much as a word, and walking off with half the food in the place. Spongers, that's what you are! When I was your ages, I was out at work. It's time you girls learnt to look after yourselves and stopped coming pinching things in my kitchen."

"We are trying to look after ourselves," Imogen pointed out humbly.

Mrs Gill flung round in her chair. The cigarette wagged

fiercely. "Well, you better try harder than this! I've had about enough of you girls coming in here and walking off with things. I'm going to speak to your mother about it." The cigarette wagged on, and with it went Mrs Gill's voice, shrilling and skirling. The tirade was so familiar that no one needed to listen properly. Hopefully, the ghost put herself where Mrs Gill could see her. Mrs Gill certainly saw her. Her face turned to the ghost, to Imogen, to Fenella, and the cigarette wagged fiercely her way every third sentence, like a punctuation mark. But Mrs Gill had evidently decided that her strange appearance was intended to annoy and just one more cross to bear. "You and your silly tricks!" the cigarette wagged at her. "I've had enough!" it wagged at Imogen. And at Fenella, "So I'm going to your mother this minute!" Mrs Gill seemed to mean this. She started to get up from her chair.

Fenella spoke. "Go if you like," she said carelessly. "And I shall go and tell her all the things you take away in your green and orange bag."

Mrs Gill's face became utterly still. It was hard, peaky and red, and her eyes stared into Fenella's venomously. "I see," she said. "Right." She turned back to her thick cup of coffee on the table. "You do one more thing, my girl," she said. She said no more. She picked up her cup. The other ladies went back to eating cornflakes. Fenella and Imogen might have been ghosts too, for all the notice anyone took of them.

Quietly and hurriedly, they retreated to the door and backed out, clutching the milk and the cornflakes. "I wish you hadn't said that," Imogen whispered when they were outside in the passage.

"So do I," said Fenella. "But I had to, or she'd have gone to Phyllis."

"But we've got a *right* to food!" Imogen said wretchedly.

"What else can we do? Do you think Phyllis would give us the money to buy cornflakes of our own?"

"No," said Fenella.

They arrived back in their own kitchen, where Fenella first poured a large heap of cornflakes and milk in a bowl for Oliver and then another, without milk but even larger, into a bowl for herself. She sat down to eat them dry.

"Have some milk," Imogen said hopelessly, with a jug in her hand.

"No," said Fenella. "Milk makes them all soggy."

"Milk is good for you," Imogen observed, pouring milk on her own cornflakes.

"I never eat things which are good for me," said Fenella.

There was silence except for the sound of three mouths eating cornflakes. In it, the ghost hung, wondering what to do. She saw she had been silly to expect Mrs Gill to notice her. For Mrs Gill would have mentioned it in the hospital if she had understood. According to Cart, it was her sisters who had seemed to understand. So how had she attracted their attention?

One of them must be me, she said.

She looked at Imogen. Imogen was spooning up cornflakes, fast and desolately. A tear was working its way down one of her cheeks. Mrs Gill had started her grieving again, and that meant she was not likely to notice anything else.

Fenella, then? Fenella knew she was there. Maybe that was because they were the same person. The ghost floated nearer, just beside Fenella's bony shoulder and sharp munching jaw.

Fenella, she said. *I think I may be your ghost.*

Nothing came of it because, overhead, Cart came to life again. She came with a scream, which modulated to a roar, and then became a scream again, without ever once sounding like a human voice. "Will you all *stop* that horrible *crunching!*"

All jaws stopped, even Oliver's. All attention was on the ceiling.

"How can a person *sleep!*" screamed Cart. "In all this *din!*"

Fenella gave Imogen a deeply expressive look and raised her voice in return. "It's after ten," she boomed. "We're having breakfast."

"Well stop it at *once!*" howled Cart. "Or I'll come down and *kill* you!" She meant this. It was clear to everyone. Oliver lay down beside his bowl with a sigh. Imogen and Fenella looked at one another.

"No one can eat cornflakes quietly," Imogen breathed.

"Even soggy ones," Fenella whispered grimly.

"And stop that bloody *whispering!*" yelled Cart.

Imogen and Fenella looked at one another again, united in loathing for Cart. The ghost did not blame them. She had been thinking kindly of Cart — too kindly, she knew. Maybe the grown-up Cart deserved this kindness. This Cart did not. She had forgotten what Cart was like in the morning, and not just this morning, but every morning. And there was worse to come, she knew. Imogen bowed her head and gripped the edge of the table, mustering courage.

"I shouldn't," Fenella said warningly.

Imogen took no notice. It was something she did every morning. She never seemed to learn. Having made herself as brave as she could, she got up silently and tiptoed gently, gently, through the living room. She stopped at the foot of the stairs, where she cocked her head sideways and adjusted a sweet smile on her face. She was seeing herself as a ministering angel. She needed to, in the circumstances.

"Cart dear," Imogen cooed gently up the stairs, "shall I bring you up some coffee?"

A terrible growl was the answer. Imogen flinched. Oliver at his fiercest sounded like a lamb in comparison.

"I'll put the kettle on, shall I, Cart dear?" Imogen said. It was more of a quaver than a coo.

"Oh shut up!" snarled the thick animal voice upstairs. "When you start being tactful, you *really* get up my nose!"

"Cart dear—" Imogen began again unwisely.

"AAARGH!" went Cart. There was a surging sound and a heavy bump that shook the ceiling. Imogen went pale. Her ministering attitude somehow became that of someone poised on one foot ready to run. And with reason. The ceiling vibrated. The stairs shook. Cart appeared with unbelievable speed, wild haired, white faced and snarling, and dived down the stairs without apparently treading on any of them. The ghost caught a whirling glimpse of bared teeth, and swollen eyelids with little piggy eyes glaring between them, and found herself crouching on top of the piano. Imogen took a running dive and vanished into the space between the piano and the sofa. By the time Cart hit the living room floor, with a crash that shook the whole building, the room was apparently empty.

"*Aaargh!*" snarled Cart, glaring pig-eyed. She made for the kitchen in huge strides.

There was a crash, a yelp from Oliver, and the sound of big bodies falling about. Fenella bolted round the door, running on hands and knees like a spidery monkey, and came to join Imogen behind the sofa. "I *told* you not to!" she whispered.

"Come out, you cowardly little creeps!" Cart bawled. There was a series of awesome bangs.

"What's she doing?" Imogen whispered, as Oliver too crept into the living room. His blurry tail was wedged down between his great hind legs. He was shivering.

"Breaking another chair, I think," said Fenella. She sighed. Sure enough, the bangs became splintering noises and the sound of pieces of wood clattering on to the stone floor. All the same, Cart's growls showed signs of becoming slightly less animal. Once, there was even the gasp of a human being with a splinter up its thumbnail. This was followed by a thick human voice, swearing. And this in turn was followed by a last clatter, then silence. Eventually, there came the sound of cornflakes pattering into a bowl.

Imogen relaxed a little. She dared to sit up. "Cart's blood sugar is low in the mornings," she explained to Fenella.

"Is that what it's called?" said Fenella. "I thought it was bad temper."

They sat side by side on the floor, listening to the sounds of an ape woman chomping cornflakes in the next room. The ghost descended to them.

Fenella, you know I'm here. Please help. I've only got six and a half hours left now.

Unfortunately, Imogen spoke at the same moment. "Fenella," she said, "what am I going to do? I can't do my practice without going through there." She pointed to the kitchen door.

Fenella spoke to Imogen. She did not hear the ghost. "You could wait an hour till she's human," she said.

"But they'll be using the music rooms in an hour," Imogen wailed. "I'll be turned out again."

"Shut up!" Cart growled from the kitchen. "Let me have breakfast in peace!"

Fenella and Imogen shut up. They were forced to hold the rest of their conversation in signs, which left them no attention for a ghost.

"Oh all right," Imogen whispered dismally at length. "Everything's horrible anyway. But I bet she'll kill me."

"I'll guard you, I promise," Fenella whispered back.

Sighing, Imogen scrambled to her feet and pulled the legs of her trouser suit out from under her shoes. She began gloomily clearing away the picture, the papers and the jar of paint-water from the yellow keys of the old piano, and dusting it with the front of her suit. The suit was big enough for Imogen to take a bunch of it and use it as a cloth, without even leaning forward. Fenella, meanwhile, dragged an armchair in front of the kitchen doorway and took up a post cross-legged on the back of it. She made signs to show that Cart was now reading a book.

Imogen nodded and arranged music on the yellow stand. Then she arranged herself on the frayed and wobbly stool and sat staring at the music.

"It's OK," Fenella whispered encouragingly. "Get on."

But Imogen seemed to be in the grip of gloomy apprehension. She just sat. The ghost did not blame her, knowing what Cart was like. She tried to use the silence to catch their attention.

Imogen! Fenella! she screamed. *Help me!* It felt as if it ought to be as loud as the roars of Cart. But even she could tell that it made no sound at all. She stopped, despairing.

"This is going to sound excruciating," Imogen murmured.

"Well, it's a crucial piano," Fenella murmured back.

"I don't mean that," said Imogen. She sighed. Her face was bloated with misery as she put both hands to the yellow keyboard and began to play.

The ghost listened, rather amazed. It was a piece of music which the ghost knew as well as Imogen evidently did. Imogen did not bother to look at the music. Her elbows were stiff and her head slightly bent, and she seemed to be attending to something away beyond the music. Maybe she was waiting for Cart to erupt again. But there was more wrong than that. The ghost had always thought of that particular piece as a soaring electric rumble, with a tune edging sideways from the rumble. True, Imogen was playing it on a cheap old piano which was rather out of tune. But she was playing it like a machine, and the music was simply a collection of notes.

Oh, come on, Imogen! she said, without meaning to. *You can do better than that!*

"No I can't," Imogen answered as she played, without looking round. "I think I hate it."

Imogen had heard her! It must be because Imogen was playing and not really attending. Terribly excited, and trying not to let the excitement show and distract Imogen, the ghost said, *You must have been on this piece too long then.* That seemed likely, considering how well they both seemed to know it.

"Only a fortnight," Imogen said gloomily.

Well then, said the ghost. *Try something else you like better. And while you're playing, listen to something I—*

"It's not that!" Imogen interrupted irritably, rattling notes off like a pianola. "I've a brilliant memory for music. I don't deny that. But—"

"Shut up!" Cart bawled from the doorway. A book, heavily thrown, caught Fenella in the stomach and knocked her backwards off her chair. Cart followed up the book with the packet of cornflakes. It hit Imogen on the head and burst all over her. Cornflakes whirled in the air and pattered down on the piano keys. "Take that!" Cart howled. "For making a horrible noise! I told you to be quiet!"

Imogen turned, with immense dignity. A cornflake, lodged in a tear, slid down one of her cheeks. While it slid, Imogen examined Cart's glaring face for signs of humanity. She seemed to decide Cart was joining the human race by now. "I have to practise," she said.

"Yes, but you don't have to babble to yourself like a lunatic while you do!" Cart snarled, and breathed heavily and threateningly through her nose, like a bull ready to toss someone.

"I shall talk if I like," retorted Imogen. "And you've wasted all the new cornflakes. Clear them up."

"You made me do it! Clear them up yourself!" roared Cart.

"And you've murdered me!" Fenella boomed, crawling out from beyond the armchair. She knelt up, holding her stomach. "When I die, my ghost will come back and haunt you."

By this time, all three of them were shouting at once. Imogen was keeping time to her shouts by banging her hand down on the piano. The noise was horrible. Jangle, crash, scream.

The ghost quivered among the yells and the discords. She was very shaken − not by the quarrel: she was used to those − but by the way she had known that music Imogen was playing so well. It ought to mean she was Imogen. But, if she was Imogen, why on earth had she gone to Art School? Everyone knew Imogen was going to be a concert pianist. And then Fenella had thrown it all in doubt by threatening to come back and haunt Cart. Fenella had meant that. And here she was, a ghost.

Oh, how shall I find out? she wailed to herself, moving away backwards from the noise. It was a great relief to hear the screams getting fainter and fainter. But this was not helping her attract their attention. She was getting too far away. She could see a monstrous mummified leg again. And, as the narrow torch beam of her attention turned back to the hospital, it caught a memory of a grey crisp paper with words swimming on it. ONTARIO... HOWARD IN THE HEDGE.

CHAPTER TEN

Of course! she said. *Howard was in on it. He's the one to get in touch with.*

She was whirling through the orchard as she said it. Through the hedge to the trampled garden she went, under the lime trees and in by the pointed door in the red-brick school. The hum of the building told her that lessons were still on – but, surely, it would be Break any minute now. She floated her way to the arched door labelled IV A. And stopped. She could hear Himself's voice beyond it.

Well, that doesn't matter, she said. *He didn't know I was there before.* She pushed herself through the wood of the door into the warm classroom beyond.

Himself was striding sideways up and down in front of the row of faces, ruffled and beaky, with his hands clasped behind his back so that his jacket humped out like two folded wings. He resembled nothing so much as an eagle sidling up and down its perch. He was ready to peck at anyone who came near, too. He was in his worst mood – his morning mood: Cart's bad temper was hereditary. With a snap and a dart of his head, he was saying, "So you can't see the use of learning grammar, can you? So you've been infected with this modern nonsense, have you? You think there's no point in knowing a noun from a verb. I repeat, Filbert: What is a preposition?"

In front of him, the gap-toothed face belonging to Nutty Filbert wore a bemused grin. At the sight of it, Himself's head jerked, in pecking position, ready to rend Nutty Filbert. The grin left Nutty Filbert's face. "I know what it is, sir," he said hastily, "but I can't explain, sir."

"It's impalpable, sir," someone at the back suggested cleverly.

Heads turned to see who had dared be this clever. Among them was the smooth otter-head of Will Howard, with, beside it, the sandy brush of Ned Jenkins. The ghost darted to them. *Howard, please—!*

"Impalpable!" roared Himself. He sounded worse than Cart. "What's that supposed to mean?" His arms spread. The eagle mantled, ready to take off and destroy. "Impalpable means it can't be touched. I suppose that means you intend to leave the preposition severely alone. Let me tell you, boy... ."

As Himself roared on, the ghost beat unavailingly round the smooth otter-head in its electric field of life. But Howard, like all the rest, was staring at Himself mantling and roaring, waiting for the blow to fall.

And here it came. Himself folded his wings, re-clasped his hands and went quiet. "Very well," he said. "We must see how wilful this ignorance is. Boys are not going to leave my hands without knowing basic grammar. Open your books at page forty-nine and write me out translations of sentences one to five."

"But, sir," someone had the nerve to protest, "it's nearly Break time."

"Is it?" Himself's head shot savagely round that boy's way. "What a shame. Then you'd better get to work quickly, because no boy is leaving this room until he has handed me in those five sentences."

The room was thick with held-in sighs and moans no one dared make. Pages tumbled and rustled as everyone sought for page forty-nine. It was odd, the ghost thought, how teachers always talked as if you could open your book at the exact page they wanted. No one ever could. Exercise books were spread open, pens picked up and heads bowed. She looked down on Howard's smooth bent head. This was impossible. Howard's yellow ballpoint pen was poised in the air, making irritable scribbling movements, as Howard tried to work out what sentence one could possibly mean. Howard's mind was on Latin and Break, and not on ghosts or even his friends the Melford sisters. Now his pen went down. He was writing.

I. We point at the elephants—

But this was it! It could be done just as she had done it at the séance. She threw herself against Howard's fizzing hand and the pen held in it.

—advancing towards Rome, Howard wrote stolidly. She had not been able to shift his hand a millimetre. Now his pen was up, scribbling in the air, while he worked out sentence two. She waited, dithering. When he started to write again, she *would* push the pen. The pen went down. She threw herself at it, shoving mightily.

2. The soldiers walked out of the temple and marched round the forum, Howard wrote imperviously. And up went his yellow pen again. The ghost moved up with it, nearly in despair. One thing kept her hovering, ready to try again. Howard had sent that

telegram. And that meant she had got through to him somehow. But he was being a long time over sentence three. It must be difficult.

There was movement on the other side of her. Ned Jenkins' red pen in Ned Jenkins' left hand was coming slowly and doubtfully down towards a blank page. *I didn't know you were left-handed*, she said to him. *Hey——!* Howard's yellow pen was still scribbling in the air. So why not try pushing at Ned's hand while she was waiting?

She threw herself at Ned's red pen, just as it met the paper. He was holding it slackly, listlessly, obviously wishing the lesson would be over. And it moved. Under her push, it jerked sideways and drew a long curved line. Ned muttered something exasperated. His arm fizzed against her as he went to lift the pen up. But she could not let him do that. She held it down with all her strength. There was more fizzing, as Ned fought to get his hand up and move the pen off the paper, and wild electric heat higher up, as Ned's face first went bright unwholesome red and then drained to yellow-white, blotched with freckles the colour of cornflakes. She went on holding his hand down. It was suddenly limp. He was holding the pen laxly and staring down at it, white and unblinking. She was afraid he had fainted. But she could move the pen.

It was still immensely difficult. Ned's hand was like a dead weight, white, freckled and bony. And it was used to writing Ned's way. It was not good at someone else's writing. She had to heave and force and thrust at it, and, try as she would, she could not make writing of an ordinary, small size. Her letters were huge, sprawling and ungainly. Because of that and because of it being so difficult, she kept it short.

IM ONE MELFORD GIRL DON'T KNOW WHICH
7 YRS OFF NEED HELP MONIGAN HELP

The message ended in a sharp scribble because Ned, still white and staring, seemed to expect her to go on writing. She had to wrench herself away from his limp hand and then give it a sharp shove the other way to show him she had finished. Ned jumped. A faint pink came back to his face. She saw him look hastily round. One or two boys were already going out to the front to hand their exercise books to Himself. Almost at the same time, there was the immense shrill dinning of the bell for Break. That made Ned jump again and seemed to galvanise him into action. Deftly, so deftly and swiftly that it was clear this was something he often did, he took the page out of the exercise book. He did not tear it. He flipped open the staples in the middle of the book and took the whole sheet out, the page from near the beginning of the book as well as this one near the end, and folded it into his pocket in one quick movement. Then he pushed the staples shut again and began to write on the next clean page as if for dear life.

I. Elephants eat porridge in Rome, the ghost read. 2. It is miles round the temple yard. *Oh dear!* she said. *You're just guessing. I've got you into trouble.* She hung over Ned and watched him miraculously finish five wild sentences at the same time as Howard completed his five careful ones. They both got up and went to hand their books to Himself together.

Himself took Howard's book with a simple grunt. But he looked up at Jenkins, no doubt because of the way his freckles shone yellowish in his ashy white face. "Are you feeling well, Jenkins?"

"Yes, sir," said Jenkins.

"Hm," said Himself. "Then your pallor must be the result of inspiration. No doubt your sentences exhibit your usual wild creativity." He made as if to open the exercise book.

No! cried the ghost.

Howard seized Jenkins by the arm and leant towards Himself with a cheerful, cheeky grin. "He needs some fresh air, sir. I think Latin disagrees with him."

"That, or school breakfast," Himself said. To everyone's relief, he laid Ned's exercise book down on top of the growing heap and put out his hand for the one the boy behind was holding out to him.

Howard shoved Jenkins in front of him out of the open door into the seething, racing crowd in the corridor. The ghost went with them. Because of the jostling and the fizzing, she found it easier to hang in the air above the smooth head and the sandy one. She heard Howard say, "Seriously, Jenk, what's up. You look as if you've seen a ghost."

Jenkins gave a short gulp of a laugh. "Not exactly *seen*," he said. "Come on, Will. We've got to go through the hedge again. But quick."

She felt Howard stop short. The two made a still island in the fizzing crowd. "Semolina?" he said.

"Yes," said Jenkins. "I think so. And I think it's urgent. Come on."

So it had worked! In the greatest relief, the ghost sped back to the sisters to wait for them.

And there in the kitchen was Phyllis, a harassed grave angel. Cart, Imogen and Fenella were standing in a sullen row in front of her. Someone had hidden the broken chair under the table, but there were still cornflakes, thick as autumn leaves, making a trail through to the living room.

"I'm not discussing the rights and wrongs of your meals, Imogen," Phyllis was saying. "It's just unpardonable the way you keep annoying Mrs Gill. She complained yesterday, and she's complained again this morning—"

"And so do I complain," said Fenella. "Mother, Mrs Gill takes food away every day in her green and orange bag."

"I'm not discussing that either, Fenella." Phyllis turned to Fenella. She had her eyes shut with displeasure. This must have been why she failed to notice the two knots at the front of Fenella's hair. "What you four girls—" She had not noticed Sally was not there either. "What you girls don't seem to understand is that it's almost impossible to get staff for the kitchen these days. I can't *afford* to have Mrs Gill annoyed. If she were to give notice, I should be absolutely stuck."

This scene again, the ghost said dismally. Then she realised that she need not stay and listen to it. It was almost the first advantage she had found in being a ghost.

She whirled off again. She had meant to go back to Howard and Jenkins, who must be pushing their way into the secret path in the hedge by now. It might be that she could warn them about Phyllis somehow. But she found herself with Oliver instead. Oliver, in the bleak grey sunlight, was rooting around in the kitchen garden. He was engaged in digging, gently and not too actively, in the nice soft dungy earth where the rhubarb grew. The hole was already quite large. Broken pink stalks and dying rhubarb leaves lay all round Oliver's massive, meditative form. He put out a huge three-clawed foot, parted the earth, set another clump of rhubarb toppling, and then turned, mildly interested.

The unpleasant Mr McLaggan was standing three feet away, flourishing a rake at him. "Shoo! Get out of my rhubarb, you brute!"

Oliver meditated on Mr McLaggan for a second, and turned back placidly to demolishing rhubarb again.

"Gerrah, you brute!" Mr McLaggan shoved at Oliver with the rake. It met Oliver's side. Mr McLaggan leant on it with both wellingtons braced, and pushed. Oliver, rather wearily, put his fourth foot down for balance and looked round again at the leaning, pushing Mr McLaggan. The rake did not seem to affect him at all. After a moment, annoyed at being interrupted, he let out a gentle rumbling. Mr McLaggan hastily took the rake away and stood back. Oliver went back to his digging.

Mr McLaggan waved the rake in the air. "You! You may have a lucky foot!" said Mr McLaggan. "But that won't help you when I go to Mr Melford. You'll get what's coming to you then, foot or no foot!"

The ghost whirled on. Oliver could look after himself, but she was not so sure about Howard and Jenkins. She meant to go back to them. But, perhaps because of what Mr McLaggan said, she found herself with Himself instead.

Himself was in a large smoky room filled with other men and some women. It must be the Staff Room, a place she had never before even seen the inside of. But she did not see much of it. Her small ray of attention was focused entirely on Himself. He seemed to have recovered his temper. Anyway he was laughing, with his teeth closed on the stem of a smelly black pipe. In the blue smoke from his pipe was the flapping shape of an exercise book.

"Listen to this," said Himself. With his other hand, he was stirring a cup of coffee. He had a particular, obsessive way of stirring coffee, with the spoon held between his finger and thumb, and the finger and thumb nodding, nodding, making the spoon go round and round and round, like a machine. "Jenkins," said Himself through his teeth, stirring and stirring. "That boy is some kind of misguided genius, I think. He can conjure a howler out of the air. Listen."

Still stirring, Himself tried to spread the floppy book out one-handed in the air. It half closed. The page he was trying to read flipped over, revealing another. This was a page Jenkins had evidently forgotten to take out. On it was one of Ned's good-bad drawings, one of his best: Himself as a great black eagle, tufty of head and fierce of eye, chained to a perch by one claw and holding a book in the other.

"Hm," said Himself, staring rather grimly at it.

The ghost had a glimpse of the man Himself was talking to doubled over, laughing. But her attention was on Himself and Himself's finger and thumb, nodding, nodding, sending spoon and coffee smoothly swirling in the cup, round and round and round...

It was dragging her away, that nodding and swirling. Through it was appearing a great white leg, mummified in plaster. She had a sense of people round her, doing things. Someone, a stranger, was leaning over her calling her "dear".

"Will you move your hand if you can hear me, dear."

She lay there, considering this, as grimly as Himself had considered Ned's drawing. She had been dragged away – dragged seven years away – she was sure of it. That was Monigan's doing. Monigan did not want her prying about school. Something was happening, or about to happen there, which was important. If she was there, she might even have a chance to get the better of Monigan. So she must go back. At once.

She set herself to go. The person was still leaning over her entreating her to move her hand, but she did not dare obey. Anything like that would keep her there. She pushed and strove and thrust instead, to get herself seven years back in the past again. It was far more difficult than pushing Ned's hand. She felt like Mr McLaggan leaning on the immovable Oliver. Monigan was resisting her. To Monigan, it was not a question of moving seven years in one direction or another. The time at school and the time in the hospital were running side by side to her. This was what it meant to be a goddess. It was an easy matter to stop a ghost moving from one band of time to another.

As soon as she realised this, the ghost struggled harder than ever. For this meant, whatever Cart said, that she *had* a chance of changing the past. As far as Monigan was concerned, the next thing in the past had not happened yet. And she must get there. She must.

She felt Monigan yielding, bit by bit. At first she gave way peevishly. Then with a shrug. The final yielding was in a rush, with nasty amusement. She felt Monigan think, *And much good will it do you!* And she was back with a jolt, confused and anxious. *Am I too late?*

She almost was. Phyllis had gone. In the kitchen, Ned Jenkins, still very pale, had the double page out of his exercise book spread on the table. Round it were spread other papers: a letter from Sally, a school essay of Cart's, a poem in Imogen's writing and a scrawl in Fenella's. Evidently, they had been trying to decide whose writing the ghost's was. Cart, Imogen, Fenella and Howard were leaning over the papers, but rather as if they had stopped being interested in them.

"So all we can tell," Howard was saying, "is that it's not Ned's writing. It could be any of yours. You all write a bit alike, even Sally."

"Well, it's not Sally," Imogen said firmly. "You all heard me talking to her on the phone."

"And the ghost went away anyway," said Fenella.

"Having set us all by the ears," Cart said crossly. Unlike Himself, she was not yet in a good temper, though at least she was dressed now. She was a blue bolster in jeans today – and the jeans were much larger and wider than the old patched jeans of seven years ahead.

Ned Jenkins raised his pale face. "I think the ghost's back."

Fenella looked up to deny it, and paused. "Yes, he's right. It's here again. I can feel."

Imogen suddenly became hysterical. She backed away from the table, shaking her hands as if they were wet. "What do we *do*? *Do* something, somebody! I'm not going to live with a ghost all my life! I refuse to!"

"Shut up, Imogen," said Cart. "That ghost is in trouble. Of course we'll do something — particularly as it's obviously one of us."

"Or thinks it is," said Howard. "What do we do?"

"What *can* we do?" Imogen demanded, shaking her hands wildly. "Even exorcism didn't work!"

"That was too religious," Fenella said gloomily. "We're not religious enough for it to work."

"Then," asked Howard, "anyone got any ideas that aren't religious?"

In the silence that followed, Ned Jenkins murmured, as if he hoped no one would hear, "I could try writing again."

"Yes," said Cart. "But—" She stopped. She stared at the ceiling, and her eyes bulged slightly. "Wait," she said. And she was suddenly off at a gallop. Cornflakes crunched as she raced to the living room. Things fell over. There were thumps and sharp bangs. Then suddenly she was back, red and breathless, hurling fat paperback books on to the table. Thump — *The Odyssey* — thump — *The Iliad* — thump — Virgil's *Aeneid*. "There!" she said. "Somewhere in these there's a way to make them speak — it tells you how to make a ghost talk — I know there is! Do either of you two know which book?"

"Who us? No," Howard said blankly.

"I've never read the things," said Jenkins.

"Oh!" Cart was feverishly opening first one book, then another. "I thought you two were supposed to be having a classical education. I *know* it's in one of these somewhere. He made a ghost speak — whoever he was — by letting it drink blood."

She gave up her feverish search and threw the books back on the table. "I can't find it, but I know it anyway. Let's try it. Everyone go and get some blood. Quick!"

"Blood? Where?" said Howard and Jenkins, gazing dimly at one another. "And why?" added Howard.

"Thickhead," said Cart. "If the ghost can talk, it can tell us how to help it."

"Don't be so stupid," Fenella said severely to Howard. "People are full of blood. Cut yourself. Then go and see if they've got any in the Biology Lab."

"You silly fool!" Imogen said to Jenkins. "I never go past any of the little boys without seeing at least two of them with nose bleeds. Go and get them to make them bleed here."

"Yes," said Cart. She fetched the enamel bowl from the sink and dumped it with a *boom* on the table. "Get everyone to bleed in this. Tell them all contributions welcome. I'm going to raid Mrs Gill for some. Hurry. Break will be over before we've got any at this rate."

Howard and Jenkins caught the idea at last. "General call for blood!" Howard said excitedly. "Come on, Jenk!"

Everybody scattered, except Fenella. Fenella climbed on the table and knelt there, leaning over the bowl, where she commenced hitting herself rhythmically on the steep bridge of her nose. The ghost went with Cart, through a whirl of banging doors, once more to raid Mrs Gill. She was rather nervous of what Cart intended to do to Mrs Gill.

Cart stood with her back to the silvery metal of the school kitchen door. She had a blurred polite smile on her face, as if she did not mean Mrs Gill too much harm. "Oh good," she said.

On the table, there was now a silvery tray, out of which stood the rounded glistening hulks of two ox hearts. The tray was swimming nearly brim-full with weak blood from them. The sight cheered the ghost as much as it seemed to cheer Cart. No one would have to bleed Mrs Gill now. Cart went over to a white cupboard and helped herself to a thick white jug. It looked as if her method with Mrs Gill was halfway between Imogen's and Fenella's. Mrs Gill, who was slicing brassy yellow lumps of margarine into a mixer bowl, turned her face and her cigarette to watch Cart, but she did not say anything. Cart did not say anything either. She gave Mrs Gill another smile and held the tray so that blood poured out from one corner into the thick jug.

Naturally, the two slippery ox hearts began to lumber down the sloping tray, bringing a wave of blood with them. "Bother!" said Cart. She put the jug down on a chair, pulled the chair over to hold up one corner of the tray, and used her free hand to hold the slippery brown hearts in place.

"And just what are you two doing now?" said Mrs Gill.

"Only getting some blood," Cart said airily.

"And dirtying lunch," Mrs Gill threw down her lump of margarine and advanced, wiping her hands. Having done that, she took the cigarette out of her mouth, showing she meant business. "Out," she said. "This minute."

Cart was keeping a wary eye on her. "In just a moment," she said. "Which two of us do you think this is?"

"You know who you are as well as I do," retorted Mrs Gill. "Did I say Out, or did I not?"

She was now near enough to grab the tin, and she reached out to do it. Cart let go and backed off hastily with the nearly full jug.

"And see you bring that jug back!" Mrs Gill said.

"Are you accusing *me* of dishonesty?" said Cart, and backed out between the thumping doors again. The ghost did not like the last glimpse she had of Mrs Gill's face.

Back in their own kitchen, Fenella was kneeling by the bowl, wiping her upper lip with toilet paper. One of her knots of hair was red and sticky. "I managed a bit of a nose bleed," she said. "But it's not one of my best."

"Every little helps," Cart said cheerfully. There were now a few bright red splashes in the wide bottom of the bowl. Cart emptied her jugful in it. It made a watery mixture.

"It looks a bit weak," Fenella said doubtfully.

"We'll thicken it," said Cart. She took a steak knife from the untidy rack on the sink and held her wrist out over the bowl. She began prodding at it with the steak knife. "Oh, I forgot," she said as she prodded. "What he did in whatever book it was, was to keep other ghosts off with his sword, so that only the one he wanted got to drink."

"I'll do that," said Fenella. She climbed down and fetched a mighty triangular carving knife out of the table drawer. She stood waving this back and forth across the bowl while Cart prodded. "Unwanted ghosts keep away!" she intoned. "We only want *our* ghost here."

"Ow!" said Cart. "It isn't only that it hurts – I can't seem to get any blood out at all. Yet I *know* the Ancient Romans were doing this all the time. They used to commit suicide like this regularly in their baths. Do you think there's something different about modern veins?" She stabbed at her wrist and was rewarded with a swelling red blob. "Ah! Ooooh-ow!"

"Squeeze it," Fenella suggested critically, waving the knife. "Before it sets."

Cart had just succeeded in detaching several red blobs from her wrist into the bowl, when Imogen crashed in through the back door. She had two small boys each by a shoulder. One was holding a red-smeared handkerchief to his nose. The other had his head bent carefully over a paper cup. "I promised them ten pence each," Imogen said. "Go on. The bowl's there. Bleed in it."

The boy with the handkerchief obediently shuffled across and bent over the bowl. The one with the paper cup looked round and selected Cart as the one in authority. "There's a lot in here," he said, holding out the cup. "It's worth at least a pound."

"Nonsense," said Cart, giving the contents a brief glance. "I've just given more than that for nothing."

"Blood donors always give it free," said Imogen. "I told you."

"They get a cup of tea," the boy argued, clutching the cup defensively. "One pound twenty. It's *my* blood, after all."

"But that little drip's not worth one-twenty," Cart said. "Proper blood donors give at least a pint."

The boy glowered at her, still obstinately hanging on to his cup.

"If you really want to give a pint," Fenella said, flourishing the triangular knife, "I'll help you. Just hold out your jugular, and I'll make you a cup of tea afterwards."

The boy stared at her, the knife and the blood-stained knot in her hair. Then he put the cup down and fled. The other boy was given ten pence, which proved to be all the money anyone had.

"I hope the rest don't ask for money," Imogen said as with jerky, clumsy, distasteful movements, she too punctured her wrist and, with surprising efficiency, let quite a trickle of blood run into the basin.

Unfortunately, everyone asked for money. The two small boys proved to be the first of a rush of donors. Jenkins and Howard both came back with two more small boys each. Howard, in addition, had hopefully brought the corpse of a rabbit from the Biology Lab. It proved to be pickled. They laid it on the table, stinking of formaldehyde, raw and drowned-looking, and supervised the nose bleeds of their four donors. All four of these demanded at least a pound. Cart sighed and wrote them out IOUs for the money.

"The rabbit will do to stand for a sacrifice," Howard said, needling at his finger with his tie pin. "We ought to have one if we're going to be properly pagan."

By this time, word had got round the school. Boys – mostly smaller ones – began to arrive in numbers, cautiously tiptoeing through the orchard, or sliding furtively round the green door, carrying paper cups and tinfoil tart dishes each containing a precious drop of blood. It soon emerged that the market rate for a donation of blood was one pound twenty pence. No one would take less. Some demanded more. These were usually the ones who arrived without a trace of blood and expressed themselves willing to be punched on the nose for money. The price for this was one pound forty pence. Ned Jenkins did the punching. He was good at it. But if no blood resulted – and not everybody bleeds easily – the boy was given a steak knife and asked to produce his own. The price then went down again to one-twenty. Cart wrote out IOUs – a good sixty poundsworth, it seemed to the ghost. But not everyone wanted only money. Most of the donors had heard there was a ghost. About a quarter of them gave blood at a reduced rate of one pound on condition that they were allowed to stay and watch what happened when the ghost drank the blood.

"Wait out in the orchard then," Cart told each of these. "It ought to be outside anyway," she explained to the others. "It was outside in the book. I think they dug a trench for the blood."

The orchard began to become rather crowded. The level of cloudy red liquid in the bowl rose encouragingly. Fenella waved her carving knife above it with increasing glee.

"Lots of lovely gore!" she chanted. "No foreign ghosts wanted."

The ghost hovered above, looking down at Fenella's dishevelled head and waving knife and, below that, the grubby bowl of ropy red blood. *I can't be you, Fenella,* she said. *I'm not enjoying this at all. It's quite disgusting. I must be Imogen.*

But Imogen did not seem particularly disgusted. "It's a funny thing," she was saying, from the middle of the crowded kitchen. "Apart from the rabbit, I have a feeling of rightness about the whole thing. I know it's going to work."

"Well, I think it's quite disgusting, frankly," said Howard. "Don't you, Ned?"

"Yes," said Jenkins. "But Imogen's right."

A number of people seemed to agree with Howard. A group of bigger boys – Nutty Filbert was amongst them – was now standing in the orchard among the waiting donors, expressing their opinion. Mostly they did it with jeers and boos, but every so often they broke out into a chant. "We think – you are – disgusting! We think – you are – disgusting!"

"Take no notice," advised Imogen. "They don't know a serious emergency when they see one."

The chanters were in full cry when the back door opened and Julian Addiman put his head into the kitchen. "What *is* going on?" he asked, laughing. His eyes gleamed and his wet red lips shone. "I hear you're calling for blood."

"Of course. It's a way to make ghosts speak," Cart answered briskly.

Julian Addiman looked at Fenella waving the knife over the bowl, at the rabbit lying beside it, at Howard and Jenkins, and at the latest pair of donors. He seemed full of sly amusement. At that moment, the bell shrilled for the end of Break. "Ooops!" said Julian Addiman. "Let me know if it says anything." And he slid away laughing.

"Hey!" called Fenella. "Give us some blood first."

But Julian Addiman, to the ghost's relief, was gone. The donors in the kitchen sped after him. The chanting group in the orchard was going away too, and so were most of the waiting donors, slowly and disappointedly. But quite a number seemed determined to hear the ghost and lingered on hopefully under the trees. And a further party of fresh donors was just arriving — eight or ten of them — advancing across the orchard from the hedge, carefully carrying paper cups.

"Doesn't it matter to them that Break's over?" Imogen wondered, watching them advance through the window.

"Most people can think of an excuse if they really want to," said Howard. "Oughtn't we to be going, Jenk?"

"I want to know what the ghost says," Jenkins answered. His pale chin was bunched mulishly.

That was the moment when Mrs Gill pushed open the green door, saying, "You come and take a look, Mr Melford. They've got enough blood in here to float a battleship."

CHAPTER ELEVEN

Himself was in the kitchen doorway. Howard, who was nearest to the living room, made a running rugby dive through its door and vanished in a faint crunch of cornflakes. Jenkins, who had been with Imogen by the window, had no choice but to bend down and cram himself under the sink. Imogen stood in front of him. Cart hastily joined her, and the ghost joined the pair of them, with the idea of getting as far away from Himself as possible. Fenella, out of pure bravado, looked Mrs Gill unlovingly in the eye and went on waving the carving knife.

"Weaving spiders come not near," Fenella intoned. "Spotted snakes with double tongue – one of which is in this room now – must get out of here or get down on the floor and wriggle."

Himself took her, and the bowl of blood, and the rabbit, in

as he advanced into the room. He looked ready to do murder. Outside in the orchard, his silhouette was recognised and caused consternation. Those waiting to hear the ghost dived for cover. The party of donors advancing with paper cups first backed away, then ran in panic for the hedge, throwing down the paper cups as they ran.

"Oh well. We'd got about enough blood," Cart murmured.

"You see, Mr Melford?" Mrs Gill asked triumphantly.

"Yes, thank you, Mrs Gill," Himself said cordially, and he went back to hold the green door open for her to go away.

Mrs Gill, however, ghoul as she was, pretended to misunderstand him. She moved over to the table and folded her arms, where she stood eyeing the bowl of gore with strong expectation.

Himself was forced to come back into the kitchen. This caused an uncertain pause. Everyone well knew that Himself wanted to let rip in one of his screaming rages. He wanted to roar and shout and hit people and call his daughters bitches, but he did not want to do it with Mrs Gill looking on. So he stood there mantling and glaring, an eagle ready to rend, and nobody else knew whether to be scared, relieved or embarrassed.

He settled at length for sarcasm. "I seem to have spawned a coven of witches," he remarked. Mrs Gill nodded brightly at this. Himself shot her an irritated glance. "Put that knife down, Imogen – er – Selina – er – Fenella," he commanded. It was a curious fact that Himself, while he never forgot a single boy he had ever taught, could never remember which of his daughters was which. He always had to go through at least three of their names before he chanced on the right one. As Fenella laid the knife down, he said, "I shall confiscate that. It's murderous. What is that disgusting rabbit doing there? Charlotte – Imogen – Fenella, take it back to the Biology Lab at once."

Fenella glowered at him uncertainly. She was not sure he meant her.

"I said *take it back!*" thundered Himself, letting off some of his rage in a shout.

Fenella hurriedly snatched up the rabbit and set off for the door with it.

"No! Wait!" thundered Himself. "I haven't finished yet."

Fenella stopped and stood clutching the rabbit against her green sack. "What do you little bi— beastly girls think you're doing with this – this bestial display? Answer me. Don't just gape. What's this bowl of disgusting blood supposed to be for? Answer me!"

"Ancient Greek ghost work," said Fenella. She was almost always the only one who dared speak when Himself was in one of his rages. "It was in a book by Virgil. It's educational. You teach Greek and Virgil in School."

"Virgil," growled Himself, "was not a Greek, you ignorant little bi— beast. If you must scour the classics for disgusting acts, at least get them *right*. Who was Virgil?"

"A – a Roman poet," quavered Imogen.

"Right," said Himself. It seemed to be becoming a lesson. Himself realised it was. He shot Mrs Gill another irritated glance and turned it back to rage again by pointing a quivering finger and a glare at the bowl of blood. "This," he said, "this disgusting object must be got rid of at once. I do not care if you are attempting divination or sacrifice to the gods, but it must go. Selina – Fenella – Charlotte, take it outside at once and throw it away."

"But we need it," protested Fenella. "It's cost us pounds by now."

Himself whirled round on her, ready to rend. But he remembered Mrs Gill was standing there and roared instead. "I told you to take that rabbit back! How dare you disobey me! Go and do it at once!"

Fenella did not wait to protest. She dived for the door, swinging the rabbit by its hind legs, and disappeared before Himself could change his mind again. Himself swung round on Imogen and Cart.

"Imogen – Selina – Charlotte, I told you to take that horrible bowl away! Do it at once. Take it out into the orchard and pour it away."

"If you mean me—" said Cart. She was not anxious to move. If she did, it meant losing the hard-earned bowl of blood. And she was afraid to go near Himself. He had a horrible habit of delivering a swinging slap as soon as you were within range. But the worst of it was that she knew that, once she moved her bulk from in front of the sink, Himself would be able to see Ned Jenkins crouching underneath it.

"Of course I mean you, girl!" bellowed Himself. "Didn't I *say* so?"

"No," snapped Imogen, in the funny way she had of suddenly going brave. "You may have *said* Charlotte. But you also said all the rest of our names too! Can't you ever remember which of us is *which*?"

"That," said Himself, "is pure impertinence, Selina."

"I thought as much!" snapped Imogen. "How would you like it if I kept calling you Phyllis?"

Himself's eyes widened. He stood poised to rend, glaring at Imogen in what was half a glare of rage and half a stare of bewilderment. He did not see her point at all, but he knew she was being rude. His stare rapidly became all rage. At that, Imogen opened her mouth to say something else. Cart tried to shut her up by kicking her ankle.

Imogen promptly uttered a loud cry and sank to a crouch,

clutching the flowing yellow ankle of her trouser suit with both hands. "Oh! My leg!"

She did it so convincingly that Cart misunderstood and bent down to her anxiously. Imogen was forced to turn round and try to wink. Now, it was a peculiarity of Imogen that she could not wink. Not to save her life – and certainly not to save Ned Jenkins'. Perhaps it was that her features were too regular: neither of her deep blue eyes shut any easier than the other. Nevertheless, she tried. She screwed up first one side of her face and then the other. All that happened were two furious grimaces. Mrs Gill and Himself must have thought she was in agony. And at last Cart understood that Imogen was crouching like that to hide Ned Jenkins.

"Oh!" Cart exclaimed, understanding, and then had to add hastily, "I'm so sorry, Imo." And since Himself was now glaring at her, she set off sideways round the room, to keep the table between her and Himself. Mrs Gill's eyes flicked between Cart and Himself, calculating when Cart would come within hitting range. She looked a trifle disappointed when Cart managed to arrive on the opposite side of the table, facing Himself. Her eyes turned to the bowl of blood then, expectantly. Cart looked at it too and said, with a blurred placating look, "It seems a shame to pour it on the orchard. It's such good manure. That's what made the poppies grow in Flanders, you know. Suppose I take it to the kitchen garden and—".

At that, Himself plunged forward, with both hands on the table and his face only inches from Cart's. "Your damned dog," he said intensely, "has just ruined the kitchen garden. I said *pour it away!*"

His shout was at point-blank range. Cart jerked back, snatching up the bowl as she went. The blood swirled, and, as liquid swirled in an enamel bowl often does, it let out a long note, a low melancholy moan.

Mrs Gill's eyes widened. And the sound seemed to draw the ghost, just as it drew Mrs Gill. With Mrs Gill's eyes on it and the ghost hovering beside her, Cart carried the bowl to the back door and out into a fine mist of rain in the orchard.

"Has he gone yet?" said a deep whisper from behind a clump of nettles.

"No." said Cart. Indeed he had not. Himself's voice could be heard raging at Imogen now. "I think Ned's had it," Cart muttered. She carried the bowl up the orchard to Monigan's hut, and bent to push it inside.

No! screamed the ghost.

Cart paused, considering. "Yes, but I can't let it get too diluted with rain," she said, just as if she had heard. She pushed the bowl inside the hut and walked away behind it, where only the upper half of her would be visible from the kitchen window, until she came to a smaller enamel bowl which was sometimes used for feeding the hens. It had a small quantity of dirty water in it. "Good," said Cart. She picked up that bowl and made great play of pouring the water away where she would be seen. Mrs Gill would be looking, even if Himself was not. Then, with the bowl bumping against her leg, so that it was not obvious that it was rather smaller, she went back down the orchard and opened the kitchen door.

"The blood is disposed of," she announced.

Himself swung round from glaring at Imogen, who was still squatting on the floor. "Good," he said. "Right. And if there is any more disgusting nonsense like this, I warn you, the trouble will be terrible. Have you little bi— beasts got that into your thick heads?"

"Yes," said Imogen and Cart in chorus.

"Very well." Himself went and swung the green door open for Mrs Gill. "After you, Mrs Gill," his voice came courteously. Mrs

Gill, looking rather let down, was obliged to go through it in front of Himself. Himself followed, trying to bang the door to relieve his feelings. Since it was a swing door, all it did was thud back and forth all the time Imogen was unwinding herself from the floor.

"Where's the blood?" Imogen asked, as soon as the door stopped.

"In Monigan's hut," said Cart. "I'm sure that's ill-omened, but—"

"Shut up!" Ned Jenkins said hollowly from under the sink. "He has a horrible way of coming straight back again."

"He only does that to boys," said Imogen. She put her hand down to help Ned crawl out, which he did, somewhat mucky. "You've got custard all over your back," Imogen told him severely. "Hold still." She was wiping him down when Howard crunched cautiously out of the living room. A second later, Fenella put her head round the back door.

"The rain's stopping," Fenella said. "Shall we do it here or outside?"

"Outside," said Cart. "All old witchcraft was done outside. Besides, there are more places there to run away to."

So, a minute later, the bowl rested carefully propped on a clump of wet grass against the slope of the orchard. Around it, wet nettles and baby apples in the trees winked in the sallow sunlight. Monigan's hut steamed dankly. In a ring round the bowl stood Cart, Imogen, Fenella, Howard, Jenkins and all who remained of the blood donors. These were four smaller boys, each rather damp in the trouser legs and sprinkled over the shoulders, with traces of blood round their noses.

There was an expectant silence. In the distance, the hens pecked busily, not in the least interested.

"Nothing's going to happen," said one of the donors

disgustedly. "They ripped off our blood for nothing."

Fenella gave them a look of deep contempt and raised both skinny arms. "Ghost!" she boomed. "Ghost, come and drink."

At that, with varying degrees of awkwardness, everyone else raised their arms too. Howard did it limply, with both hands drooping, as if he hoped no one would notice. Ned Jenkins stretched up, like someone reaching something off a shelf. Imogen contrived to look like a priestess. "Come and drink," they all said, not quite together.

The ghost hovered miserably over the bowl. Under the shiny surface, ropy tendrils of thicker blood were slowly dispersing in the thinner liquid from the ox hearts. She was not sure she could even try to drink it. It was like cannibalism. And Cart had put it in Monigan's hut, as if it were an offering. Monigan was there. She could feel Monigan, pressing down in the orchard, watching with a sly, sarcastic amusement like Julian Addiman's, daring her to drink. It was like the dead hen all over again.

All the same, it seemed her once chance to explain to them and get them to help. But if it meant that Monigan could take her once she drank— She did not know what to do. And she could not bear to drink anyway.

Monigan was highly amused. In the circle round the bowl, people's arms were going down. They were ready to give up. The smaller boys had their hands in their pockets and were showing signs of shuffling away. And still the ghost hovered, unable to do anything. She might have done nothing, had she not suddenly been interrupted by something in the hospital, seven years in the future.

A voice by her ear said faintly, "We need another bag of blood here."

Another bag of blood? she asked, bewildered. Then she remembered. All the time she hovered here, she was having blood transfusions. She was being given life from blood that unknown generous people had given because they knew it was needed. Was that so different from drinking blood? It was the same here, except that she knew whose blood it was. And although the small boys had given their blood for money, Howard and Jenkins and her sisters had been just as generous as the unknown hospital donors. And what a waste of both gifts if she were to refuse them and let Monigan take her away at midnight.

She lowered herself in a rush, in order not to have to think about it. The shining pool in the bowl came up to her, full of reflections of leaves and baby apples, with no sign of a reflection of her. It was, she found when she was near enough, fizzing faintly with the same electric life-feeling that people's bodies had. But it was weaker. It did not stop her lowering herself into its sticky, prickling surface.

It felt as if she was having a bath in soda water. She fizzed all over. She tried to do something which would be like gulping the stuff in, but it did not work like that. It was more as if she took the blood in through her whole surface. She could feel it going in, tingling all over what now felt definitely like a body.

She stood up, fizzing. There was a curious roaring in her ears, a blur of green pressing on her eyes, and a sharp rainy smell to her nose. None of it was clear, but she knew what it was. For just a short while, she was hearing, seeing and smelling as people do in bodies. At the same time, she could feel Monigan going away. Monigan was sarcastic, angry and not defeated yet, but she was leaving the orchard. Something had been done there which was outside Monigan's power.

Around her, they were all staring. Most of their faces were white. The smaller boys managed to be leaning backwards and forwards at once — backwards in terror, forwards in fascination.

"Standing in the bowl!" one was whispering. "It looks like a girl."

"Hanging. It's all blurred," said Howard's voice. "Who is it?"

Yes, said the ghost. *Who am I? Don't you know?* This was what she said. But what she heard, and what the others certainly heard, was not so much a voice as a moaning, like the noise of liquid swirling in an enamel bowl, only with words in it. And the words were broken patches of words. It was like a faulty radio circuit. "Who I— Who I— Oh who I?" she went, like a broken owl.

Everyone made a movement to run away, and then stopped. A smaller boy said, "I heard that."

"What did it say?" asked Imogen, craning forward irritably.

"I think," Cart said slowly – her mouth was jibbering a little – "I think it doesn't know who it is."

Fenella said, "It looks like you, Cart."

"Or like Sally," said Jenkins. "Why is it wrapped in white like that?"

Imogen said, violently and shrilly, "I'm *intensely* scared! I think we've conjured up the devil!"

"No, the dead," said someone. "That's its shroud it's wrapped in."

No, said the ghost. *You don't understand. I'm not dead yet, but I'm going to be if you don't help me.* And like her first speech, it came out broken and garbled to, "Understand dead help— Yet will be."

"I don't understand you," said Fenella.

The great shaggy shape of Oliver hove into sight, with his face plastered with earth. He saw the ghost at once. He uttered a squeak of pleasure and set off towards the bowl at his fastest pace, wagging his tail madly. But three feet away he stopped, shivering and whining, staring piteously at the apparition hanging over the bowl. He plainly dared not go any nearer. To make up for that, he swung his great tail faster than ever.

Oliver's behaviour seemed to make everyone feel better. "Oliver knows it," said Howard. "I think it really is one of you four."

"Well, it said it was," said Cart. "Please – whoever you are – tell us what you want and why you're here."

The ghost knew she should have started explaining at once. The tingling of her blood-given body was growing less already, particularly lower down. She tried looking down. She could see a tall vague length of human body, mostly blurred white, with the green of the orchard grass showing through. The white puzzled her as much as it puzzled the others. Perhaps it was what they had put her in at the hospital. But the more alarming thing was that there was a gap between the blurred white and the shining blood in the bowl, where her feet should have been. She could not feel any tingling there at all. Frightened, she tried to summon all her strength and concentrate it in the part of her that seemed to be speaking.

Meanwhile, Imogen was saying ferociously to the four smaller boys, "Don't *you* know who it is? Can't *you* recognise her?"

They shook their heads. In spite of Oliver, they had lost their voices from sheer terror.

The ghost spoke. She gave them, as far as she was able, a perfectly clear explanation. She told them about Monigan, Julian Addiman and the hospital. She told them how she had found herself seven years back in the past as a ghost. But, while she spoke, she was listening to a strange broken mutter and moaning pieces of words, and she knew it was what everyone else was hearing.

"Monigan – Monigan – seven years' claim – life help. Help. Help future now – only you – help blood Monigan – seven years help life – dying – seven – help..."

The moaning mutter of her voice seemed to go on and on, but she could feel it fading even from the first word. Within seconds, she knew it was too faint for anyone to hear. Behind that, very distant, she could feel Monigan's amusement at how little she was saying, and how she had wasted this opportunity. So she kept on desperately forcing out words. And the tingling of the life the blood had given her grew less and less and fainter every moment. She felt it travelling from her chest, up out of her arms, up through her neck, up into her head. Until it was gone.

It was gone. She was lying, greyly aware, in the hospital bed again.

Cart's voice said, "She's only allowed one visitor at once. I'll go. But I warn you..." The voice fell to a murmur. She lay, hearing it, wondering about that blood. Had it been a mistake? Cart had put it in Monigan's hut, and that troubled her. Was this perhaps how the dedication of Sally had got passed on to her?

There was somebody else beside her bed now. She was chiefly aware at first of the enormous bunch of red and white roses which this someone was busy arranging in a vase.

"Those must have cost a bomb!" she remarked, deeply impressed.

"They did," said this new person. "Nice, aren't they? I like spending money. I got it out of Himself to stay in a hotel with, but I shall have to sleep on your floor instead now."

"Cart seems to be doing that too," she said. She was beginning to focus on this new person. It seemed a total stranger, as bad as Mrs Gill. This was a highly glamorous young woman, much better dressed than Cart. Her hair was beautifully cut, in a tumble of glossy brown curls, and her face was beautifully and carefully made up. Delicate scent breathed off her, and the hands arranging the roses had long egg-shaped red nails. Yet the voice was definitely familiar, deep and refined and grown-up though it was.

The young woman turned from the roses, saying, "Cart says you're concussed and don't remember a thing, but that sounded quite alert to me. How are you?" And, with the words, the pretty lipsticked mouth spread in a smile full of affection, uncovering a pair of large front teeth with a wide gap between them.

"Good God!" she said weakly. "You're Fenella!" It made her wonder if more than seven years had passed by this time. This Fenella *could* not be only seventeen. "Why are you so glamorous?"

"These," said Fenella with dignity, "are my coming-to-London clothes. I worked in Boots over Easter to earn them. I thought you'd like them. Mrs Gill's sister did my hair for me."

"Oh," said her sister. "Er – you've left school now, have you?"

Fenella sighed, and followed the sigh up with a scowl which was pure ten-year-old Fenella again. "No," she growled. "I meant to. I told you. I wanted to leave like anything, but Himself wouldn't let me. I told him I was going to fail all my A Levels on purpose if he made me stay on – I may still, I don't know. But I don't mind so much now I'm going to be an opera singer."

"Opera singer!"

"Yes," said Fenella. "Listen." She faced the glass wall and opened her mouth. Out of it came a long clear note. It was one of the most beautiful sounds her sister had ever heard. But it was also most powerfully loud. It made her throb, from her head to her hoist-up leg. Beyond the glass wall, bandaged heads craned and visitors turned round. And it brought to mind the way Fenella had always been able, without the least effort, to produce that deep booming shout that was twice as loud as anyone else's.

"Ow!" she said. "Lovely, but please don't do it again. You'll get turned out."

"I know," said Fenella. "I only did it to show you I really have a voice. I know you kept worrying about me. But you needn't any longer – truly. I'm having proper singing lessons now. I got the money out of Himself."

"Out of Himself—?"

"Yes," said Fenella, with just a trace of smugness. "Last month. I'm almost as good at getting money out of him as you are. In fact, I may even be better than you. What I did was, I went to him with the cost of the lessons all added up, and, next to that on the page, the cost of all the other things other fathers always have to pay for and he never does — you know, clothes and food and heating and pocket money and all that. Even for a year it came to a huge amount. I was quite scared to show him."

Fenella paused, looking a trace surprised. "I thought he'd be furious, being shown how mean he is. Wouldn't you? But the first thing he did was multiply it by four to find out how much money he'd saved over the four of us. And it was such a lot that he was ever so pleased. Then I threw in a bit of cajolery. That's one thing," Fenella declared, "that you three never noticed. Himself loves to be cajoled. The boys know. They cajole him all the time. But none of you three realised — you just had rows with him all the time. But I imitated the boys and cajoled him, and I got him to pay for singing lessons in five minutes flat.

"That was clever," the patient said admiringly.

After that, as so often happens in hospital visits, they seemed to run out of things to say. Fenella sat down and stared at the bag of blood in an alarmed, observant way. Her sister lay and thought.

I am Imogen, she thought. This settles it. I don't feel like Imogen, and I don't particularly want to be a concert pianist, but I must be her. I wonder, she thought, with a trace of hope, if my concert career is ruined— Oh no. I went to Art School, didn't I? How odd. Wait a minute—

"Fenella. Who painted that picture of you that used to be propped up on the old piano?"

"The one with the blackberry bushes?" asked Fenella. "You, of course." At that, they both began to speak at once. Fenella, being in full health and with by far the strongest voice, naturally won. "By the way, if you see Mrs Gill before I do, will you let her know that I came on the later train because I couldn't get the money from Himself in time."

"Why—?"

"I got it straight after the hospital phoned, of course," said Fenella. "But I couldn't bear to come with Mrs Gill. If she's not talking about illnesses all the time, she's sort of taking charge of me. She makes me feel as if I'm a human version of her green and orange bag. So could you very kindly?"

"Of course. She's sitting in Casualty now. Cart sent her there."

At this, Fenella gave a sharp chuckle, as startlingly loud as her singing voice. And they relapsed into silence again.

This won't do, thought the patient. There are so many things I don't know. "Fenella, what time is it?"

Fenella looked at the gold watch on her wrist – no doubt she had got that out of Himself like the singing lessons. "Four – just after."

Another hour gone. "Fenella, do you remember the ghost?"

Fenella's head turned sharply. Her eyes, large to start with, and splendidly enlarged by her make-up, now seemed enormous. "We got rid of it," she said. "It went in the afternoon."

"How? What did we do?"

Fenella shrugged. It was now a pretty gesture, but it meant what Fenella's shrugs had always meant: she knew, but she was not going to say.

"Please, Fenella. It's terribly important. I was the ghost – don't you realise?"

"If you think," Fenella said grudgingly, "we haven't all realised that by now, you must be a fool. But it was all years ago. There's nothing any of us can do now."

"Yes, there *is!*" cried her sister. "I know I can do something!"

"You'll make yourself ill," said Fenella. "Even iller, I mean. All right, but I don't really know how it happened. We all went on a cycle ride because of something Cart said, and it worked somehow, though I don't know how. Anyway, the ghost wasn't with us on the way back — but we all got soaked, and Will and Ned got caught because they were wet."

"And where did we go?"

Fenella clearly did not want to say. She hated answering questions. She hated it even more if the questions were important. In the normal way, she would have clammed up, or pretended to forget. It was because she found it so difficult to explain anything. But, since she was being asked by a very ill sister, she forced herself to answer. "We went where Monigan was supposed to live, of course."

Her sister understood the effort Fenella had made to say this. She tried to smile, and Fenella smiled in reply, a gap-toothed grin which matched better with freckles and hair in two granny-knots than with the modern elegant Fenella. "Thanks. Where did she live?"

And Fenella made one more effort and answered exactly as she might have done seven years before, "Through the Dream Landscape and behind the Back of Beyond, of course."

CHAPTER TWELVE

She sped back, once more a ghost, in triumph. She was certain that going to confront Monigan was not Cart's idea, but hers. It looked as if she had managed to guide her sisters – or perhaps the boys – into some kind of attack on Monigan. She could hardly wait to be back there in the orchard, with the bowl of blood.

She was there. Here was the orchard, still in sallow sunlight, and the baby apples were still glinting with drops of moisture. But something had happened while she was away. The enamel bowl beneath her was upside down in the grass. She looked down at black patches flaked out of its underside, and a brown ring of grease. The hens, lifting their claws with tiptoe, delicate caution, were moving away from it not to be near her.

Beyond that, Monigan's hut was in ruins. Pieces of carpet lay scattered flat round the oblong of yellow grass. The clothes horse and the two deckchairs which had supported the carpet were snapped in pieces, with yellow raw wood showing where they had been broken. Cart did that, she was sure.

She was terrified. The sisters had understood, but they had still not seen the horror of Monigan. She had told them it was Monigan's doing, and their answer had been to desecrate Monigan's temple. That would make Monigan angry.

She hung over the pieces of sodden carpet, listening, or feeling – or whatever it was she did – waiting somehow for Monigan and Monigan's anger. And there was nothing. The orchard felt blank. Monigan was not there. Then where—?

Of course Monigan was not there. The old sodden doll that had stood for Monigan for over a year now was gone. There was no sign of it among the carpet and splintered wood, or anywhere in the orchard. What had they done with it? Where had they taken her?

She sped indoors to find out. There was no one there. In the kitchen, flies were circling over three plates, hastily scraped and not quite empty. The back door was open. That had to mean that they had hurried outside, but she felt she had to make sure. She whirled through into the living room. Nothing. The cornflakes still lay there. Books, papers and a map of North Hampshire had been tumbled out of a bookshelf on top of them. The painting of Fenella stared up at her from the seat of an armchair, and dust slanted in a gloomy bar of sunlight.

Cart! Imogen! Fenella! she shouted, uselessly and soundlessly. The only sound was the buzzing of flies.

She was speeding to the stairs when something moved. A great brown heap of carpet raised a large furred face and then heaved itself up, groaning. Oliver stood staring at her, gently swinging his tail. He was whining, a small and troubled sound, through his massive nose.

She knew that sound. It was Oliver's unhappy noise. He meant they had all gone off and left him. She had heard it, often and often, if she came in quietly from school and Oliver still thought he was alone.

Oh, poor Oliver! she said.

Oliver's ears pricked a little and his whining died away.

He could hear her. He was the only one who could hear her. But would he, even so, do as she told him? *Good dog, Oliver,* she said. *Come along. Let's find them then. Find them, boy!* She sped out of the room to the open back door and waited there.

To her relief, Oliver came shambling through after her. He stopped beside her in the doorway and stood with his head down, patient as a pit pony and almost as large, waiting to see where she would go next.

Find Cart, she said. *Find them, boy. Go on.*

Oliver did not move. She remembered, with exasperation, that Cart always said he was as thick as two short planks and had no sense of smell anyway. *Well, I'm going anyway!* she said, and went whirling out into the orchard again.

Oliver made his unhappy noise. He did not like going for walks, and he always resisted mightily if people tried to take him, but he hated being left alone in the holidays even more. He could see his last chance of company, peculiar as it was, drifting away from him among the trees. He heaved up a sigh and resigned himself to exercise. He plodded to the shed at the corner of the orchard. Hopefully, he thrust his huge face round its open door. And sighed again. It was empty, except for the rusted remains of a very old tricycle.

That meant they had taken all the bicycles and gone somewhere, just as Fenella had said. It had clearly not been her idea after all. But where had they gone? The Dream Landscape meant nothing to her, although the Back of Beyond did seem to bring a misty memory. *Come on, Oliver,* she said, and set off again.

Oliver went too, with his face set in a blurred look of protest. Together they went round the side of the school, and round a further corner, and arrived at the long shed where the boys' bicycles were kept. Dutifully, Oliver plodded along the row of cycles until he came to the bright red one at the end. There, he sketchily raised a leg and peed on its red back wheel. Having done that, he sat down. He had done enough.

The ghost hovered up and down, nearly screaming. *Yes, I know the boys went too. WHERE? Oliver, show me, please!* She had been cheated. She was sure of it. Monigan had kept her talking to Fenella to make sure that she came back too late to catch them all. Which meant it must be terribly important that she did. *Oliver – please!*

Oliver saw he was being pestered. The only way to get some peace seemed to be to keep moving. Grudgingly, he heaved up and set off. This time, he went along the path round the kitchen garden and down the school drive to the big metal gates. There outside was the road. Oliver looked at it with distaste – it was hard on the feet – and stopped again.

Which way, Oliver? To the right was the way to Chipping Milton, where they went to school. Country lanes turned off that to right and left and ran to a hundred remote places. If they had gone that way, she would need every bit of help Oliver could give. To the left was Audrey's farm, and the Downs were beyond that. *Show me, Oliver.*

With a long-suffering grunt, Oliver shambled out into the road and turned left. *Oliver, are you sure?* She was certain he was wrong.

To show he was sure, Oliver broke into that peculiar gait of his, which Imogen said was like a camel, that was the nearest he ever came to running. His front legs swung round and out, round and out, and his huge body swayed. Up the hill he went, and the ghost kept pace with him, until they came to the entrance to Audrey's farmyard. Oliver slowed to a loiter. This time he really had gone far enough. Somewhere behind a barn, a sheepdog sensed he was there and burst out barking. The dog seemed the only living thing in the yard. It looked dead and empty in the grey light, as deserted as the rusty harrow propped up in a corner.

This can't be right, Oliver, she said. *There's no one here.*

The unseen dog heard her and barked frantically.

The noise fetched a lady out of the stable where Audrey's pony lived. She seemed a total stranger, youngish and darkish and pretty — but then she would if I'm Imogen, the ghost thought — but she was clearly Audrey's mother. She saw Oliver slouching in the gateway. She knew Oliver. Everybody did. Once you saw Oliver you never forgot him.

"Hallo, Oliver old boy," she said, and she came over and rubbed Oliver's head. The ghost had to jerk back from the lively, energetic tingle of her. "Did they leave you behind then?" said Audrey's mother. "It's no good looking here for them, old fellow. They've all gone off to the Downs. They called for Audrey and Sally quarter of an hour ago. You'll never catch them now. You go home."

Oliver sighed. The ghost darted on up the road. *This way, Oliver!*

"Go on home, Oliver," said Audrey's mother.

Oliver decided. Not even for company was he going any further. He had already had a huge walk — nearly a mile. He turned round and shambled home down the hill.

She was forced to go on alone. She had no idea of the way. There were at least three places where the road forked, and her only hope seemed to be to catch them before the first fork. In a panic, she went faster and faster. That was one good thing about not having Oliver with her: she could go at an inhuman speed. The hedges whirled by. The whitish road hurtled under her. She was going as fast as a bicycle – faster – as fast as that car when she was thrown out. No. She had to slow down. She could not go as fast as that awful car. It brought it all back, and this time she saw it as it had happened to her, not as a spectator. The road rushed under her eyes. The door was pushed, and so was she, until the road came up at her face. She had to stop.

But there they all were, thank goodness! They made a big group of bicycles, with people standing astride them, just beside the first fork, where the signpost said MANGAN DOWN ONLY. All of them looked drab in the dull, ominous light. Fenella was brightest in her shrill green sack, and she looked a dismal little urchin. She was on a fifth-hand kiddy cycle, which had long ago been repainted baby blue when it was Sally's turn for it. With her was a hot-faced Howard on a smart grey bike. Ned Jenkins was beside him on a much more battered cycle. It had FILBERT painted on its back mudguard. She wondered if he had asked Nutty before taking it – probably not.

Imogen was a little aside from them, looking irritable and frightened. A lot of Imogen's irritation must have been due to the fact that she had been forced to ride the second smallest bike, the one which would have fitted Fenella better. But nobody ever wanted to ride that one. Its chain kept coming off. Imogen had had to have it, though, because Sally had taken the one reasonable second-hand bike when she went to visit Audrey, and was riding it now. And Cart was the only one who was big enough to ride the other remaining bike. It was a vast black one called the Atomic Heavy Bike – with good reason.

In fact, apart from Howard's, there were only two decent

bicycles in the group. One was Audrey's. It was the kind with small thick wheels, which Himself had roared were far too expensive for children. The other was Julian Addiman's. The ghost looked at it, and at Julian Addiman, in dismay. She had no idea how he came to be there. But there he was, with his trousers in shining cycle-clips, leaning on the handlebars of a gold-coloured lightweight cycle, which had so many gears that the chain seemed to turn a dozen corners before it reached the back wheel. Julian Addiman, with a superior, sarcastic smile, was listening to Sally, who was arguing, typically enough.

"But you haven't told me a thing!" Sally was saying. "I don't move a step further until you do."

"You're not stepping, you're pedalling," said Fenella.

"But I *have* told you!" Cart said angrily. She was bright red from the work needed to move the Atomic Heavy Bike. "We're going to Monigan's Place because we've had a ghost all the time you've been away."

"I still don't see why you need me," Sally argued. She seemed quite untroubled by the mention of Monigan, and Julian Addiman did not turn a hair either. "What has a ghost got to do with me?"

"It may be your ghost," Howard called from the rear. "We saw it. It looks a bit like all of you. And it kept saying 'Help' and 'Monigan'."

Even this did not trouble Sally. She tossed her fair hair. "You all have too much imagination. Or you invented it. You made up Monigan, after all."

"We did not!" Imogen shouted indignantly.

"So we decided," Cart said, in a patient way which usually maddened Sally, "that one of us must have got into Monigan's clutches in the future somehow, and come back to now to tell us."

"We thought it came back because there's something we can

do," Ned Jenkins added. "And now we're going to try and do it."

Sally looked at Cart in exasperation and at Ned uncertainly. Julian Addiman laughed and pointed to the handlebars of the Atomic Heavy Bike. "Is that the ghost there?"

"No," Cart said gruffly. The mildewy Monigan doll in its grey knitted dress was tied there with string.

"So," said Ned, "shall we go?"

Sally still looked uncertain. She could not think of a dignified way to say either Yes or No.

"Let's go, now we've started," Audrey suggested. "It makes something to do. I'm bored."

"And I'm dying to see a real live goddess," laughed Julian Addiman.

"All right," Sally said wearily.

"Don't sound so keen, will you?" Cart said. She stamped heavily on one pedal to get the Atomic Heavy Bike moving. As always, it stood on the spot, trembling. "Someone might think you meant it," she added, as she balanced. The bike moved at last, as if it had been designed for doing something else completely and was only moving as a by-product. Cart pedalled it, clanking, into the road marked MANGAN DOWN ONLY, leaving Sally glaring after her.

The rest pedalled after her. It was a fairly narrow road, winding uphill, and they made a crowded and toiling procession of it. It was understood by everyone that Cart was leading them, so nobody liked to pass her, despite the fact that the Atomic Heavy Bike had not been designed to move. Even so, Fenella and Imogen were left in the rear. The legs of both flashed round and round furiously. Both zig-zagged from side to side. This was partly to help them get up the hill, and partly because both bikes were so dreadful that it was impossible to ride them straight.

The ghost followed the procession, feeling deeply grateful.

They were all being so kind, even Audrey and Sally – though she was not so sure about Julian Addiman.

Audrey was moving smoothly beside Sally, tick-tick, tick-tick. "It's a nice idea to rescue a ghost, isn't it?" she said.

"Very nice," Sally said curtly. "If Cart hasn't made it up."

"You will keep criticising!" Audrey complained.

"So what?" said Sally.

It looked as if Sally and Audrey were not getting on together. Sally put on a spurt and caught Cart up. Julian Addiman was gently and easily pedalling beside Cart as Cart puffed and clanked in the lead. Cart was plainly finding his gentle superior cycling an irritation. "Why don't you go on in front?" she snapped as Sally came up. But Julian Addiman stayed, gently pedalling beside them both.

Sally gave Julian Addiman a look which meant that she too wished he was not there, but he took no notice of that either. Sally turned to Cart and they exchanged a look of annoyance. "How's the Plan going?" Sally asked, in as near a whisper as one can manage while pedalling a middle-aged cycle uphill.

"Not at all," Cart puffed. "Neither of them has noticed a thing."

"Not even Fenella's knots?" said Sally.

"Nope," puffed Cart. "Himself came and told us off, and he went through your name in the list as usual, and he still didn't notice you weren't there. And he looked straight through Fenella."

"Oh well, it was worth a try," Sally said. She pretended to consider. It had plainly only been important to her to spend just that one night away. "Let's scrap the Plan," she said. "I might as well come home."

Behind her, Audrey had heard. Her face showed nothing but plain relief. She smiled and, letting herself be caught up by Ned Jenkins and Will Howard, she cycled between them, talking in a polite, social sort of way. She had not met either of them often. "Have you got the afternoon off School?" she asked.

"No," said Ned, who was annoyed by her social manner.

"'Fraid not," said Howard, who did not mind it. "We'd got Games this afternoon and we sneaked off."

"Won't you get into trouble?" Audrey asked Ned.

"Only if we're caught," Howard answered cheerfully. "Then it'll be hours in Detention at least, I suppose."

Here, everyone except Imogen and Fenella reached the top of the hill. Imogen and Fenella, pedalling furiously back and forth, tried to go faster in order not to be left behind. The result was that each zigged when the other zagged. And of course they collided. The chain of Imogen's bicycle, with the ease of long practice, promptly fell off. Imogen stood in the road, looking from the chain to the black oil on her trousers, and swore her strongest swear word.

"Oh!" she said. "*Bloody!*"

Everyone stopped.

Julian Addiman laughed condescendingly. "Here," he said. "Let the expert."

Imogen looked at him consideringly. In spite of what Cart had said, seven years in the future, Imogen at least seemed quite immune to the charm of Julian Addiman. "Since you think yourself so superior," she said, with considerable dislike, "I *defy* you to get this censored chain back on."

"Easy," said Julian Addiman. He leant his beautiful cycle on the hedge and got down to work. The rest of them stood round and watched. The chain fell off as soon as it was on. And again. And yet again after that. Julian Addiman got steadily oilier and steadily more annoyed.

While Julian Addiman worked, Cart was standing on the bank where the hedge grew. "We're quite near Monigan's Place

186

now," she announced. "Down there, there's the Hole of Mouldy Dough, and there's the Nasty Tree, with the Nasty Place underneath it."

The ghost rose up there to see what Cart was pointing at. There was a dip in the field behind the hedge, where the ground was the colour of putty. The other thing was a twisted oak tree growing in the hedge. The ghost looked at both with consternation. She had forgotten that Cart had this habit of enlivening the landscape by giving everything names. No doubt it showed Cart had a vivid imagination, but it was nothing at all to do with Monigan. *Have you dragged us all on a wild goose chase?* she demanded. *I thought you were doing something real to help me!*

At this, the chain fell off Imogen's bike for the tenth time. Imogen tried not to laugh. "Oh, I give up!" Julian Addiman said disgustedly.

Fenella gave her most booming chuckle. "Let the expert," she said.

Imogen knelt down beside Julian Addiman and took hold of the bicycle chain in both her large clumsy-looking hands. She gave the chain two clumsy flicks and wound the pedal of the bicycle. The chain went on and stayed on. Everyone laughed.

Julian Addiman was viciously annoyed. He knelt and glared at Imogen. It was hardly a human look. It was more like the stare of a dangerous wild animal. The ghost backed away from it, behind Ned and Fenella. He had looked like that in the car, before he threw her out.

"The ghost's here," Fenella remarked.

Imogen stood up and wiped the oil off her hands on to a grey handkerchief with little jerky, disgusted movements. "It's no good looking at me like that, Julian Addiman. *I'm* not one of your worshipping girlfriends!" She looked meaningly up the hill where Sally and Cart were now leaning, with their elbows on their handlebars, talking quietly and eagerly together. They looked glad to see one another again.

Julian Addiman's face went deep red. He stood up, snatched his cycle from the hedge and rode off.

Everybody else got on their bikes again and rode after him. The road dived down and round a corner.

"Here we are in the Dream Landscape," Cart announced.

They saw what she meant. The road led through unreal-looking rounded hills — the sort of hills you might draw by pencilling curves on paper. Each hill had a clump of trees somewhere on it. Some had a ring of trees right at the top. Some had the same sort of ring on one side. The rest had a line of wood precisely halfway up. The hay had just been cut here, so that each hill was striped grey and green, like corduroy, and the stripes made a swirl round each different clump of trees. As the procession of cycles came round the corner, the sun felt out in long fingers from behind the grey clouds and touched round knobs of green grass which stood out of the cut hay on the lower slopes of every hill.

Sally said, "If I were to paint this, everyone would think I'd made it up."

Audrey said to Cart, "How imaginative you are. It *is* just like a dream!"

Cart looked irritated, and more irritated still when Julian Addiman rode to and fro in front of the rest of them, cackling with laughter. "Dream Landscape!" he said. "I've never had a dream like this."

"I have," said Howard. "Often. Those clumps of trees."

"Those," said Julian Addiman scornfully, "are planted on purpose to act as windbreaks. They're called hangars." And he continued to ride scornfully backwards and forwards, laughing rudely at anything anyone said.

188

Not that anyone spoke much. There was a curious stillness about the Dream Landscape which no one liked to interrupt. Even Julian Addiman's laughter and the clanking of the Atomic Heavy Bike did not disturb the stillness much.

Behind the last hill, the road just stopped. There was a white fence across the way and, behind that, a long wood standing against the sky. There was nothing behind the wood. It looked as if it was standing on the edge of the world.

"And this is the Back of Beyond," said Cart.

"Very interesting," laughed Julian Addiman. "Shall we go home now?"

"We have to leave the bikes and walk," said Cart.

They laid their bikes down in a heap beside the notice on the white fence. Howard said nervously, "It says PRIVATE."

"There's never anyone about," Cart said, ducking under the fence with the Monigan doll clutched to her chest. There was a chalky path leading round the left edge of the wood, under the hillside. As they all followed Cart, the wood was beside them on their right, rustling and surging with a wind no one could feel.

"It sounds like the sea," Ned Jenkins remarked, looking at the wood. This close, you could see nothing but leaves, tossing and rustling.

"All this land used to be under the sea at one time," Cart said. "When the wind blows, it remembers."

"Yeah, yeah!" said Julian Addiman.

"I find that boy very irritating," Imogen said to Fenella. "Why did he come?"

"He always skives off Games," said Fenella. "Then he has to find something to do."

Though it looked as if they were walking straight into the frowning grey sky, the path led them down a gentle slope beyond the wood. It was thick and still and hot there. On one side was a field with three bright chestnut horses in it. On the other, the ground was broken into more of those round grassy knobs – a whole crowd of them. Each one was a small hill higher than anyone's head. The ghost looked at them, terrified. Audrey gave an expert exclamation at the sight of the horses and loitered, staring.

"I think she's really a horse herself," Sally whispered to Cart. Julian Addiman laughed loudly, but the sound seemed to get buried in the hot, heavy silence.

Howard was interested in the crowd of mounds. "What happened there? Giant moles?"

"Those are barrows," said Cart. "Old graves from before history began. Every single person buried there was a mighty king once, but that was so long ago that they've all been forgotten."

The ghost wondered how Cart knew. She knew. Because she was a ghost herself she saw the invisible shadow over the mounds. In the shadow flickered thin wreaths of thicker shadow, and from them came whispers and sad snatches of things that had once been important. Occasionally she caught a murky glimmer that could have been a crown. The heat and the stillness centred on that shadow and horrified her so that she clung close to the crowd of living people. Something of the same fear fell on them too. Audrey and Julian Addiman were the only ones who looked happy.

A lark went up. It rose out of the centre of the mounds, fluttering and twittering. The song had no joy in it. It was like an alarm clock going off. The ghost jumped and stared. That looked like a warning to Monigan that she was coming. Sure enough, as the lark worked its way into the sky, fluttering as if every wingbeat was an effort, a second lark went up, from beyond the barrows, and a third beyond that. The alarm notes of their songs pattered down like drops of lead.

Monigan knows I'm coming, she said.

Imogen tipped her head back to look at the larks. "They did that when we came before," she said to Cart. "You'd almost think they were warning someone."

"You'd almost think," Julian Addiman said, in jeering imitation, "they were up in the sky twittering!"

At this, Imogen's dislike of him came to a head. "I've had enough of you, you stupid rude boy!" she said. "I refuse to stay near you one moment longer! I'm leaving this minute and going home!" And she set off running, back towards the wood.

Come back! shouted the ghost. This was a disaster. Imogen had to be there when they came to Monigan's Place. But here she was, running away at top speed. Her sturdy legs were flashing as fast as they had flashed on the bicycle, and her yellow figure was getting smaller and smaller against the dark leaves of the Back of Beyond.

Get her back! she shouted to the others. *She's me. I have to be here too.*

CHAPTER THIRTEEN

Sally and Fenella shouted after Imogen. But Imogen just kept running as if she had not heard.

"Leave her," said Cart. "She didn't want to see Monigan anyway."

"You mean she was scared, so she made an excuse to leave," Julian Addiman said, laughing.

He was probably right. Though nobody else laughed, they all seemed to think so. They stood uncomfortably beside the green mounds, while the larks twittered remorselessly overhead.

"These barrows make me depressed," said Howard. "Let's go."

To the ghost's relief, Cart led the way on again. She had been dreading Cart would lead them among the barrows. It seemed such a likely place for Cart to imagine Monigan living. But

Monigan's Place proved to be a short way ahead, where the path tipped over the edge of the hillside and, like the road, stopped. Below them lay a big, bowl-like hollow. Round the bowl's rim there ran a green track of turf, carefully chained and fenced. A notice hanging on the chain said, PRIVATE GALLOPS KEEP OUT.

"This is where they train those racehorses," Audrey explained.

Inside the gallops, the valley was an oval of rough grass. Monigan was there. Cart must have an instinct, the ghost thought. This had been truly Monigan's Place from time immemorial. She felt Monigan, first of all, filling the hollow like a pond of dense gas. Then, as the seven living ones slipped under the chains and crossed the bouncy turf of the gallops, she began to see things sliding and changing and dissolving in the gas. These were things which had been done in honour of Monigan. Dim blood flowed. An axe, and now a knife, glinted as it struck. Phantom mouths opened to scream. All these, and hundreds of others like them, melted and moved and reappeared as they went down the slope. Always there, melting and changing with the rest, were great wooden posts. Sometimes the posts stood in a line. More often they stood in a ring. But, however they stood, the posts were where the victims of Monigan were put to be killed.

Cart's instinct did not lead her quite right. She stopped in the centre of the bowl, where the ghost knew they were neither in one of the shifting rings of posts, nor quite in front of any of the melting lines. But Monigan was there, anyway, all round them.

"Nothing to be scared of here," said Julian Addiman, with his hands in his pockets. "Not a goddess in sight."

"What do we do?" Fenella asked Cart.

"Speak the Invocation," Cart said. "It's very dangerous, but we have to do it."

Cart raised the Monigan doll up in both hands and led the

others in a ragged chorus. "Oh Monigan, mighty goddess, come forth and show thyself…" The ghost watched them all, trying not to see the phantasmagoric slaughter going on all round. Howard had forgotten most of the Invocation. Ned remembered only about half, and Fenella kept going off into her own private version of it. "Spotted tongues," she said several times. Much the same happened to Sally. Several times she said things like "Let thy blood-lust inflame—" and then caught herself up, looking guilty. Audrey, of course, did not know the Invocation, but she stumbled on after Cart, trying to be polite, although she was beginning to giggle by the end. Luckily Cart had a good memory. It must have been a year since she had spoken the Invocation, but she led them in a loud voice, word for word, and cut ruthlessly through their stumblings. The result was like being in church when nobody knows the hymn tune and everyone waits to hear what note the organ will play next.

Julian Addiman said nothing, and gave no sign that he had heard the Invocation before. When it was finished, he said sarcastically, "Is that all?"

"We sit down and wait for Monigan to manifest herself," said Cart.

Julian Addiman threw himself down in the hot grass. Everyone else sat or knelt too. The grass was full of flowers, more kinds and colours of flowers than the ghost had seen in a field before. Ned Jenkins began nervously picking one of each kind and, after a while, Audrey helped him. They crawled about muttering, "You haven't got this blue kind," and "This one's a wild pansy."

Julian Addiman, meanwhile, shifted over near Cart. He did not seem to realise that whatever had happened by the telephone had been final. After a minute, he tried to hold Cart's hand. Sally saw him, but she did not seem bothered. Cart, however, pulled her hand crossly away. "This isn't a picnic."

"You could have fooled me!" said Julian Addiman, and lay flat on his back with his eyes shut.

The ghost wished they would all be more serious. Monigan was gathering herself. Slowly, she was moving in from filling the whole valley to the centre of the nearest ring of phantom posts, where she hardened, swelled and grew. The ghost could not see her, but she could tell what was happening from the way the ghostly killings and the other posts melted away from the sides of the hollow and grew sharper in the centre. Shortly, she could feel Monigan like a heavy shimmer, growing thicker and thicker. Because Cart had slightly misjudged the place, it was happening to one side of them, almost behind their backs.

But they must have felt something. One by one, they glanced over their shoulders. After a while, all of them except Sally and Julian Addiman were sitting uneasily bowed over towards their right. Sally was picking flowers now, humming a tune. She seemed to have no sense of Monigan at all. Julian Addiman was pretending to snore. The ghost marvelled at them. She wondered if they even remembered the midnight dedication. She had a feeling it had gone hazy in their minds as a silly, fantastic joke.

At last, Monigan was like a thick pillar of nothing, breathing out heat and quivering depression. She stood almost behind them, as high as the heavy sky.

Cart stood up and half turned round. She was still not quite facing the right way. "She's here now," she said.

"How do, Monigan!" Julian Addiman called from where he lay.

The others ignored him. Everyone except Sally left him lying there and scrambled up to face not quite the right way with Cart.

Cart said, "Monigan, mighty goddess, we have a ghost, and the ghost is in your power and has asked us for help. What do we have to do to redeem this ghost from you?"

Monigan answered. It was like heavy pressure, or heavy heat. It had no sound, and it was remote and scornful. *Please yourselves. I have the right to claim a life seven years from today.*

Have you heard? asked the ghost. Sally had not even looked up, but the others looked as if they were straining to hear something.

"Sort of vibration," Howard muttered.

"She says she has the right to claim a life in seven years," said Fenella.

"That's what I thought," said Cart.

"Anything can happen in seven years!" Julian Addiman called out from the grass.

"Whose life?" Ned asked, not quite in Monigan's direction.

But Monigan was dealing only with Cart, as priestess. It amused her to keep up her old ceremony. Nothing but a thick hush pressed on them.

"She won't say who," said Fenella.

"But what are we going to do about it?" said Howard. "I think one of you is in horrible danger. Can we give her something instead? Suppose we all offer her something."

"Good idea," said Cart. "You go first."

"Gold tie pin," Howard said promptly. He took his tie pin off and threw it in the grass. It glittered there in a clump of clover, almost as well known to everyone as Howard himself. Howard always wore it, despite the fact that Himself threatened to confiscate it a dozen times a term. It had a small Union Jack enamelled on the gold.

Monigan meditated on it. It was very distant, the time when she had been given gold. She did not exactly refuse it. But it was not worth much to her.

Howard! said the ghost. Now she knew why Howard had gone away to Canada. *Be careful, all of you!* she called out.

"Me now," said Fenella. She carefully put her hands to the

sides of her head, and then carefully pretended to lower something invisible to the grass beside the tie pin. "A piece of brain," she said. "Not all of it – I can't spare it – just the bit old girls do A Levels with. I shall be too old to care then."

"What a daft idea!" exclaimed Julian Addiman, looking expressively up at the sky. He blinked. "I felt a drop of rain."

The piece of brain did not seem to the ghost to be there, but the heavy shimmer of Monigan considered that too. It was not worth much to her, either.

It seemed to be the turn of Ned Jenkins then. He felt quickly in his top pocket and produced a folded piece of paper, which he seemed rather embarrassed about. "No need to unfold it," he said, as he tossed it on top of the tie pin. "She'll know."

Monigan must have known what was in the paper. She considered that too. It appeared to be worth more than the rest, but nothing like so much as a life.

Cart looked at Audrey then. That seemed to the ghost a little unfair. Audrey had nothing to do with any of it. But Audrey, who clearly thought she was taking part in some creepy kind of game, gave a snort of laughter and threw the bunch of flowers she and Ned had picked down on top of the folded paper.

The quiver of Monigan at this was so sarcastic and so amused that the ghost was afraid for Audrey. Audrey had certainly done a very silly thing.

Cart looked at Sally and Julian Addiman then, and so did everyone else. But both of them pretended not to see. They were not going to play. So that made it Cart's turn. She stepped forward anxiously, still not really facing Monigan's presence, holding the Monigan doll under her chin. Wet grime from the doll was oozing through her fingers as she said, "Please, Monigan, if you need a life, would you consider having Oliver instead?"

Cart! exclaimed the ghost. Ned Jenkins gave a grunt, which was obviously a bitten-off protest, and Fenella glared at Cart.

"I know," said Cart, and a tear slid down one of her cheeks. She did not think this was a game, whatever Audrey thought. "I know he's only an animal," she said to Monigan, "but there's an awful lot of him."

Monigan's thick silence was total contempt.

"It's all I can think of," Cart said.

Monigan's silence shimmered with anger. An offering had to be perfect. Oliver had only three toes on one foot. She rejected Oliver utterly.

The ghost was not sure how much of this Cart understood. Cart was turning away. "That doesn't seem to be any good," she said. A sad, wobbly relief showed through her despondent tone. "I think we've done all we can now." She turned back and laid the grey Monigan doll beside the other gifts.

While she was doing it, everyone seemed to jerk in a double blink of white light. As Cart straightened up, thunder crashed into the valley and rolled tremendously round it. Julian Addiman was at once on his feet, fishing in his back pocket. As the first drops of rain spat, he unrolled a plastic cycle-cape and rather smugly clothed himself in it. He took a matching waterproof hat out of its pocket and put that on too.

"I wish I'd thought to bring mine," said Howard.

Then the rain came down. The bowl was cancelled into a grey-green space by lashing white lines of rain and hail. The ghostly slaughters were hidden in it and the phantom posts dissolved.

Monigan was dispersed. All the ghost could see was a turmoil of soaking people confusedly trying to keep some part of themselves dry as they put their heads down and ran, with a further turmoil round their legs, where the rain and hail were bouncing up off the grass. They vanished behind the rain. One reappeared. A shiny plastic shape darted back, picked up the Monigan doll and ran back into the rain again.

She opened her eyes to see Fenella's beautifully made-up face looking sick and troubled. "Thank goodness!" Fenella said. "I thought you'd gone and died on me. I was going to shout for a nurse."

The smell of rain on grass vanished behind the scent of roses which overlaid the smells of the hospital. She was back, with nothing done. No one had been able to give Monigan anything which was worth a life. And Monigan had taken everything she could and given nothing in return. She could have cried at the waste: Will Howard forced to go to Canada, Fenella about to fail A Levels, and Ned and Audrey losing whatever it was they had given. And Cart's generous offer of Oliver thrown back in her face. That was the only good thing she could see. Maybe it was because she had run away – Imogen had run away. She knew that had been a disaster.

Cart came striding into the glass room, as shabby and natural as Fenella was smooth and groomed. It was hard to tell they were sisters. "They're beginning to turn visitors out, along there," Cart said. "I thought I'd sneak back for a few minutes."

"I'm so glad!" said Fenella. "Cart, I thought she was dead!"

She was telling Cart how it had seemed, which was most unusual for Fenella. Fenella must have been very frightened. But the patient did not want to listen – she was frightened enough about herself as it was. She looked beyond her hoist-up leg into the ward, where there was a slight bustle as some of the visitors there collected themselves to go. Quite a few of them looked relieved. They had done their duty and run out of things to say. But there were others, like Cart, coming back at the last minute to say goodbye. Most of these looked anxious and urgent. One of them, a tall pale young man carrying a bunch of flowers, looked lost as well. He seemed to have mislaid the bed he was meant to visit and was wandering up and down among the patients, looking increasingly upset.

"What did Julian Addiman do with the Monigan doll?" she asked.

Cart and Fenella broke off their talk. "What do you mean?" said Cart. "He never had it, as far as I know."

"Yes he did," she said. "I saw him pick it up just now, beyond the Back of Beyond. He came dodging back after the rest of you had run away in the rain."

Fenella stared at Cart. Her eyes had gone all large. "I'd no idea he did that," Cart said. "I haven't seen it since we left it in Monigan's Place."

Out in the ward, the young man had turned back towards the door. He had obviously come to the wrong ward. She hoped he would find the right one soon. He looked so upset.

"Is Will Howard hating it in Canada, do you think?" she said.

"No," said Fenella. "He wrote to me last month. He wants me to go and visit him there. He made it all sound like Heaven, so I may go. He says he wouldn't come back to Britain if they paid him."

"That's something——" she was starting to say, when the lost young man appeared beside her bed. He was with a nice-looking nurse, who seemed to be mothering him.

"Here you are," said the nurse. "You haven't left yourself much time, but I'll turn a blind eye here for as long as I can. Make the best of it." She winked at Cart and Fenella. "And neither of you are here," she said.

"Thank you," said the young man humbly, as the nurse left.

"Ned!" exclaimed Cart and Fenella.

Ned Jenkins smiled at them and held his bunch of flowers out towards her. They were geraniums and pansies, and those little white flowers she could never remember the name of, and small blue ones, and stiff yellow ones — all the kinds of flowers you would expect to see growing in a window-box. In fact, that was just what they were! She remembered now that Ned Jenkins rented a room in a rather smart house just down the road from her own flat, and the people who owned the house took enormous pride in their window-boxes.

She began to laugh. It was not easy to laugh, but she could not help it. "Ned! That looks like most of one window-box!"

"I picked a handful from all of them, actually," Ned said. "I thought I'd better leave them a few flowers or they'd throw me out. But I didn't have any money to buy any, you see."

Fenella gave vent to her huge chuckle. Cart said, "Same old Ned!"

She stared up at Ned, wondering how she had managed not to recognise him. It was, she supposed, that she was thinking of him as a sandy-haired schoolboy. Ned's hair was more light brown than sandy these days and the freckles had largely gone. But she knew him so well! Ned had been at the Art School almost as long as she had. He could not talk about Art either. Because of this, he was always ready to sit drinking coffee with her — coffee she nearly always had to pay for, because Ned never, ever seemed to have any money — and wondering what made all the other students so clever. Despite this, she was a little awed by Ned. He was a success. What she had thought were his good-bad drawings were much admired. And only last week, he had sold a set of cartoons called *Oliver!* to a magazine. She wondered what was making him look so worried now.

"How are you, Sally?" he asked.

She stared at him. Who was mad? Or was she Sally after all?

Things fell about in her head, and the confusion seemed to get into the rest of her body, in a mass of distant aches and numb prickles. She was Sally. Phyllis had known after all. But this was crazy! That meant the drab lady had been *Imogen!*

Ned did not seem to notice her amazement. He said anxiously, "I'm sorry I got here so late, Sally. I'd have been here an hour ago, only I ran into Imogen outside the Music College. She said she'd just been to see you, and you seemed to think she was you. She was in an awful state about it. So I brought her back here with me. Would you mind seeing her, Sally, and setting her mind at rest? She's sitting down the corridor, crying her eyes out."

"Of course," Sally said guiltily.

"Fetch her in," said Fenella. "If they say there's too many people, we two can go."

"But tell her I'll kill her if she starts grieving in here," said Cart.

"She won't," said Ned. "She promised. I'll get her." He passed his window-box flowers carefully to Fenella – they were rather wilted – and went.

While he was gone, she lay not really listening to Fenella telling Cart about her singing lessons, and to Cart saying things in reply about Cambridge, and thinking about the person she now knew was herself. It was not good. She had painted a picture of Fenella: that was the one good thing she knew. For the rest, she had taken Audrey over from Fenella, purely in order to spend a night in Audrey's farm, and she had done that in order to meet Julian Addiman secretly for the midnight dedication to Monigan. That had been so foolish. It was not that she had been under Julian Addiman's spell, either – not then. She had known he had a craving for dark doings and bloodthirsty excitement which was not quite normal. That was why he had made the rest of them hold the séance. But she had been determined to be the one who helped him find his dark excitement. She remembered her disgust, now, when he had killed that poor black hen. She could even remember, dimly, running through the moonlit mist to the dead elms that night – it was a memory queerly overlaid by the more recent memory of herself as a ghost, watching the girl run through the fields. Why had she gone? The hen had almost been too much for her. She could only think that, as the most normal one of four truly peculiar sisters, she had been trying to prove that she could go further than any of them.

The worst bit was after that, when she had got rid of Audrey the next day. She had watched herself doing that just now. True, she had paid for all that after seven very dreary years, but she was not sure now that this Sally she was, was worth saving from Monigan. And she wondered if this was why she had forgotten she was Sally: she did not like herself.

"What happened to Audrey?" she asked.

"Hush," said Cart. "Ned's coming back."

Then she did not need to be told. She remembered. Audrey had made a fool of herself over Ned Jenkins. For seven years, she had sent him letters and Valentines and declarations of love. She had embarrassed Ned horribly by turning up in London and making scenes. Ned said Audrey was the most boring girl he knew, and he swore he had never once given Audrey an excuse for her devotion. But now, Sally wondered about that. There was not only that bunch of flowers Ned and Audrey had picked. There was that nice-looking nurse too. Ned was rather given to turning on a kind of helpless charm. He had got round Himself that way – in fact, he managed Himself even better than Howard. And no doubt he was going to get round the window-box people the same way too. All the same, Monigan had a lot to answer for. So did Sally. Poor Audrey. She had only been roped in because she happened to live in the farm up the road.

She looked at Ned as he came back with the melancholy grown-up Imogen. No charm now. He simply looked extremely anxious. She looked at Imogen, and was still unable to believe that this drab lady had once been an angel-faced little girl with blazing blue eyes who wore yellow trouser suits and frilly green pyjamas. What had happened to make her like this?

Imogen's eyes were puffy, but she was making an evident effort not to grieve. She managed a smile when Cart and Fenella said, "Hallo, Imo!" And she smiled again when Ned pushed her towards the bed. Sally looked up at that dismal little smile and braced herself to bear Imogen's discontent again — exactly the same discontent, she was now aware, that Imogen had borne from her. She had been as dismal as Imogen these last years.

"I'm sorry, Imo," she said. "I couldn't remember anything when you were here first. I was being a ghost—"

"I know," said Imogen. She gulped on a sob. At that, Fenella and Cart both started to speak, explaining the ghost in order to prevent an attack of grieving. Ned, however, cut through the explanation.

"We know all about the ghost," he said. "Imogen thinks there's something she can do."

"But Sally says she saw Julian Addiman sneak back and pinch the Monigan doll," Cart said. "That really worries me. I'd no idea—"

"It doesn't matter. We can still cheat her," said Imogen. She sat down in the chair, leaning over Sally, breathing out a faint lavenderish smell. Sally knew that smell so well. It hung in the bathroom of the flat she and Imogen had shared these last two years. How could she have forgotten! Imogen was, of course, at Music College, training to be a concert pianist.

"Listen, Sally," Imogen said. "I tried to explain before, but you didn't seem to hear. I was terrified. I thought Monigan had been too clever for us. But I think she's too – too primordial to be clever. She just blocked your mind off and hoped. Do you remember how I ran away?"

"Back to the Back of Beyond," said Sally. Once again she had one of those memories, overlaid with her memory as a ghost – Imogen's running yellow figure, herself as a girl crossly shouting after her, and herself as a ghost utterly dismayed.

"Yes, well I want you to go and find me," said Imogen. She had those two earnest creases above her nose. "Find me before I decide to go home. Can you do that? Try every way you can to make me go back to Monigan. Make me give her something too. You won't have to tell me what. I'll know."

Cart said doubtfully, "But aren't you trying to change the past, Imo? I don't think that can be done."

"I know it can't," said Imogen. "It's the future I'm trying to change."

"But did you go back to Monigan?" Ned asked. He was equally in earnest. "It's important – because, if you didn't, there's no point Sally trying to make you."

Imogen ran her hands through her drawn-back hair. Some grey-blonde locks of it fell down round her face, making her look a little more like the Imogen of seven years before. "I – think I did," she said. "I think something made me go. But it's all muddled in my head, because there was a thunderstorm. I was terrified of thunder in those days. But I think there were ghosts in the storm somehow." She leant earnestly down to Sally. "Try it, Sally. For my sake as well as yours."

"I'll see what I can do," Sally said.

Doubtfully, she closed her eyes and tried once again to become a ghost. Nothing happened at first. She seemed to have forgotten how. She lay there with a prodding sort of ache in one leg, and niggling pains all over the rest of her, listening to the quiet voices of the others. They were exchanging news again. She heard Cart say, delighted, "You mean Oliver's going to be a comic strip! That's marvellous!"

That was the last thing she heard. She faded into a ghost.

But it was wrong. She was in the low light of evening, instead of the afternoon. And it had stopped raining. Soaked grass and drips on brambles were catching late beams in red and orange twinkles.

She was facing Himself. That was quite wrong.

Himself was in such a towering rage that he made all other rages seem almost peaceful. His eyes popped with anger. He was roaring. His white face pecked and stabbed with fury. He kept pointing, stabbing an eagle-talon down towards the earth, where a soaked clump of dandelions had been heaved out of the grass. Mr McLaggan's spade lay there, beside a metal detector, and there was a ragged hole by Himself's feet. In it lay the black hen on top of a pile of chains. Insects were crawling on the hen. Above all this, the rooks were going noisily to their nests in the dead elms.

"Evil!" roared Himself. "*Evil!* This – this is the veriest Black Magic! This is wicked, destructive, perverted, loathsome, horrible, devilish! Evil, I say!"

In front of him, Cart, Sally, Imogen and Fenella stood in a scared line. They all looked bewildered, but Cart, Imogen and Fenella, because Himself was so angry, were looking guilty as well. Sally was looking rather pained. She could not understand why Himself should rage so at what had only been a macabre sort of experiment. It had not done any harm, her face said.

"And a perfectly good hen!" bawled Himself. "How many innocent boys have you corrupted with this – this Satanism? Howard and Jenkins. Who else? Answer me, Selina – Imogen – Charlotte!"

"Julian Addiman," said Fenella.

"Nonsense!" yelled Himself. "You malicious little hag, Charlotte – Imogen – Fenella! Addiman is above reproach!" And Himself was so incensed at what he thought was a downright lie, that he commenced swinging impartial, heavy slaps at all four, roaring furiously at the same time.

The ghost was forced to back off from his fury. Himself, in his extreme anger, seemed to have expanded his field of life until it was sparking and fizzing for yards round him. But what made her even more uncomfortable was that she did now actually remember this scene. She remembered being fetched from a supper of custard – which was all Mrs Gill would spare that evening – by Nutty Filbert, looking so smug and righteous that they all felt he deserved to have two heads, and being marched over the field to confront Himself across the grisly hen. And it was the strangest feeling, to be having the same experience twice at one time – once as an unseen watcher, and once as the real Sally's memory, wincing to each remembered slap.

She decided not to stay. Once was enough, and it was the wrong time anyway. This was hours after Imogen had pedalled home, soaked and grieving. She knew what was due to happen after this too. Phyllis would put them all, and Oliver, in the school minibus, by which they knew how badly they were in disgrace. Himself had never allowed them near that minibus before: it belonged to School. But Himself had said he never wanted to see any of them again. So Phyllis was allowed the minibus to drive them all to Granny's.

After that, everything had gone quiet. Granny was a gentle tyrant. She took one look at Fenella and fetched her scissors and cut Fenella's knots off. She had made them all wash their hair. She insisted on a bath every evening and proper table manners. Granny's house, anyway, was the kind of place where you naturally walked quietly and did not quarrel. And there were regular meals and constant attention. Granny bought Fenella and Imogen new clothes out of her own pocket – nice clothes. She gave Sally her good old paintbox and Cart a silver box for jewels. And she had fallen in love with Oliver. They were all secretly very grateful. Even Oliver had behaved well. But the only bit of excitement had been when Will Howard turned up.

She opened her eyes.

They had all been waiting for her. She saw a line of anxious faces. "Well?" said Cart.

"It's no good," she said. "I don't think Monigan's going to let me get to the right time. I got back to the hen row."

Imogen, Cart and Fenella all began unconsciously rubbing their arms. The hen row was a painful memory. "What time did you try for?" Imogen asked.

"Just after I left before," said Sally. "But—"

Imogen plunged forward. She intended to plant both hands on Sally, just as she so often plunged both hands down on the yellow piano. But she stopped, realising it would hurt Sally. "No, no! That's too late!" she cried out. "You must get there before I panicked in the thunder!" With the jerk, and her eagerness, hairpins slid from the back of her head and tinkled on the floor. Long pieces of ash-blonde hair flopped down on the shoulders of her drab coat.

Sally smiled. Hairpins fell out of Imogen all the time. Ever since Imogen had decided she would look more like a pianist with her hair pulled back, there had been hairpins all over the flat. You found them buried in the sugar and stuck in the butter. "But I was there when the thunder started before," she objected.

"But have you tried to be there twice at once?" Fenella asked.

It was the deep arresting voice Fenella used on Mrs Gill. It stopped Sally in the middle of saying No. She remembered the strange feeling she had had during the hen row, as if she was there twice. And she had been there twice with herself running through the fields at midnight, in a way. She remembered doing that now, as a real person, with her hands to her face and the owls making noises, almost too terrified to go on – but going on, because she had decided that her whole character was at stake. And so it had been, in the wrong way.

"I suppose I could try," she said. "But if Monigan notices—"

"But that's *it!*" Cart said. "Aim for a time when Monigan was busy – when we were all in Monigan's Place!"

"When we were all giving her things she didn't want and took anyway," Ned said, very bitter about it.

"And another thing," Imogen said vehemently. More hairpins tinkled on the floor. "You find me, and we'll help. Move this hand when you've got to me, and we'll all *will* me to hear you. Won't we?" she demanded, whirling round on the others in a sheet of hair.

"We can try," Fenella said dubiously.

CHAPTER FOURTEEN

Monigan had taken from Audrey, and from Will Howard, and probably from Ned too, things they had never expected to give. Now she knew that, Sally did not feel at all bad about cheating Monigan. She sauntered back seven years, pretending this was only a visit of curiosity. She was going, she let Monigan know, to see what happened to Howard and Ned when they were caught soaking wet trying to get back into School. Monigan let her go. It was not important. Sally waited until she had a glimpse of a master – it was not Himself – sarcastically watching the two boys drip on the floor of a corridor, and then she slipped away sideways, ten miles off and an hour or so back.

She almost went too far. She found herself in the ring of private gallops, under twittering larks, looking down into the bowl of the valley. There was Julian Addiman lying in the grass, and someone sitting some way from him who had to be herself. The rest were all standing up, looking slightly the wrong way. She could not find herself as a ghost there. She was lost among the unreal, shifting posts, and the screaming and bleeding phantoms, which surrounded the thick invisible presence of Monigan. At the moment when she looked, Fenella, shrill in her green sack, stepped forward and carefully put her hands to her head. She could feel Monigan avidly concentrating on what Fenella had to give. She slipped quickly back over the brow of the hill.

Oh help! she said. She had forgotten those barrows. There they humped, to her left, a crowd of small green hills, old and peaceful enough to living eyes. But she could see them shrouded in unseen shadow and full of flitting half-faded scraps of denser shade.

Half faded though they were, those shadows had sent that lark up to warn Monigan before. They had been Monigan's people. That was why they were buried so near to Monigan's Place. And, if they saw her, they would send a lark up again.

But she had to go past. Imogen had run towards the wood. There seemed nothing for it but to get by as fast as she could. She gathered all her strength and fairly whizzed up the path. From her left, as she whizzed, she could hear the muttering of the old ghosts. It was a blurred mumble, like talk in the next room which you have not quite heard, of old things, old troubles and arrangements for old crises that had gone by long ago. On her right, the three near-red horses in the field knew she was going past. They broke into a sudden gallop and went, with streaming tails and level backs, from one end of the field to the other. Terrified that this would make the old shadows notice, she went faster still, faster even than Julian Addiman's car, and hardly knew she was doing it. She only wanted to get by.

The mumbles faded, the wood flashed past, and she was beside the heap of bicycles. Imogen had not been there. Her bicycle was in the midst of the heap, with its chain trailing off on the grass. So where *was* Imogen? She wished she had asked in the hospital – but it had seemed, from the way Imogen talked, that it was muddled in her mind anyway. Perhaps she did not know where she went. The most likely place seemed to be the heaving, surging wood.

She drifted into the Back of Beyond. It was unexpectedly open inside. It was all tall young beech trees, rising like grey pillars to the green and tossing roof. Close by the end where she came in, the trees stood aside to make room for a long sloping mound, overgrown with moss. The mound was not natural. She knew at once that this was another tomb – a different kind of barrow from another age – of someone very important. It was so hushed and cool in there, and the trees so like pillars, that the wood might have been a church built over the bones of an old king.

As she drifted past the barrow, a voice spoke out of it. *I wait here under the hill. Has the time come when I am needed?*

I – I don't think so, she said.

I hoped you had come to summon me, said the voice. *You are both living and dead, as is fitting.*

This alarmed her considerably. *I – I'm really not a messenger,* she said. *I'm looking for my sister Imogen. You – you haven't seen her by any chance, have you?*

Imogen? said the voice. *Long ago. Lost. Long gone.*

Oh no, she said, hoping it was not a prophet lying there under the long mound. *My sister's alive. She has fair hair and she's dressed in yellow.*

There was a pause. The voice spoke sombrely. *That one. Corn yellow and running, came past me just now, the one bearing within her the power to give life in the realms of death. I took her for the harbinger of my summoning. Am I needed among you now?*

I — really don't think so, she said. *Er — who are you? A king?*

There was a longer pause. Then the voice said, *I have forgotten.*

She knew how that felt. She was sorry for it. *I'm sure you will be needed in the end*, she said. *Tell me, do you know Monigan?*

This time the pause was long and cold. Finally the voice said, *Leave me in peace.*

She knew it would not speak to her again. It knew Monigan all right. Still, she thanked it politely. It had given her more hope than she had had since she woke up in hospital. *The power to give life in the realms of death*, she repeated, as she set off down the cool aisles of the church-wood. It was so open in here that she would have seen Imogen at once, had she been there. But Imogen was not in the wood.

Imogen was outside the wood at the other end, where a bank sloped down into a field. There was a mass of wild strawberry plants there. Imogen was squatting among them having an eating orgy. It was a thing she did when she was not happy with herself. Her mouth, and her hands, and the front of her trouser suit, were stained pale pink with strawberry juice. She was eating strawberries as fast as she could pick them. "Very exquisite flavour," the ghost heard her saying as she came upon her.

The relief of finding her was so great that, for a minute or so, the ghost simply hovered, watching Imogen eat. Then she remembered that she was supposed to do something when she had found her. It took her another minute to recall that she was supposed to raise one hand in the hospital so that the others could help in some way. She hovered there, trying to raise her hand. She tried mightily, but there seemed no way to do it. She did not seem to be in touch with her seven-year-distant body at all.

For five frantic minutes, she struggled to find some way to work those distant muscles, while Imogen ate strawberry after strawberry. Then it was too late. The tree beside her stood out green in a double blink of lightning. A moment later, thunder crashed.

Imogen dropped a handful of strawberries and sprang up under the first patter of rain. "Oh – oh!" she cried out. "I mustn't stay near trees in a thunderstorm!"

Lightning came again. Imogen heard it smicker and screamed. Her scream was drowned in the thunder, but the ghost knew she was screaming, because her mouth was open, pale in the lightning. Then she had almost vanished in a wall of rain. In the rain, Imogen turned and ran, out into the field. The ghost almost lost her. She streaked after, and found her by the merest luck, running and floundering and trying to hold up her trouser legs in blind panic. The ghost kept up with her, in a panic quite as great. Where they went, neither of them knew. The rain drowned everything. The ghost did not dare do anything but keep Imogen in sight. She knew she could only move her hand in hospital by going back there, and that would mean losing Imogen. Imogen did not dare stop running. Once, she tore through a hedge, screaming, "I mustn't stay here! It's wooden!" And then she ran again until her foot slipped on a wet slope and she rolled down it, wailing.

Foreign. There was a dim mutter through the pelting of the rain. *Tell – beacon lit – No chance – negotiations – Warn—*

Now the ghost knew where they were. The slope Imogen had rolled down was one of the round barrows. And its occupant had noticed they were there. Monigan was alerted. She had sensed trickery. The ghost, despite all her efforts to stay beside the crouching shape of Imogen, felt herself being pushed away. At the same time, she found lying beside her a floppy heavy thing, which seemed to be somebody's hand. She dropped it with a shudder.

Ned's voice said, "She's found you! Concentrate."

She was lying in the hospital bed again, too dejected to tell them it was no good. And she seemed to be more firmly and definitely there than before. She could feel the weight of her hoist-up leg. The rest of her hurt quite badly.

Cart said, "I don't believe this!"

All four of them were staring at something on the other side of her bed. Sally turned her eyes that way. There was a blurred yellow shape there. It was a soaked and waif-like little girl in a yellow trouser suit. Phantom rain was lashing down around her, soaking her further, and she was staring at them all in evident terror.

The blurred lips moved. Sally heard what they said, but no one else did. *I shall look upon it as some fiendish futuristic experiment. I refuse to think I've gone mad.*

Poor Imogen! she thought. It must be terrifying for her.

Fenella, with great presence of mind, dug her beautifully manicured hand into the grown-up Imogen's back. "Quick! Explain to her."

Before the grown-up Imogen could do more than lean forward, ready to speak, the nice-looking nurse appeared in the doorway. "Five o'clock—" she began briskly. She looked at the blurred yellow apparition. She jumped slightly. Then she turned round and went out again, with the quiet, shut look on her face of someone pretending something has not happened.

"Get on, before she comes back!" said Cart.

"Imogen," said the grown up Imogen. "Please believe this. I'm you. You grown up. You're seven years in the future. Do you understand? This is how you'll be then."

The blurred blue eyes turned to look at her. The ghostly

Imogen seemed to understand, but she did not seem to like what she saw.

"And this is Cart and Fenella and Ned Jenkins," grown-up Imogen said hurriedly. The blurred eyes moved from face to face and seemed to recognise them. She's doing better than I did, Sally thought. "And this is Sally," said Imogen. "Monigan's trying to take Sally."

The blurred Imogen considered Sally. Her lips moved again. *It's not Sally. Her hair's wrong.*

Fenella leant over the grown-up Imogen. "I know what's the matter. It *is* Sally, honestly, Imo. Her hair went dark as she got older. Lots of people's hair does that. Do you believe me now?"

So that's why I thought I had dark hair! Sally thought. The blurred Imogen was nodding and looking carefully at her. She believed Fenella.

"You've got to stop Monigan," the grown-up Imogen said. She was so anxious that she looked ill. "Only you can do it. You've got to go to Monigan *now* and give her something – you know what. Can you do that? For all our sakes."

This seemed to strike the blurred Imogen as rather a good idea. A faint smile spread on her waif-like face. She nodded again, firmly and cheerfully. Everyone let out a long sigh of relief. And, as their concentration went, the blurred shape of Imogen blurred further and dissolved away like paint in water.

Sally leapt to follow her. How she did it she did not know. She seemed stuck in her aching body like someone stuck in tight clothes. She struggled out of it frantically, and managed to catch Imogen crouching between two barrows with her hands over her face.

"Oh, ghosts!" Imogen was saying.

There were ghosts, but not the ones Imogen meant. *Raiding party,* said the old ghost in the mound. *Hostile band war-party – sentries report—*

Oh be quiet! Sally snapped at it. *We're not hostile. We come — come bearing gifts.*

Merchants from the East, muttered the ghost and, to Sally's relief, it went on to mumble about corn and jewellery as if it had forgotten them.

Imogen climbed to her feet, shivering. By this time, the thunder was rolling back into the distance. The rain was slackening, but it had by no means stopped. Imogen's hair was grey with it, and plastered to her head. Her yellow trouser suit was so wet that her body shone through it, in pink streaks. But she was looking very determined, in a frightened, hectic way. She pulled her sopping trouser legs from under her soaking shoes and plodded through the barrows to Monigan's valley. She knew the way. She must have been here with Cart, when Cart first found it. Over the edge of the hill, she plodded through the rain, under the chains and across the gallops.

As Imogen started going down into the grey, drizzling valley, Sally hung back, afraid that Monigan would notice she was here again, trying to cheat her. Monigan was watching Imogen coming. She was filling her valley, but not very strongly. The posts and the phantoms were faint behind the rain.

At that, Sally understand a little how things like Monigan worked. For Monigan, all times ran side by side, but there were times — like the time of the barrow people — which were in front of her, and other times, like this one, which were off at the edges of her attention. At these edges, Monigan only sopped up all she could get. She did not give them her full attention. She had a greedy interest in what Imogen might give her, but she had not noticed that Imogen had been, for a few minutes, seven years in the future. The ghost of Sally did not bother Monigan at all. She thought there was nothing more Sally could do.

In the middle of the valley, Imogen stopped to pick up a

sopping piece of paper. It was Ned's drawing. Howard's tie pin was lying not far off, but Imogen missed seeing it. "What's this?" she said, and unfolded the wet paper.

Sally came boldly down beside Imogen and looked over her shoulder. She saw herself. It was unmistakable, even faint and spread by the wet. Ned's drawings were always so like the things they were meant to be, that she knew it was herself. Now she knew why Ned was always so ready to sit drinking coffee with her. And she hoped Imogen would be able to cheat Monigan very thoroughly indeed.

"That was very careless of him," Imogen said. "I must give it back to him." She held the paper up in one hand and recited the Invocation. She knew it almost as well as Cart. She only stumbled twice.

Monigan did not draw herself together in answer to Imogen. She was only going to do that if she was likely to lose something. She simply waited, greedy.

"Can you hear me, Monigan?" said Imogen. It was the special clear, quick voice she used when she was very much in earnest. "Listen. I'm going to give you something you're going to like very much. I'm going to give you the supreme sacrifice." Monigan began to be interested. So did Sally. Imogen flourished the drawing and began walking up and down in the rain, making a speech. "The supreme sacrifice," she said. "It's better than a life. I'm going to give you honour and glory, Monigan. You'll get cheers from the masses and the applause of huge audiences. You'll win prizes and have people writing your life story, with all sorts of glorious experiences for you and other people. I'm going to give you years of hard work, Monigan, and the prospect of my serene profile contemplating beauty and relaying it to others—"

Imogen paused dramatically, pointing Ned's picture to roughly where Monigan was. She was certainly doing some good hard advertising, Sally thought. But what did it matter? Imogen thought she was alone, and it was definitely the way to talk to Monigan. Monigan's greed filled the valley.

"The supreme sacrifice," said Imogen. "The rise of my beauty into the limelight. I'm giving you my musical career, Monigan. Do you want it?"

Yes, said Monigan and moved in and took it.

Sally could have cheered. She wanted to hug Imogen. But Imogen had turned away, shivering again, looking thoroughly deflated. "I think Monigan might have the politeness to answer at least," she said. "And it was the supreme sacrifice too!" With that, she burst into tears and ran away up the side of the valley.

Sally longed to be able to go after Imogen and tell her that Monigan *had* answered, and had said Yes into the bargain. But she was sure Imogen would not be able to hear her. And, while Monigan's attention was still on this time, she had to speak to Monigan for herself at long last.

Monigan, she said. *You can't take me. I'm not a perfect offering now. I'm all in bits. You'll have to make do with Imogen's career. That's perfect because it's all in her imagination still.*

Monigan pushed her aside, peevishly wondering why those two leap year days had got in the way and prevented her having Sally already.

Sally was pushed, rejoicing seven years on, into the hospital bed again. "You did it!" she said to Imogen. "You gave Monigan your musical career! And she took it!"

The relief on their faces astonished her. Imogen astonished her even more. Imogen flung back her head – losing the last few hairpins in the process – and laughed.

"Oh marvellous!" she said. "What a joke! She can have it. It's no good to me. I was never any good anyway. I only took up the piano because Phyllis said I looked beautiful playing it. I hoped

Monigan would take it. I took a chance and resigned from the Music College just after I first saw you, but I was afraid it hadn't worked. Now I can go and do something I want to do!" She was looking like the Imogen Sally knew as a child. The drabness was gone. The keen and vivid light was back in her eyes. Sally knew, just from looking at her, that Imogen was truly capable of doing great things. She wondered what the great things would be.

Then she looked at Ned, wondering what had become of that rain-sodden drawing, and found that the change in Ned was almost as great. That worried her. "Are you sure it was worth it – all you've done – just to rescue me?" she said.

"Oh, come off it, Sally!" all her three sisters said together. They sounded so bored, that Sally gathered that this kind of self doubt was as well known in her as grieving was in Imogen. Perhaps there was no need for either now. She, like Imogen, had taken a wrong turn – a very wrong one, in her case. Both of them had wanted something to cling to, and they had both clung to something which was no good to them. She could go and do what she wanted now, too.

And what did she want? Unlike Imogen, she wanted what she had always wanted: to paint – to paint well – to paint better and better. And she had seen so many things in her time as a ghost that were just itching to get painted: the Dream Landscape, Fenella waving the knife over the bowl of blood, Cart in her morning fury, Imogen dangling from the beam and later holding the fungoid candle, Himself like an eagle, and those queer times when the world had split into ribbons, to name just a few. She was so excited at the thought of all she could paint, that a sort of flush ran through her, bringing a kind of easiness with it. And that easiness told her that she was going to get well.

The nice-looking nurse was back, this time determined to send all the visitors away. "It really is time—"

newspaper. "Listen! I bought the evening paper," said Mrs Gill. "You'll forgive me a minute, dear," she said to the nurse. "I'm just coming in to say goodbye."

"I give up," said the nurse.

"It says here," said Mrs Gill. "Oh, hallo, Mrs Melford. Fancy seeing you here. Listen, everyone. That boyfriend of hers got himself killed. It says, 'After a long car chase – ' I won't read it all out, my eyes won't stand it, but he ended up almost next door to the school, up on Mangan Down. Went up that dead end and hit a post by that wood there. Crashed the car. He was dead when they got to him. Now what do you say to that!"

Nobody said anything. Monigan had got her life after all. She had cheated again. Perhaps she had meant to have Julian Addiman all along. He had been hers as much as Sally.

In the silence, while Mrs Gill stood enjoying the impression she had made, the nurse pulled herself together and told them they must all be going now.

But someone else was trying to push past behind the nurse, saying in a tired, flurried way, "But I've driven all the way up from the country to see my daughter. Please let me just say hallo."

Phyllis was there. Sally stared at her. Phyllis was a silver angel now, hollowed and lined like a silver tool from long, long years of heavenly battling. Here was another thing she must paint, Sally knew. But she was surprised that Phyllis's eyes should be full of tears.

"Five minutes then," said the nurse, and she stood there to make sure.

"Hallo, everyone," said Phyllis. "Sally darling." She bent and kissed Sally. It hurt rather. "I had to come," Phyllis said. "It's almost the end of term, and I got the trunks packed, so I can stay in your flat till you're better." The flat was going to be crowded, Sally thought. "And I brought this," said Phyllis. "I know how you used to love it."

She held out the Monigan doll. It was only a doll, dry, floppy, grey and stitched, with very little face and a badly knitted dress. A faint scent of long-ago mould breathed off it. Sally rather wished it was not there.

"Where did you get that?" she said.

"I've had it for years in the towel cupboard," Phyllis said. "I found it in the school drive that day you were all sent to Granny's in disgrace."

She turned away to tell Ned she remembered him very well. Sally found Fenella had been pushed by the crowd round to the other side of her bed. "What do you want done with that?" Fenella whispered, jerking her head to the doll.

"Burnt," said Sally.

"Shall do," said Fenella, and then looked up, along with all the rest.

Mrs Gill burst excitedly into the glass room, waving a